HANDYMAN

ARON BEAUREGARD

Cover Art by Marc Schoenbach

Interior Art by Anton Rosovsky

Edited by Spencer Hamilton

Printed in the USA

WARNING:
This book contains scenes and subject matter that are disgusting and disturbing; easily offended people are not the intended audience

FOR EXCLUSIVE OFFERS AND UPDATES JOIN MY MAILING LIST AT:

substack.com/@abhorror

FOR SIGNED BOOKS, MERCHANDISE, AND EXCLUSIVE ITEMS VISIT:

www.ABHorror.com

To the many overlooked men who have built, fixed, and continue to develop this impossible infrastructure that everyone in the United States of America has the privilege of using.

And for Mike.

The greatest deception men suffer is from their own opinions.

— Leonardo da Vinci

MEASURE TWICE, KILL EVERYONE!

HANDYMAN

ARON BEAUREGARD

1939

THE SIBLINGS

Blanche Edwards stared across the table into her frail brother's eyes. Alfred's eight-year-old body mirrored hers—scrawny and underdeveloped. While he was only a year her senior, to the naked eye she probably looked much younger. The overall lack of protein in their diet wasn't helping things.

"And in light of the violent crime spree perpetrated by Bonnie Elizabeth Parker and her lover Clyde Chestnut Barrow, President Roosevelt vows to propose new laws around firearms," the radio droned on from the other room.

"You still feel the same?" Blanche asked.

Alfred nodded. "Of course. I brought Father's tobacco."

Furrowing her brow, Blanche fidgeted in her chair. "Are you sure?"

"Yes," Alfred said.

"Sure about what?" Elaine asked, shutting off the radio.

The siblings looked at each other.

As their mother returned to the kitchen, she persisted. "Well?"

"Uncle Rooney tells us scary stories whenever we stay over," Blanche said. "And I—"

"Let me guess," Elaine said. "You're not sure if you want to hear another?"

The siblings nodded as their mother set modest bowls of stew in front of them before fixing herself one.

Elaine grinned. "Well, just remember what he's telling you is make-believe. But I suppose your uncle does have a few stories that rival the radio."

She took her seat at the table, clasping her hands together.

"Now, who wants to say grace?"

Before anyone could answer, a loud pounding on the front door interrupted.

Elaine sighed. "It appears your uncle is early again."

The pounding continued.

"Just a minute!" Elaine yelled. She turned to Blanche. "Go let him in."

Blanche left her place and unlocked the door. Smiling in the rain, holding an umbrella, stood her Uncle Rooney. Protection from the elements was paramount, as evidenced by the smoking pipe between his perky lips. His bushy sideburns snuck out the edges of the black top hat he used to hide his baldness. An equally bushy mustache hovered above his crooked teeth as he bent over slightly and tipped his cap.

"So good to see you, dear," Uncle Rooney said.

"Hello, Uncle," Blanche replied.

"Come inside already," Elaine hollered.

By the time they reached the table, Elaine had brought out another bowl of stew. She gestured toward the pipe in his mouth. "Put that thing out."

"Monty smokes in here, so why can't I?" Uncle Rooney asked. "Cripes, we even smoke the same brand."

"Because we're about to eat. Not that I should be forced to explain myself to you in my own house."

Uncle Rooney chuckled. "Speaking of your old ball and chain, where is he?"

"He's working overtime," Elaine said. "And that's not the point. We're about to have stew, and since you insist on arriving unannounced, you may as well join us."

"Ah, I see!" Uncle Rooney exclaimed, eyebrows jumping. "Lovely, I'm starved."

Shaking off the droplets from his coat, he put his finger over the pipe, starving the embers of oxygen. Gliding his tongue over his lips, Uncle Rooney took his seat.

Elaine waved her hand, prompting her brother. "Since you're our guest, it's only proper that you say grace."

Blanche's eyes widened slightly as her gaze darted over to Alfred then to Uncle Rooney.

"But of course," Uncle Rooney replied, bringing his palms together. "Bless us, dear Lord. We thank you for providing us with this offering during a time when many go hungry. We are *forever* in your debt . . . Amen."

"Amen," the others replied in unison.

"So," Elaine said, "what will the three of you be doing this weekend?"

The siblings anxiously looked at Uncle Rooney.

"I think I'll take them to see a picture," he replied, plunging his spoon into the stew and slurping some up.

"Another one?" Elaine asked.

Uncle Rooney grinned. "That's one of the perks of being a projectionist."

Elaine swallowed a piece of potato and cleared her throat. "And what shall you see this time?"

Uncle Rooney raised his eyebrows. "Oh, I've gotten my hands on something special. This film isn't even being played in the theaters . . ."

Elaine brandished a slight frown of disapproval. "Well, don't show them anything too frightening."

Uncle Rooney's crooked smile crept back up, his yellow teeth now visible. "Of course not."

PERVERSE PROJECTIONS

The train ride and weather had made Blanche and Alfred quite tired. But as they stood in the dark alley on the side of the theater, they were suddenly wide awake. Listening to the rhythmic patter of the raindrops, they both shook, the chill of the night only amplifying their nerves as they awaited their Uncle Rooney.

"So, what do you think Uncle is going to show us?" Blanche asked.

"I don't know," Alfred replied. "Does it matter?"

A squeaky door swung open, revealing Uncle Rooney. He waved them in. "Come."

As Blanche and Alfred entered, Uncle Rooney secured the door, locking it behind them.

"Why must we come in this way?" Blanche asked.

"Because . . . I'm not supposed to be in here at such an hour," Uncle Rooney answered. "A man and two children just strolling into a closed theater after midnight is quite conspicuous. Just because I work here doesn't mean I own the place." He beckoned them again. "Follow me."

Uncle Rooney led the siblings through the dark hallways of the theater until they reached a small staircase. The area was enveloped in eerie darkness.

4

"What is the film you mentioned before?" Alfred asked.

"It's not just a film that I plan to show you," Uncle Rooney replied. "It's *proof*."

"But we already believe you," Blanche said.

"As you should," Uncle Rooney replied. "But, if we are to move forward with our arrangement, both of you must see it with your own eyes."

"See what?" Alfred persisted.

Uncle Rooney turned his back on them and started up the staircase. "You'll find out soon enough."

When they entered the projection room, Uncle Rooney turned on the lights. The primary piece of machinery sat in a fixed position, pointed into the theater, to their left. On the opposite side of the room, a much smaller projector stood aimed at a private screen on the wall. There was already a reel set up inside. Two chairs had been placed in front for the siblings.

"Take your seats," Uncle Rooney said.

Blanche and Alfred did as they were told while Uncle Rooney powered on the smaller projector and dimmed the lights until they were barely visible.

"Beyond all the other lessons I've taught you over the last several months about Oswald, this is by far the most important."

Uncle Rooney activated the projector.

As the reel began to spin, the title of the documentary appeared: "Fueled by the Damned." A British man's voice narrated over a montage of archival footage. The story was mostly autobiographical, following an infamous musician and magician from the 1800s who Uncle Rooney had shared many details about previously: Oswald Hitchens.

The words spliced in between explained how, despite having an entertainment career that lasted a half century, the mechanics behind Oswald's magic tricks still remained a mystery, unable to be debunked. The narrator elaborated to explain that the magician claimed the reason for this was that they weren't actually tricks.

"The warlock performer's esoteric practices were rooted in dark magic," the narrator said. "On more than one occasion, he proposed the idea that demonic entities might be the force behind his ability and musical success."

Black and white archival footage of a nefarious man violently slicing the hair of his violin bow against the crying strings of the instrument was accompanied by the wicked, brooding music bleeding out from the speakers. The look in his eyes was every bit as sinister as the song he played.

"Oswald boasted that the portable darkness he roosted in was only growing," the narrator continued, "and as the ghosts he'd seduced over time multiplied, he would soon have a vast army of the damned at his beck and call. So vast, in fact, that Oswald claimed he would one day compete in popularity with the Prince of Darkness himself."

The film continued, showing what was rumored by many to be the transmitter of Oswald's secrets. The front face of the compact onyx pyramid box was removable. Within stood a metronome needle. The end of the sharpened tip impaled a false eyeball, black, the center of which was illuminated by a crimson pupil.

After discussing the details of Oswald's death—a drug overdose only fitting for an entertainer—the short film abruptly concluded.

"I don't understand, Uncle," Alfred mumbled. "You said beyond all the prior lessons that you've taught us, this would be the most important. But we haven't been shown anything new."

"But you're about to be." Uncle Rooney grinned. "You heard what was said: Oswald aspired to compete with the Devil. While he was a brilliant man, a fountain of knowledge for arcane material who solved many riddles, he was no visionary . . ."

"What do you mean?" Blanche asked.

"I mean, why compete with the Prince of Darkness?" Uncle Rooney asked.

A silence fell over the room.

Blanche watched Alfred carefully, knowing he wanted to speak up. And he didn't disappoint her.

"Because this world we walk in seeks only to starve us and bury us," Alfred said. "The powerless are self-cast. *We* can be something more with this knowledge."

"Certainly," Uncle Rooney said.

"And—and it is better to live a life of guilt than agony," Blanche eagerly added.

"You both listen well," Uncle Rooney said. "But allow me to now extend that riddle a bit further. Why compete with the Prince of Darkness . . ."—his eyes glimmered with an orangey spark—"when you can replace him?"

Uncle Rooney opened a locker in the corner of the room and removed a satchel. He approached the table a short distance away from the siblings and opened the bag.

"All I require is enough influence," Uncle Rooney said. He set an aged leather journal on the table, followed by an obsidian, pyramid-shaped object. "I've been waiting my entire life for this moment. I've spent decades in pursuit."

Blanche watched as Uncle Rooney popped the front of the device off, revealing the same black eye and red pupil from the documentary. Mouth open in awe, she couldn't resist asking him a question.

"How did you get that?"

"Never you mind," Uncle Rooney said. "Just know, I took on much darkness to do so. But even so, the darkness I absorbed will pale in comparison to that which I harvest as a result."

Making his way back to the projector, Uncle Rooney carefully placed the metronome in front of the light and set it in motion.

Click . . .

Click . . .

Click . . .

The ominous sphere swayed left to right, the dim light on the wall manipulated by its shadow. Blanche and Alfred looked on as the object continued to bounce and the sinister mass morphed.

Within the strange illumination on the wall, the darkness began to take on strange shapes. Sharp, crooked limbs melded with twisted expressions of agony and rage. The obscured faces of the shadowy entities looked like they were conjured from cigarette burns. The disturbing grimaces and frowns weren't merely a nightmare for the eyes: the hellish wails they released from their mouths could be heard echoing inside the room.

The siblings sat wide-eyed, analyzing the anguish of the wicked spirits closely. As they absorbed the bad vibrations, they listened to their Uncle Rooney like a pair of pupils would their teacher.

"You are the black mass," Uncle Rooney said to the countless beings imbedded in the wall. "The Nexus. The core of the new abyss. I shall nurture you alongside murderers, rapists, and madmen. Until you are a shade of darkness the universe can't fathom. Until I am strong enough to siphon the damned from the other side—from He who shall not be named. You will obey my every command . . ."

The demonic voices sounded like an army of hoarse vocal cords wailing inside a furnace, their increasing cadence appearing to be an immediate acknowledgment of Uncle Rooney's orders.

"But not only will you obey me," Uncle Rooney said, turning to Blanche and Alfred and grinning. "You will also obey my minions."

A BLOODY BLUEPRINT

"Why did you show us all these things?" Alfred asked.

Uncle Rooney knelt in his attic using a piece of chalk to create symbols on the dusty planks of the floor. The largest drawing was a circle with a tuning fork overlapping it, the handle sticking out over the top curve. Uncle Rooney double-checked the countless other signs surrounding the focal point, then, wiping the sweat off his brow, he looked up at the siblings.

"I have always felt close to you children," Uncle Rooney confessed. "I feel our trinity is the missing link to my destiny."

Blanche looked at Alfred, as if waiting for him to say something.

"Uncle, please," Alfred said. "There is no reason to shield us from the truth."

A smug, almost proud look swept over Uncle Rooney's face. "Why do you not believe me?"

"As a man, you are many things," Alfred said, "but one thing you are not is a slave to destiny."

Uncle Rooney's eyes widened.

"If you aspire to be worse than the worst," Alfred continued, "who is there left to control you?"

Uncle Rooney's round face beamed. He set the chalk aside and stood.

"You are wise beyond your years, my boy."

Blanche stepped closer, anxious to add her two cents. "Do what thou wilt, not as you're told."

"I see you've both been listening," Uncle Rooney said, approaching his desk.

"We have," Alfred said. "Now will you tell us why?"

Uncle Rooney looked down at the desk, where Oswald's black, triangular metronome and worn leather journal lay. Beside those items sat three rectangular structures—two smaller boxes in front of a much larger one. Each of them had an off-white shroud cast over the top, obscuring the contents.

"I shall," Uncle Rooney replied. "But first, we must review your results. That last time the two of you were here, I asked you to blend a powder of decay. For one to become a collector of darkness, they must first understand their atmosphere. People like us operate in secrecy, using our knowledge to mask ourselves from the public's distrust. People like us must pay attention to the details."

Uncle Rooney opened the tobacco tin on his desk and started to pack his pipe. "The suspicious eyes must go blind, and we shall leave no evidence behind." Opening the box of matches, he noticed they were empty. "Drat. I'll have to wait until after the reveal, I suppose."

Setting his pipe aside, Uncle Rooney lifted the shrouds off the smaller boxes at the same time. The pair of oversized rats revealed to be inside had many lumps under their flesh—some still covered by hair and skin, others ripping through the elasticized tissue. Blood was smeared all around the cages. Their malformed bodies lay motionless.

"Again, it's obvious that you've both been listening quite closely," Uncle Rooney said. "The results are good. Almost too good . . ."

Alfred furrowed his brow and leaned in. After studying each of the monstrosities, he turned back to his uncle. "I'm sorry, Uncle. Did we do something wrong?"

"Well, the idea was to make these cancerous growths develop naturally, so as not to arise any suspicion. While you both certainly accomplished that feat, the increase was too rapid. Exponential growth the likes of which I've never witnessed before. It's quite impressive, but also reckless. If this were a human specimen, such a fiasco might draw the attention of the medical and scientific communities. It isn't our goal to create panic and attract the eyes of scrutiny. We must be smart."

The siblings nodded in unison, absorbing the critique emotionlessly.

"But we have much time to perfect your dosage," Uncle Rooney continued. "After all, this was your first attempt. I don't foresee any future failures from such bright pupils."

"If that is your belief, then will you tell us why you've actually chosen us to work alongside you?" Alfred asked.

Uncle Rooney exhaled. "The root of the truth is that to accomplish such a lofty goal, I require help. This is a long-term proposal. To acquire the land, privacy, wealth, and carnal currency required to burrow deeper than those before us—deeper than Oswald or anyone else—will entail a monumental effort. One that may or may not go beyond my years in this realm."

He reached for the final shroud and yanked it away. Under the veil stood a model-size, compact structure. But the formation was not comprised of traditional materials; instead, the house-like outline was made up of many sick and dismembered rats.

The crimson bones dripped.

The bulbous tumors glistened.

The flesh, meat, organs, eyeballs, and teeth of the deathly ill rodents came together to create a hellish home. The foul, bleeding structure had been carefully conjoined—some rat parts were burned, some nailed, some sewn, some glued. The amalgamation of mutilated vermin was a hideous sight to behold.

"I give you . . . *The Nexus*," Uncle Rooney whispered.

"It is glorious, Uncle," Blanche said. "Far more beautiful than we could've imagined."

"This is nothing," Uncle Rooney corrected. "It took me just a short time to construct this model."

Glancing at the pipe on the desk, his gaze drifted back toward his jacket on the chair. He walked over and patted the pockets, eventually retrieving another box of matches. When he returned to the abomination, he lifted his pipe.

"The true marvel will come to exist when we've erected it in its proper form," Uncle Rooney continued.

"I can only imagine," Alfred said, grinning as he watched his uncle strike the match.

"The human form," Blanche added.

Uncle Rooney took several puffs from his pipe, inhaling, and nodded in agreement. "But acquiring human husks is a far greater chore than a few rats." He blew out a cloud of smoke in a heavy sigh.

"Is something wrong?" Blanche asked.

"It's just a shame," Uncle Rooney said, taking several more puffs.

"What is?" Alfred asked.

"Had I been able to—" Uncle Rooney coughed several times before continuing. "If I had only known what I know now when I was your age, things would be different."

"How so?" Alfred asked.

He took several more puffs until a thick plume of smoke leaked out of his mouth. "I'd have been a hell of a lot more motivated. Instead of enlisting you, I might've already evolved. I might've been ready to stand upon the final foundation inside The Nexus. I might've—"

Blanche and Alfred watched as Uncle Rooney seemed to lose his balance. His hip slammed into the table, knocking the tobacco tin to the floor. The aggressive coughing only got worse as his eyes started to water. Falling to his knees, he dropped the pipe and slumped onto his side.

"Wha . . . what's happening to me?" Uncle Rooney managed to say amid his choking fit.

As crimson oozed out of his ears and eyeballs, Uncle Rooney's body began to quake and balloon.

Blanche felt her heart start to race.

Apple-size balls began to crop up under Uncle Rooney's skin. Some of the swollen growths were solo while others came in clusters. Between his coughs came wails of anguish and horror.

Alfred grinned. "You thought you were looking at dead rats in a cage, but actually, *you* are the dead rat, Uncle." He looked down at the spilled tobacco tin on the floor, then pulled a separate one from his pocket. "We'll have to bring the rest of the untainted 'baccy to Father. I'm sure he'd be upset if it didn't turn back up."

Stepping beside her brother, Blanche brandished a sinister grin of her own, echoing her sibling's excitement. "But not to worry. As you know, we listen and observe quite closely. Your aspirations are not lost. It's more like they've been . . . transferred. They shall be polished, and then pursued."

The tumors bubbled like lava under his flesh, many having already doubled in size, stretching him to the breaking point. With his body over capacity, the cancerous tissue began to rip through its strained casing.

When Uncle Rooney opened his mouth this time, blood exploded up his gullet and onto the ground beside him.

"W-w-whhyyyy?" he wailed.

"Because," Alfred said, "why would we escape this earthly enslavement only to agree to another form? To be crushed under the heel of a new master? But once you're gone, we shall take all you've taught us, and with that knowledge, we shall govern ourselves as equals."

Blanche locked eyes with her brother, the two of them nodding in agreement with the pact.

"And with Father Time on our side," Alfred continued, "we shall accomplish what you waited far too long to."

Blanche approached the desk and took hold of Oswald Hitchens' metronome and the leather-bound journal before returning to her brother's side.

14

Taking the journal from Blanche, Alfred flipped open the arcane artifact to a page that read *Conjuring a Handyman*. He grinned as he skimmed the text.

"It seems that the signs are showing themselves," Alfred said. "Instead of being the helpers, it appears we can manifest our own. I can only imagine what else we'll learn with our gate-keeper removed."

As Blanche watched the life drain out of her uncle's bleeding eyeballs, she felt the urge to share a few final words.

"If there is no longer anything left for you to take comfort in, take comfort in knowing that we shall make you proud."

1996

HELP WANTED

When Vinny Fowler pulled up to the halfway house, he got the creeps. Stroking his beard from the confines of his van, he had to will himself forward.

It's part of the gig, Vinny thought. *Just get it over with.*

He got out of the van and made his way to the door. Most of the facilities created to help people get back on their feet that he'd seen were in cities. From what he already knew about the place and its isolated surroundings, that made it even weirder. After ringing the bell twice, Vinny waited patiently for someone to answer.

It didn't take long for the owner of the property to open the door. Len Anderson was a scrawny but fit older man.

"Hey, Vinny," Len said. "Good to see you, come inside. You want a cup of coffee or something?"

"Nah," Vinny said. "If it's all the same, I can just talk to you out here."

"Okay . . ." Len nodded, stepping outside and closing the door behind him.

Vinny glared through the window at a woman and several other men that he could see inside the living room.

"You know, they don't bite," Len said. "Nothing to be afraid of."

"I'm not afraid of them," Vinny said, eyes darting from the window to Len's face. "This is just my preference."

"They're not monsters, they're just misunderst—"

"I'm not tryin' to be an asshole, Len, but I ain't here to talk about anything but filling jobs. So, let's just cut to the chase and be done."

"Fine." Len pointed through the glass at a Hispanic man in his mid-thirties. "So, Martinez don't exactly speak perfect English, but he speaks enough. Fuckin' guy's a Swiss Army knife, he can do a little bit of everything."

"That sounds like what Curtis is looking for," Vinny said. "If we can keep the finder's fee the same as last time, then we'd be happy to take him off your hands."

Len squinted. "Seeing that I've fed you all so many good hands now, some might say that would entitle me to an increase."

"Maybe so, but others might counter such an idea and say that if you press your luck, we'll look elsewhere. However, if you were to play your cards right, King's Construction would be willing to continue to come to you for workers . . . exclusively."

When Len scratched his face and sighed, it made Vinny chuckle. The hesitation was all he needed to go at him even harder.

"C'mon, buddy, you think I'm stupid?" Vinny asked. "I know you're taxing these boys on top of your finder's fee. The paycheck you've got coming in monthly is only gonna grow. Or I can pull the rug out from under you and walk away. The choice is yours, but just remember, it ain't no sweat off my back."

"All right, all right," Len said. "Relax, you know how much I value my relationship with you and Curtis."

"Then show me, instead of trying to upsell me on shit every time I talk to you."

"Okay, point taken."

Vinny reached inside his jacket and pulled out a knot of cash. As he counted out a few bills, another van pulled down the driveway.

"One other thing while we're on the topic," Len said. "I'm supposed to have a few more guys that are gonna be available soon. So, just keep that in mind."

Vinny nodded as he handed Len the wad of cash.

"And this . . ." Len pointed at the man in the van. "This fuckin' guy's a legit pro. He can handle an entire crew by himself."

"How do you know that?" Vinny asked.

"Because, that's what he did . . . before he got caught up."

Vinny scoffed. "Is that what you call it?"

"Hey, man, I thought you said you wanted to just cut to the chase?"

Vinny smiled, knowing he had him.

"But if you ain't interested then that's—"

"No, I'm interested," Vinny said. "We're probably not ready for anyone else yet, but you're right, I may as well meet him now."

Len looked at the van, stuck his dirty fingers in his mouth, and whistled obnoxiously. "Yo! Come here!"

The clean-cut young man brandished a friendly smile as he opened the door and approached them.

"This is Vinny Fowler," Len said. "He's in charge of hiring at King's Construction."

"Oh, wow." The man stuck his hand out. "Name's Ryan Clements, it's a pleasure. I heard you guys are by far the top company in the state."

"You heard right," Vinny said. "Listen, I don't have a ton of time right now, but it's good to meet you." Vinny drifted back over to his van. "Maybe if Len keeps his head in the game, we'll see you on the job soon."

"I sure hope so," Ryan said.

Vinny looked at Len. "Tell Martinez to show up at five. Not a minute after. Understood?"

"Loud and clear," Len said.

"All right," Vinny replied. "You boys take care."

Opening the door to his van, Vinny slipped back inside, started the engine, grumbling in his head.

Can't get the fuck away from this place fast enough.

Backing out of the driveway, he took off down the road. He drove for a few minutes before reaching the gas station, pulling in, and parking beside the payphone. Vinny slipped out of his car and fed a pair of dimes into the coin slot.

It didn't take long for the ring to be answered.

"Hello?"

"Hi, sweetie," Vinny said, smiling naturally at the sound of Kelly's voice. "So, how was *Dragonheart?*"

"It was actually maybe a little scarier than I would've hoped," Kelly said.

"Come on, you're afraid of dragons? Such a wimp."

Kelly giggled. "Not me, silly. I mean for Ashley."

"Well, she's the one who asked to see it. That's what she gets for liking mythical creatures, I guess."

"Dragons and robots, that's all she seems to talk about anymore. That and how she misses her daddy."

"Yeesh, way to make me feel like a scumbag."

"I'm not trying to, it's just . . . she really looks forward to spending weekends with you. But you've been so busy lately, and I think it's wearing on her."

"Well . . ." Vinny ran his fingers through his hair. "It's wearing on me too. Did you remind her about the trip we have planned to Capron Pond for her birthday, and how excited I am to spend time with her then?"

"I did, but she wants you now." Kelly's tone suddenly shifted to something more seductive. "I might want you now, too, actually."

When she talked dirty to him on the phone it drove Vinny nuts. He couldn't help but picture Kelly biting her lip after dropping that little line on him.

"Damn, I want you too, baby."

"Then come and get it."

"Fuck . . . you know I want to, but I've gotta go and start prepping for this side-gig thing that Curtis wants to get going."

"Vin . . . he wants you to do more on top of what you're already doing? How is that even possible?"

The payphone gave Vinny a warning. He fished another two dimes out of his pocket and dropped them into the slot.

"I don't know, but he's trusting me with a lot. He doesn't have any jobs secured right now, but he wants us to be ready. Something tells me if I nail this, it could be the start of something big."

"I get it," Kelly whispered.

"I'm sorry, sweetie," Vinny said. "I promise, if we can just get through a few more weeks of this, it'll be worth it."

"And if nothing comes of it?"

"Then I'll put my foot down and tell Curtis to lay off."

"Okay. Whenever you do decide to come home, can you pick up my prescription on the way?"

"I would love to."

A brief silence filled the line.

"Baby, you promise that you'll mention it to him if he doesn't ease up?"

"I promise." Vinny couldn't get enough of the sound of her voice, but he knew he needed to get moving. "And you know what else I promise?"

"What?" Kelly asked.

Lowering his voice, Vinny spoke to her like she was the only person in his world. "I love you to the moon and back."

HALFWAY TO HELL

Alfred Edwards turned to his sister, Blanche, as she looked at the cage. The siblings stood side-by-side in the basement of their manor, looking at the symbol chalked onto the floor behind the steel bars.

The circle with the tuning fork overlaid on it was at the center of the cage, and sitting atop the outline was a weasel. The creature was calm and quiet, staring forward as the black and red pupil of the metronome bobbed from side to side.

Click . . .

Click . . .

Click . . .

"First Willis, now this," Alfred said, disgust clinging to his tone like stink to feces. "I'm running out of time."

Blanche squinted her eyes at her older brother, remembering a time long ago when it was "us" instead of "I."

We shall govern ourselves as equals, Blanche thought, recalling his final speech to Uncle Rooney.

Blanche couldn't help but wince at the bitter taste her brother's choice of language left in her mouth before looking down at the pendulum needle of the metronome, then above the cage. A young man and woman were strung up over the weasel's enclosure, mouths gagged, hanging by their ankles.

"Just because they don't harbor the darkness required to replace Willis doesn't mean they can't be of assistance," Blanche said. "We mustn't think pessimistically. We must prepare and look toward our next opportunity."

"Jack and Jill?" Alfred scoffed. "You should've known better."

"The man sounded troubled on the phone," Blanche said. "How was I to know they'd be such lovely people?"

"Well, next time, I don't care how they sound, we don't hire young. Young people haven't been through anything! They—they don't have what we *need*!"

Blanche looked at the terrified brother and sister. Each of their shirts read: Jack & Jill Family Carpentry Services.

"Fair enough," Blanche said.

Reaching for the table beside him, Alfred unsheathed his sword. "We need *men*, goddamnit! The gritty, the hardened, the overlooked, the broken!"

As Blanche watched Alfred move toward Jack and Jill with the tip of his sword pointed at them, she took hold of a glass jar filled with yellow liquid.

"I shall hire an entire team of workers," Blanche said. "And we shall have many men to choose from."

Biting down on his lip, Alfred looked into the terrified eyes of his captives. The lightweight sword moved forward with ease—it was the perfect density for his elderly arms.

Still, it took Alfred several hacks to get Jill's head off. As the gap oozing a reservoir of red widened with each blow, all the blood in her body covered the mesmerized weasel. But even when Alfred lopped off the head entirely and moved on to Jack's, the beast didn't flinch. Once the sword slicked through the neck tissue diagonally and the second head fell to the floor, the weasel was covered in a full-on bloodbath.

Blanche double-checked Oswald Hitchens' book before removing the lid from the glass jar.

Watching in repulsion, Alfred witnessed the yellow liquid splash over the coat of the animal. Several additional mini waves of the liquid followed, tainting the quivering heads on the ground.

The blood-covered weasel remained in the center of the cage, wholly engrossed in every motion of the metronome.

Alfred and Blanche looked at each other and nodded before turning their attention back to the weasel.

"Eat! Eat! Eat!" they chanted in unison.

In the blink of an eye, the weasel snapped. It pounced on Jill's head, chewing on the facial cartilage and skin. And just as quickly as it ripped off chunks of gore from the face, it swallowed them.

Blanche lifted the open book from the table and read a passage aloud.

"They do not hold the darkest tone, still eat their skulls, flesh and bone. A yellow slime, the sacred piss, when swallowed with, you gain the gift. To shape and shift, to change in size, to be so sick, to kill and lie."

As Blanche finished the words, Alfred watched the beast continue to feast. Its eyes turned midnight black, and with each bite of gristle the weasel devoured, its teeth grew sharper, and its claws grew longer. The animal developed in stature to the point where it looked less like a petite weasel and more like a full-grown wolverine.

"It says we must name it," Blanche said.

There was a brief silence as Alfred watched the raging, bloody animal continue to mutilate and devour the severed craniums.

He grinned. "I've got just the perfect thing."

EARLY MOURNING

Sara St. James stared at the weathered picture fixed to her dashboard. Clenching the loaf of bread, she shook her head. The tingle in her nose was fierce.

I can't believe it's been this long, she thought. *Five and six years to the day . . .*

When she looked at the photo of her, Eric, and Michael, all smiling on the farm, she tried to hold it in but instantly broke down.

I miss you so much.

Taking a few deep breaths, Sara was able to calm herself. She wiped the tears away and exited her car. Looking down at the bench near that waterfront where she usually sat, she noticed an older man with a crutch leaned against him occupying part of her favorite spot.

Hopefully he doesn't mind company.

Trudging down the hill, she crept up beside the man.

"Excuse me, sir," she said. "Do you mind if I sit?"

The man continued to stare forward into the dirty pondwater. "It's a free country."

Sara's eyes widened. She was a bit surprised by the man's frank response.

"For now, anyway," he quipped.

Plopping down beside him, Sara opened the bag of bread and started to rip a slice into pieces.

"You've been crying," the man said.

Sara tossed out several globs of white bread a few feet away and watched a mother and her baby ducklings pounce on the free meal.

"Yeah . . ." Sara said. "How'd you know?"

The man continued staring off into the distance. "I've been around a lot of pain in my time. I can sense when it's close. I know what it sounds like."

As Sara looked at the mother duck carefully nudging a piece of bread closer to one of the babies, another tear welled up in her eye.

"What's wrong?" the man asked.

She wiped her face. "It's just . . . an anniversary—well, two anniversaries, actually."

"Yikes," the man said, biting his lip for a moment. "You know, usually when people say 'anniversary,' death isn't the first thing that comes to mind. Usually an anniversary marks a date where something sweet happened."

Sara threw more bread to the baby birds and their mother, shaking her head.

"But the older you get," the man continued, "the less that's the case. Now, everyone's dead and I'm alone. And all my anniversaries are with agony."

"Boy, you sure know how to cheer a girl up," Sara said.

The man finally turned to her and grinned. "Cheer a girl up? Ha! After what I just said, you should be the one cheering me up!"

They both shared a little chuckle.

"Truth is, when you sat down here, I wanted to lie to you," the man said. "I wanted to tell you that things'll get easier with time. That you've got a lot to look forward to. That the golden years are just that . . ."

The man took hold of his crutch and grimaced as he put weight on his hip. It took him a moment to get up, but he managed.

"But that's a crock of shit," he explained.

Sara nodded. "I kind of figured."

"Good," he whispered. "I'm not especially a fan of unsolicited advice myself, but I have some if you'd like."

Sara shrugged, not seeing the harm. "Sure, why not."

"You're a beautiful young woman."

Sara immediately raised an eyebrow.

"Okay, maybe not a spring duck, but you're not so far off," he said. "It's okay to celebrate them, but . . . don't let the past control you." He started limping away. "Don't forget to live your life. Otherwise, you'll end up like me."

With glossy eyes Sara looked at the momma duck watching over her children. Just seeing the animals interacting triggered a pain that felt like a knife turning in her chest. Inside she hoped they would never be separated.

COME AGAIN

Outside the vast grounds of the estate, the gravel driveway was shrouded in darkness. Faint moonlight illuminated the shiny white paint on the construction van. The porta-potty stood several yards away from the vehicle; groans of deep discomfort and urgency slipped through the slots of the gridded ventilation panes.

Alfred and Blanche watched the toilet closely, waiting with great anticipation. After several weeks of observing the men work on the vanity project at their house, the moment they'd been awaiting had finally arrived.

As the intestinal battle concluded, the door of the shitter started to rattle. The red OCCUPIED indicator on the handle turned green, and the leader of the construction project, Vinny Fowler, stepped out of the smelly cell. He tried to swirl the scent away from his nose by waving his hand in front of his face.

"Good evening, Mr. Fowler," Blanche said.

Vinny jumped at the sound of her voice. It was clear to Alfred that he'd been caught completely off guard. He looked down the driveway, trying to play it off, like the loaf he'd just pinched wasn't so bad.

"Glad we ran into you," Alfred said.

Turning to his sister and smiling, Alfred saw her pale complexion pop in the night, like a ghost in the darkness.

"Ah, hey," Vinny said, flustered by their appearance. "Sorry, I was—uh—I was just about to get going. And tomorrow should mostly just be cleanup, so we'll be out of your hair likely before noon."

"It's quite all right, Mr. Fowler," Alfred said. "Our intent wasn't to make you feel rushed. But since I have you here, I do have a query for you."

Vinny nodded hesitantly. "Of course."

"My dear sister and I have one other project we're hoping for some help with."

Alfred joined Blanche as she brandished her stained teeth and purple gums. Even through the darkness, his sister's age showed. Her graying hair, wrinkled skin, and veiny bulges were obvious geriatric symptoms. Yet, despite her oldness, he was thankful Blanche's mind remained incredibly sharp.

"Oh, that's great," Vinny said. "This job worked out really well for everyone. I'm sure Curtis would be happy to draw up another contract for you and—"

"I'm sure he would, but . . . you see, that's the problem, old chap," Alfred said. "We wouldn't want the entire crew here, or even the company involved, for *this* work."

"Oh, no?" Vinny asked.

"No, sir," Blanche confirmed.

Alfred took a step closer to him, making eye contact before he whispered, "Just you."

Vinny's forehead wrinkled. "Why's that?"

"During your time here we've both had a chance to watch how you operate. We've been waiting for a man of your ilk for some time now. People like you don't just grow on trees. You're special."

"Furthermore," Blanche said, "the job we're seeking to fill requires a certain amount of . . . sensitivity. Simply put, there are few candidates we're able to consider, but you're at the top of our list. And let me assure you that—"

"I really appreciate the offer," Vinny interjected, working his way around to the driver's side of his van. "But as of right now, I'm under contract. I'm property of King's Construction. Therefore, if you want me to work a job, you'd have to go through the office."

Blanche's eyes squinted with displeasure. "But—"

"Now, I don't mean to be rude, but it's been a long day, and I've still got a big drive before I'm home to my family."

A snarl of displeasure contorted Alfred's face, mirroring his sister's. As he watched Vinny start up his work van, the annoyance in his voice was cutting.

"Let me assure you, we'd pay far more than anything you'd be able to earn in your current role," Alfred said.

Vinny put the van in reverse and then stepped on the brake. He looked out his window at Alfred and Blanche.

"With all due respect, Mr. Edwards, you have no idea what I'm capable of earning. If you'd like to negotiate another job, feel free to call the office in the morning. It was a pleasure to oversee the remodel. Thanks again, goodnight."

The seething seniors watched as the van kicked up a little dust on the way down their winding driveway. They both stared into the darkened path in shock. In a world as rich as theirs, money usually did the trick.

"We'll see about that, Mr. Fowler," Alfred grumbled.

Blanche hobbled sluggishly to the porta-potty, outstretching her fingers with their overgrown nails and pulling open the door. Alfred loomed just behind her. The smell of fresh shit hit them both in the face, quick as a boxer's jab. Her tarnished grin reappeared as she gawked into the pool of excrement, then back at her brother.

"It *was* a number two," she whispered.

Alfred's expression went from grim to that of a sharp grin. "Wonderful, love."

Blanche stepped up into the smelly chamber and looked past the seat into the pit. It was filled with used tissue and watery blackness.

"That it is," she whispered. "That it is."

A PROMISING FUTURE

"Got a little bit of gristle on the end here," Curtis King said, using the bloody knife to carve another piece off his steak. "That's all right though, just 'cause it's a little tough don't make me hate it. In fact, that's one of several reasons I always admired *you*."

While Vinny was beyond happy to be treated to such a meal, he wasn't accustomed to fancy restaurants with standards like the one they were dining at. Feeling out of place, he fidgeted in his seat again. He glanced at a gorgeous blonde wearing a black, sparkling dress just a table over and tried to emulate her impeccable posture.

Eyeing the whiskey and cola on the table in front of Curtis, Vinny couldn't help but wish he could have a drink by his own plate. It was especially awkward when they initially sat down at the table and Curtis asked him what he wanted. He'd ordered a ginger ale, but part of him always wanted to break his sobriety. Yearning for the sting of liquor on his tongue, he reminded himself that it was a bad idea.

You worked too long to fold now, Vinny thought. *Can't go back to that darkness . . .*

"A sturdy foundation—like the one you have—is rare," Curtis continued. "You must've had a hell of a father."

The words resonated in Vinny's head like a bell going off. That was a box that he'd prefer not to open.

"That's one way to put it," Vinny said, trying to focus on his steak instead of that topic.

"And I'm sure that when he's old enough, you'll pass the same on to your boy," Curtis said.

"Girl, actually," Vinny corrected, taking a sip of his ginger ale and smiling nervously. Despite working under Curtis for many years, the boss always had a way of making him extremely uncomfortable.

"What?" Curtis asked.

"I have a daughter, not a son."

Curtis swallowed a bite that looked like mostly gristle. "Shit, did I say 'son'? Now I feel like a fool."

"It's okay, I know you've got a hundred people who you're overseeing. It'd be ridiculous for me to expect you to remember everyone and their families."

"Understanding too, that's always a good quality." Curtis winked at him and smiled. "How old's that little girl of yours now anyway?"

"Ah . . . seven—well, actually, she'll be eight in less than a week."

"My, my, time sure does fly. Seems like not that long ago you were telling me about the baby you'd just had." Curtis shook his head and sighed. "Before you know it, she'll be old enough to date and, well . . . take it from me, that's an entirely different set of problems."

"Did you take me out for a nice steak dinner just to raise my blood pressure?"

The joke got a grin out of Curtis, but he stopped short of a laugh to transition into a more serious topic.

"Not at all. In fact, I wanna keep you healthy as a horse for the long haul."

Vinny furrowed his brow. Curtis sure did have a strange way with words sometimes. Still, he was interested.

"Why's that?"

"Because you're a fuckin' asset, Vinny."

The statement gave Vinny some relief. Feeling more comfortable, he took another bite of his steak while listening to Curtis.

"Being able to trust you to manage a separate team on the side is huge." The waiter approached the table, but Curtis shooed him away. "That gig with those old weirdos worked out incredibly well. We didn't lose any ground on the Halpert contract and made a goddamn boatload of extra cash simultaneously. Those geezers are loaded."

Vinny nodded. "I'm glad it worked out so good for the company."

"Not good, *great*. And the idea that I have someone who I can rely on, like you . . ." He shook his head with utter delight. "Well, it's put some other ideas in my head."

"What kind of ideas?"

"I'm not at liberty to share just yet. But let's just say if this Halpert deal is a success—and by 'success,' I mean their office building goes up on time and without any major hiccups—then you'll surely find out. And I promise . . . dinners like the one we're having tonight'll become a regular thing for you and your family."

Excitement filled Vinny's insides. As his heart started to beat faster, he looked down at the bloody meat on his plate and back up at Curtis.

"You can count on me, boss."

Curtis grinned. "I know I can. But one thing I'm gonna need you to do pretty soon is call up Len Anderson. We're gonna need a little more manpower to stay on schedule."

The name made Vinny's stomach turn. Just thinking about calling Len made him uncomfortable all over again. He could feel his palms starting to sweat. It wasn't as bad as seeing him face-to-face, but phone conversation was typically the precursor to an in-person meeting.

"But . . ." Vinny paused, choosing his words carefully. "Since we pulled in so much extra money off that side gig . . . do you think maybe we should invest a little more in the men? Maybe look at some with a little less . . . baggage?"

Curtis scoffed, waving the idea off. "Ah, baggage-smag-gage. What does the quality of a guy swinging a sledgeham-mer or pouring concrete matter? You don't build an empire by blowing profits."

"But, morally . . . I mean, all those guys that Len houses are released sex offenders . . . you don't find that a little strange?"

"Maybe . . ."

Curtis seemed to be listening. If Vinny was going to be able to sway him, now would be the time to make his argument.

"I looked up the rap sheets on some of those guys—guys working shifts for us right now—and it's ugly. I'm not sure what you imagine it to be, but it's not whistling and catcalls. Some of it involves kids . . ."

An image flickered in Vinny's mind. A pair of small hands holding a pornographic magazine opened to a beau-tiful woman. There was an overlaid image that covered the model's face and upper body: a gory, toothless grimace. Her underwear was pulled partially off while her arm reached around her backside, fist being swallowed by her vagina.

Vinny shook his head, trying to get the image out of his brain. He could feel his hair growing moist with sweat as the eyes of the stunning blonde sitting at the table beside them fell on him.

As their stares connected, Vinny noticed her mouth was no longer politely chewing. The woman's face was now rag-ged and scabby. A disgusting white mush rained down from her crusty mouth, her eyes glossing over, as if begging and pleading with him.

"Listen," Curtis said, "with all due respect, let me handle the financial side of things."

Curtis' words snapped Vinny out of his strange trance. The woman was suddenly stunning again. As he turned his attention back to his boss, he already didn't like where the conversation was heading.

"You hire from the pool I tell you to hire from." Curtis cut into his steak. "I can't go bleeding out money because I'm hiring men who made mistakes."

"Mistakes? I think that's more than just a mis—"

"So, what? Should we just execute 'em? Do they never deserve another opportunity in life?"

"I'm not saying that. All I'm saying is, I'm not sure we should be the ones giving them a break."

"Then who's gonna? It's not like I'm running a goddamn middle school here. This is the construction business. It's just a bunch of men. How much trouble can they even get into here?"

Vinny clenched his steak knife tight, trying to control his emotions.

"But this job might give them the means to get into some trouble," Vinny said. "Do you want to be responsible for funding that when you can find good, deserving men elsewhere?"

Curtis put the bite of meat in his mouth and chewed on Vinny's question and the steak all at once. He swallowed, took a drink, and cleared his throat.

"Why you got such a hard-on for this, Vinny?"

Vinny looked down at his plate and didn't say a word. It wasn't anything he could talk about with Curtis—it wasn't anything he could talk about with anyone.

"If I didn't know better, I'd say it's something personal. You're getting emotional. People only tend to get emotional when it's personal to 'em."

"No . . . it's nothing like that," Vinny lied.

"Well, if you're just gonna continue to fight me on cost-cutting measures, then maybe I had the wrong idea about you. Maybe I need to reevaluate my—"

"It was just a thought," Vinny interrupted. "I'm happy to call Len first thing and get some more men onboarded. I was only wanting to make sure that you looked at all your options before making a decision, that's all."

"Well, I appreciate that," Curtis said. "But I don't want these conversations to turn into arguments. Emotions and business don't mix."

"Understood, boss."

Vinny was trying his best to not seem overly invested. The idea of damaging his image in Curtis' eyes caused a bit of angst to swell inside him.

"I would hate for you to think I'm not the guy over that," Vinny said. "If something needs to get done, you know I'll be the one to do it."

As he watched Curtis grin and go back to carving his steak, a sense of relief overcame Vinny.

"I know," Curtis said. "Don't worry, Vinny. I know."

FROG IN YOUR THROAT

When Vinny got home, the girls were both relaxing in the living room. The volume of the television was cranked enough that they hadn't heard him come inside. Through the kitchen doorway, in the shadows, he admired his wife and daughter.

You're one lucky son-of-a-bitch, Vinny thought.

Ashley was every bit as smart, sweet, and innocent as her mother. Somehow those aspects and all the other things that had attracted Vinny to his wife in the first place were a part of what made his daughter special.

Glad she got her mother's genes . . .

Kelly pointed at the television screen and chuckled. "Did you know that's how I met your daddy?"

Watching the scene in the movie unfold, Vinny saw a car broken down on the side of the road. A frustrated woman checked her tire and then kicked it several times upon realizing that she had a flat.

The bursts of images instantly lit up in Vinny's mind: a dusty road; a beautiful girl; a nail stabbing through rubber.

Don't go too far down that road . . . He shook his head. *You might not come back.*

"Really?" Ashley asked.

Vinny locked on to Kelly. She was more than just his support—she was his strength. The steady reassurance he'd longed for his entire life until he'd randomly found her stranded on the side of the road that fateful day. The day that Vinny had helped Kelly avoid—unbeknownst to her—certain doom. But ever since that moment, it was the other way around. Kelly hadn't just kept him on track; she'd been his savior.

"I wouldn't lie to you," Kelly said. "I was on a trip and your daddy was going to visit his fath—"

"I think you both have watched enough TV," Vinny said. Stepping forward, he looked down and grinned at Ashley and his wife.

"Daddy!" Ashley squealed.

"Honeybun!" Vinny leaned down and gave her a big smooch. "Maybe it's time for a bedtime story right now, what do you say?"

"Yay! Yay!" Ashley cheered.

"All right, all right." Vinny laughed. "Go in your room and pick one out, and I'll be right in."

Ashley rose from the couch and bolted through the door. "Hurry, please!"

It was obvious by the smirk on Kelly's face that she loved seeing how much their child adored her daddy. But she wasn't beyond poking a little fun either.

"Geesh, did you see that? Not even a goodnight," she said. "What am I, chopped liver?"

"She's just excited," Vinny said.

"I know, I know, I'm just teasing." She stood up from the couch and threw her arms around him. When she pulled him close it felt like an angel was cradling him. "But can I tell you what's *not* a tease?"

"Please do."

She planted her lips on his, slipping her tongue against Vinny's while pressing her breasts against his chest.

"*That's* not. I'm going to take a quick shower. Be ready for me after story time . . ."

41

Vinny's heart started to race—she knew how to get him riled up. "I was born ready."

Winking at him, she disappeared into their bedroom.

Vinny found himself walking into his daughter's room more eagerly than anticipated. But when he rounded the corner, he froze. He'd never seen the book Ashley held while sprawled out on her bed so gleefully.

Frog and Toad Are Friends was fanned open in front of her face. Vinny's eyes widened as they zeroed in on the kind-looking cartoon rendition of the frog on the cover. His jaw loosened and he felt his heart sink.

Not that road . . .

"Daddy, what's wrong?"

"Oh, nothing, Honeybun. Is that a new book?"

"Yeah, Mommy just got it for me today."

Just move past it.

Vinny nodded and willed himself forward. "Okay, then. You ready to hear it?"

"Yes, please."

Vinny sat down on the bed beside her and pulled the covers over Ashley's legs. Taking the book from her, he started to read. He was grateful that Ashley seemed to be enjoying the story, but as he stared at the illustration of the sweet frog and the pond, he couldn't help but think back.

1965

DIAMOND HILL

"Gimme a chocolate frappé with extra malt, and two scoops of pineapple orange in a waffle cone," Dennis Fowler said.

"Coming right up," the cashier replied.

When Vinny's dad turned and handed him the cone, he couldn't have been more excited. Any six-year-old getting their favorite ice cream would be happy. And on a day when the weather was perfect, how could he complain? The sun was just warm enough to get the ice cream melting to where he had to lick it fast to avoid getting a sticky hand.

"Let's go," Dennis said, waving Vinny over.

They crossed the street into the surprisingly empty park. It was named Diamond Hill on account of the rocks that could be harvested from the massive stones that surrounded the area. It was mostly just quartz crystal by then, but the fancy name fit the grounds better.

Vinny and his dad walked in silence for some time. Long enough to climb the hill and finish their ice cream before they made their way back down. Through the clearing they trotted past some trees up to a small, secluded pond.

There was no choice but to stop, Vinny was so excited when he saw it. The frog was maybe the size of a strawberry and resting calmly on the rock near the water bank.

Having watched his father catch frogs on several occasions before, Vinny already knew he had to keep his voice down. Turning, he signaled his dad.

"Dad," he whispered, pointing to the frog.

Dennis had his back to him and remained motionless.

"Dad . . . ?"

When Dennis finally twisted his body around, Vinny saw the smirk. The unsettling expression was forever burned in his head along with the plum-size stone in his hand.

As Dennis brushed past Vinny and got close to the frog, the creature didn't flinch. Extending his arm outward, he held the small rock directly over the frog.

In the moment, Vinny wanted to cry out. To tell his father not to do what he believed he was about to. That frogs were nice creatures and wouldn't ever hurt either of them. But no words came out. Instead, he just watched.

The result wasn't overly violent. The stone, slightly bigger than the frog, dropped at freefall speed and smacked it on the head. The blow was strong enough to knock the frog either dead or unconscious. When Vinny watched it splash belly-up into the pond, a strange hollowness filled his gut.

He wasn't quite angry or sad, just confused. And the confusion only grew when he turned away from the dead frog and saw his father pull another rock from his pocket.

A crooked grin manifested across Dennis' face. "Now it's your turn."

Vinny looked at him, unsure exactly how to proceed.

"Go on, take it," Dennis whispered.

Putting his short fingers around the stone, Vinny felt the coarseness and weight.

His father got down on one knee and pointed to a frog on another rock a short distance away.

"Just go up to him slow, you don't wanna scare him."

Vinny didn't want to do it. It was one thing to watch his father do something, but completely different to partake in the act himself. But the feeling—and fear—that came along with disappointing his dad was what pushed him forward.

Like his father, Vinny palmed the stone tight, slowly stretching his arm until it was positioned over the frog's green skin.

Dennis licked his lips. "That's it . . . now just—"

"Hey, what are you doing?" a feminine voice asked.

They both turned around to face a woman with curly hair and glasses.

Looking up at his father, Vinny took in a familiar sight. His father's gawk fueled by hate as his face transitioned to a deeper shade of red. He didn't say a word, just kept his eyes fixed on her.

Vinny turned back to the woman, seeing the look of disgust on her face. He'd known something about what he and his father had been up to didn't quite feel right, but only then could those instincts be validated.

Shaking her head, the woman's eyes darted from the frog to the stone in Vinny's hand, back to Dennis' face. "He's . . . he's just a kid, why would you have him—"

"And this is just a park," Dennis interrupted. "A park without a lot of people inside it."

The woman seemed confused by the response. "What does that have to do with anything?"

Balling his hands into tight fists, Dennis continued to glare at the woman.

"Be smart," Dennis explained. "Sticking your nose where it doesn't belong might get it cut right off that ugly face of yours."

Her jaw dropped, the threat—and shock bleeding into her system as a result of it—instantly resonated.

Dennis stared at the woman, a tiny curve of pleasure starting to crimp the corner of his mouth as he carefully looked her up and down.

Something about his words and expression seemed to alter the woman's posture. Vinny had never seen his father do anything violent, but the confidence and coldness he spoke to the woman with convinced Vinny that his father was capable of delivering on his vow.

Taking several steps backward, the woman turned back up the trail, walking briskly in the opposite direction and never looking back.

Dennis turned his focus back to his son and let out a deep sigh. "These fuckin' bitches will never get it. Walkin' around all high and mighty, thinkin' they can just snap their fingers and the world'll change for 'em."

A nervousness blossomed in Vinny's gut. He could hear the tone of his father's voice morphing into a deeper, more sadistic timbre. But all Vinny could do was hope he wouldn't somehow be blamed for the random interaction.

"Fuckin' cunts." Dennis looked at his reflection in the pond water. "They're all the same . . . all of 'em."

Vinny anxiously chewed his lip as his father turned away from the pond and glanced back at him.

"But that's why your dad's here. I'll show you exactly what I mean—not just yet, but soon. I'm gonna make sure you're raised without blinders. Make sure you don't get fed lies your entire life. Just because everyone else in this miserable world thinks like a bunch of goddamn loons doesn't make it gospel. Ain't that right?"

Vinny nodded.

Dennis went down to one knee, placed his hand on his son's shoulder, and forced a smile. He pointed back at the frog that remained relaxing on the stone.

"Now, go on and make your daddy proud."

THEY'RE ALL THE SAME

It was a day of firsts.

Dennis had always been a bit off his rocker, but after watching the frog get stunned and slowly drown in the water, Vinny was glad to be home. Still, the thought of that woman happening upon them and his hand gripping the rough stone afterward would be forever engraved in his brain. He wondered what the frog felt when the rock came crashing down over its little head.

"Have a seat." Dennis pointed to the couch, then immediately picked up the bottle of whiskey and poured himself a drink in a dirty glass. He took a sizable swig and exhaled, as if the mere taste of the alcohol gave him relief. "I've got something I need to show you."

When Vinny sat down, his dad disappeared into the other room. Seeing his father drink was nothing abnormal, but it did instantly heighten his senses. Whenever his old man hit the bottle—which was most of the time—it added a certain unpredictability to the air. But on the other side of that coin, there was also quite a bit that was predictable. His temper would shorten, and his anger would boil. Vinny always had to prepare himself, knowing the woes of the world would be discussed in detail.

He expected to be "educated," that his neck would ache at the end of the night from nodding so much. That would accompany the ache in his head. The nagging echo that he couldn't seem to shake since Diamond Hill. The sound of laughter reverberated—not just his father's, but his own.

As the second little frog had submerged even deeper into the pond, they'd both cackled like hyenas. Dad didn't laugh a whole lot, so when he did—whether it was funny or not—Vinny always found himself doing the same. He wasn't even really sure if he knew what *funny* meant, and oftentimes he didn't know why they were laughing. But it felt so good to share a moment with his father.

Being left to his own devices in the house pretty regularly, when his father did show him attention, Vinny would tend to bask in it. But the attention as of late was different.

It was . . . darker.

From his expression, to the things he said, to his general aura, it was like his father had permanently turned the lights off. It frightened Vinny and he didn't even know why.

Turning his head, Vinny glanced out the window. The old box truck his father used to drive remained parked in the overgrown vegetation. Recently, on more than one occasion, he'd seen him stagger out into the darkness in the dead of night and disappear inside the truck for hours at a time. And while Vinny was often grateful for some distance between them, there wasn't a night that went by when he didn't wonder what his dad was doing in there.

His father returned holding a small cardboard box and sat down on the couch beside him. Dennis reached inside the box. His hand emerged with a magazine—the cover of which showed a photograph of a scantily clad woman.

"Now these aren't easy to come by," Dennis explained. "Do you know why that is?"

Vinny shook his head.

Opening the page, Dennis pointed to the crusty picture of a busty woman dressed professionally in an office. Her pose was different than any woman he'd ever seen.

"It's because they don't want you to know the truth," Dennis said. "Look at her, for example. This lady looks normal enough, doesn't she?"

His father was now so close that Vinny could smell the whiskey on his breath. Locking eyes with his dad, he nodded.

"That's 'cuz that's what she *wants* you to think." Dennis turned the page to reveal the same woman, now lying spread-eagle on the desk—her fingers toying with her overgrown bush. "But don't be fooled . . . she's just like the rest of 'em. A fuckin' whore."

Before flipping to another page, Dennis swallowed the rest of his drink and set the glass on the TV stand.

When they returned to the magazine, Vinny saw a second lady dressed like a dirty firefighter. Several pages later, she was inserting the metal tip of the firehose deep into her anus, grimacing in a mixture of agony and elation.

"They'll fuck you and leave you . . ."

The hate in his father's voice made Vinny tremble.

"Same as your mother. Same as *my* mother . . ."

A moment of dead silence lingered as Dennis stared at the page indolently. It was like he was somewhere else but still frozen in time, holding on to the weathered magazine. Finally, he snapped out of the trance.

"Have a look for yourself," he said, handing Vinny the book.

As Dennis filled up the glass again, Vinny pried the pages apart. An odd excitement started to tingle in his body—one that he'd never felt before. As strange as the sensation was, he liked it. His eyes and mind were already eager for more. While much of the pornography was redundant—just different women posing sexually in a variety of outfits—when he got closer to the back of the magazine, something caught him off guard.

He only saw it for a second before his father snatched the book out of his hands. The gnarly, superimposed image appeared sloppily laid over the magazine model's face and upper body.

The blood and wide gashes on the woman's face were a deep red, and the horrified look on her toothless face would live with Vinny forever. The ropes wound tight around her body revealed some of her skin, but not all.

The lower half of the girl's body was almost bare, and her backside faced Vinny. Pulling her underwear to the side, the model had inserted nearly her entire fist into her vagina.

Vinny's heart burned and raced all at once.

As the magazine was torn out of his hands, he looked at his father for an explanation. Even he didn't quite seem to know how to explain himself.

"I didn't realize that was in there," Dennis whispered.

Vinny remained quiet, focused on his father.

"There's always going to be things that . . . things that you're not quite ready for. Not yet, anyway. But that doesn't mean there won't come a day when you are."

Unsure how to feel about what his father was saying, Vinny just nodded obediently.

"But until that day comes . . ." Dennis reached into the cardboard box, this time flipping through the entirety of another magazine and thoroughly inspecting its pages. "You can look at this one."

He tossed the magazine on Vinny's lap.

Immediately picking it up, Vinny opened it. But just as soon as he cracked the pages, his father's hand squeezed tightly around his wrist. When they locked eyes, his father's gaze was so serious it felt like it was drilling a hole into his brain and controlling it. Vinny hoped he hadn't done anything wrong.

"Just remember what I said though," Dennis whispered.

This time, Vinny knew his father wanted him to finally speak and prove what he'd learned. "They're all the same."

1996

YOU LOOK HORRIBLE

By the time the story was finished, Ashley was sound asleep, and Vinny was wide awake. The rabbit hole was deep— deeper than he liked to admit—and once he went down, there was a good chance he wouldn't be back again soon.

Slipping out of bed, Vinny made sure Ashley was covered. He turned off the lamp and looked at her. The idea of showing and telling her the kind of things his own father had seemed beyond insane.

She deserves so much better, he thought. *And she'll get better.*

Looking down at the book, Vinny shook his head. Approaching the bookshelf, he moved beside it and slid the paperback behind it. He didn't have the heart to throw out the new book she'd just gotten, but at the same time, it was best for everyone if he didn't think about such things again.

Vinny tiptoed out of her room and quietly closed the door. When he reached the bedroom, the lights were already dimmed. Facing his wife, the sight of her asleep in her see-through negligee excited him. But it excited him in a way he didn't like to admit.

She looks . . . dead . . .

As he took his pants off, he had to maneuver his stiff cock out of the way.

It's wrong. Don't think like that.

Stripped down to his boxers, Vinny slipped into bed and jostled her. The sooner he woke her up, the sooner he could try and derail his dark fantasy. He'd been trying to rewire his brain for many years, but he knew from experience, once the foundation's set, it takes a lot of swings to even put a crack in it.

"Mmm . . . hey, baby," Kelly whispered seductively. As she opened her eyes, she toyed with his erection. She kissed him deeply and started to jerk him harder. "Fuck . . . don't make me wait . . ."

Vinny knew what that meant. He put his hand between her legs, forcing them open before rubbing her pussy. When he entered her, she wasn't quite wet, and because of his size, there were a few moments of resistance.

No, don't.

No matter how much he wanted to, there was no way for Vinny to control himself—not after what he'd just re-lived in Ashley's room. The darkness was rooted deep inside him. His imagination was starting to run wild.

After being presented with such a tight pussy, the idea entered his mind that a hole so tight could only belong to a dead person. The stiffness of the *rigor mortis* period came to mind, and he imagined the bed he fucked his wife on to be a steel examination table.

As he studied the subtle pleasure on Kelly's face, he re-membered one of the darker, more private reasons why he'd been drawn to her. A reason he'd never be able to admit to her, or anyone else.

She was a dead fuck.

The way she lay there so lifelessly, making him do all the work . . . it couldn't have been hotter. But despite the ex-treme pleasure he reaped from the sinister delusion, Vinny knew it wasn't healthy. While imagining his wife was dead turned him on, it also made him sad. It was a bizarre clash of emotions—a sort of tug-of-war between his decency and deviancy. And the dark side had been winning as of late.

After pounding on her limp body, he started to use the moonlight pouring in from the window. The bluish hue cast on her face made her look even more like a cold corpse on a mortician's table. But it wasn't just imagining her body was dead that really got Vinny worked up; it was imagining that her corpse had been desecrated.

Stop it. She's . . . she's your wife!

In an effort to stop thinking about the dead version of his wife, he decided to switch positions. Wiping the sweat from his brow, Vinny rolled her onto her stomach. Kelly didn't help him much, though, and the idea of lifting her dead weight only made his cock harder.

Looking at her back instead of her face would help him focus more. As his hips smacked against her ass cheeks, he could feel his cock throbbing. But when he glanced down, he didn't see Kelly's backside. He saw the thick, gaping slices that showed some of her ribs. As the blood oozed out, he could see one of her lungs deflating with what he imagined to be her final breath.

Damnit!

While internally he chastised himself, on the outside he continued to dance with the devil. Instead of slowing, trying to concentrate and move on from the delusion, he fucked her even harder.

ORDINARY SUFFERING

"It still feels unreal," Sara St. James said, crossing her legs in the opposite direction. "Even after all this time."

Fidgeting was normal whenever she was seated in the therapist's office. It didn't really happen at work or in the real world though. She'd found a way to galvanize her shell and not be so vulnerable when she needed to. But in front of Dr. Amber Marrow, she found the strength to peel back all those layers.

"I think that's normal," Dr. Marrow said, jotting down a few quick scribbles on her pad. "Especially with back-to-back anniversaries just passing. The reality is that it might never feel real to you. Maybe that might even be a good thing. Such profound pain and distress shouldn't ever be normalized. I actually might be more concerned if you told me otherwise."

Sara nodded. "But it's just . . . I mean . . . where do I even go from here?"

"I don't think you have to go anywhere."

"That sounds kinda boring."

"Well, boredom is a lot better than despair, wouldn't you agree?"

Sara nodded.

"Let's think of it this way," Dr. Marrow said. "You haven't had any thoughts of self-harm in years. At least you can hang your hat on that."

"True, but . . ."

Dr. Marrow furrowed her brow, clearly concerned. "Wait, is there something you haven't told me?"

"No, no, that's not what I mean. I guess . . . what I'm trying to say is, if I'm walking around like a zombie all the time, still so lost in the—in everything . . . I mean, what kind of guy is going to be interested in someone like that?"

"Oh," Dr. Marrow said. "Now I see."

Sara sighed. "Yeah."

"There's nothing to be frustrated about. Think about when you first came in here."

The doctor let a moment lapse before continuing, allowing Sara to recall those trying times. She had been a total mess. The sleepless nights, the constant crying, her bottomless depression. The stark recollection of that horrible period made her a bit grateful again.

"You sat in that very chair, telling me how it was impossible to be where you are right now. How you'd given up on every aspect of your life. That version of you I met—that Sara would've *killed* to be where you are right now."

Sara fiddled with her sleeve, embarrassed by the scar peeking out.

Dr. Marrow, noticing this, glanced down. "That's nothing to be ashamed of. If anything, you should be proud. It shows that you're a survivor. That even in your darkest hour, you were able to push through. I only dig all this up to show you that if dating's the thing you're most worried about, that should be a gold-medal victory for you."

Letting out a tiny smile, Sara nervously let her fingertips trace over the scarring.

"You're right," she said. "I guess when it happens—and when I'm ready—I'll know. But I just wonder . . ."

"It's okay to wonder." Dr. Marrow took more notes. "You can tell me whenever you feel like you're ready."

Sara gestured to herself. "I just wonder if this'll all be too much for him to handle."

"Your life was—and is—far from perfect, Sara, but without sharing any details, let me just reassure you that I've seen much, *much* worse. No one's perfect. Any person that you find is going to have their own warts and skeletons. I think that's a bridge that you and I can cross together when we get there. But until then, I'd hate to see you stress about it."

"You're right."

Dr. Marrow grinned. "That's why you pay me all that money."

Sara chuckled.

After a quick glance at the clock, Dr. Marrow put a final scribble in the notepad. "It looks like we're at time."

"Okay, I guess I'll see you next w—oh, wait. I forgot to ask you last time. I need a prescription for a refill on my sleeping pills."

"But I thought you weren't having issues sleeping any longer . . . ?"

"I'm not, but should I go into some kind of spiral, I'd like to have something to fall back on. Just as a precaution."

The doctor looked at her disapprovingly.

"C'mon, it's just sleeping pills," Sara reassured her. "You know with my job I can't afford to miss a night of sleep. People are depending on me."

"But if you were to take enough of those sleeping pills at once, that could be the tipping point for tragedy."

"Who's the shrink here? You and I both agree that outside of these anniversaries, I'm probably feeling the best I ever have. And now you're just gonna put an idea like that out in the universe?"

"You're right, I'm sorry. I'm clearly overthinking it." Dr. Marrow pulled another pad from her drawer and filled out the paper. "I believe in you, Sara. And I trust you."

As she pushed the prescription forward, Sara smiled and took the paper.

I'm glad someone does, Sara thought.

62

SERENDIPITY

It had just turned dark by the time Sara pulled into the pharmacy parking lot. Noticing her name tag was crooked, she adjusted it in the mirror until it sat horizontally over her nurse uniform. She looked at the prescription slip beside her purse on the passenger seat, contemplating her earlier meeting with Dr. Marrow.

Maybe she's right, Sara thought. *Maybe I don't even need it.*

Her eyes darted to the dashboard, where the old picture of Eric, Michael, and herself was fixed. Taking a deep breath, she picked up the slip and her purse, then opened her car door.

Better safe than sorry.

When she entered the pharmacy, she made her way to the back. She was surprised to see that there was no pharmacist behind the counter.

"Hello?" Sara said.

"Oh, she had to use the bathroom," a male voice said.

Sara turned and saw a man step from one of the side aisles holding a pack of Oreo cookies and a single flower. The man sent a kind smile and nod her way. He was handsome, with a well-groomed beard. There was something about the way he spoke that made her feel relaxed.

"I'm waiting on her too," he added.

"Okay, thanks," Sara replied.

As he approached, the man noticed her nurse uniform and gestured ahead.

"But if you've gotta get to work, you're more than welcome to go first," he said. "Your job's a heck of a lot more important than mine."

"That's very kind of you," she said, smiling. "But actually, I've got a long drive ahead of me tonight. I'm a traveling nurse, so I've gotta head up to Lakeland."

"Holy smokes, you aren't kidding. I love that area. I'm actually heading up that way to Capron Pond for my daughter's birthday this weekend."

"Huh, small world," Sara said.

The man shrugged. "Well, I guess when you're in the smallest state, that's just how it shakes out."

Speaking with the man was just the kind of comforting interaction she'd been missing. He was so easy to talk to, and it was hard to ignore his handsomeness. But as her eyes drifted to the rose again, she saw the wedding band on his finger.

Of course, the one time you meet someone interesting in the wild, he's married.

"Gotta do the right thing for her." Noticing Sara focusing on the rose, he raised it. "Happy wife, happy life."

"Smart man," she said.

"Lucky man, actually." He sighed. "Without her, I don't know where I'd be. I hate that she's stuck on this medication, so when I pick it up, I try to get her a little something to go along with it."

Ugh, why does he have to be so damn perfect?

Almost annoyed by the man's charm, Sara nodded. "That's really sweet of you."

The way he acted reminded her of how Michael had treated her when they'd first met, and how they'd carried on for many years after. He'd work all day on the farm, and no matter how tired he was, he'd always want to rub her back and feet.

Sara knew it should've been her offering to do that for him, but he'd never allow it. During the time Michael was with her, she'd always felt special. Now, she would've given anything to look out the kitchen window at sunset and see him riding that tractor toward the house again.

The large wheel of the tractor flashed in her mind, followed by the same moving tire covered in gore.

"I can take whoever's next," a woman's voice said.

Shaking off the gruesome image, forcing it out of her mind, Sara turned to the counter, where the pharmacist stared back at her.

"Please, go ahead," the man said.

"Oh, it's okay," Sara replied. "You were here first."

The man nodded. "All right, thank you."

She watched as the man picked up his prescription and paid for it. When he was done, he turned around and smiled.

"It certainly was nice to meet you . . ." He squinted at her badge. "Mrs. St. James."

"*Miss* St. James, actually," she corrected.

Sara blushed, immediately realizing the line sounded a bit forward after she heard it come out of her mouth. Despite her undeniable attraction to him, she in no way wanted to seem like she was coming on to a married man.

God, you're such an idiot.

"Not that it matters, I guess," she added, doing her best to amend the awkwardness with a small laugh. "But you can just call me Sara. And, I'm sorry, but I don't think I caught your name."

"I'm Vinny," he said. "Well . . . good luck with your drive. Maybe I'll see you around."

"Maybe," Sara said with a grin as she watched him head for the exit.

I can only hope.

THE NIGHT SHIFT

"Easy, kid! Working the spike is like fuckin'," Vinny yelled over the heavy pounding of the jackhammer. "You can't just stick it in her ass right away." He tapped Tyler on the back, then, holding up his glove, he gestured for him to pause.

"Sorry, am I messin' it up again?" Tyler asked once the deafening drilling sound had died off.

The area the men stood in looked like a bomb had gone off. The demo team had already finished bringing down the previous structure, and so far the build was in motion and going to Curtis' plan. But there was an abundance of deteriorating concrete that still needed to be replaced.

"You're doing okay," Vinny reassured him. "You just gotta have a little finesse. The handle needs to be leaned in *toward* you. If you keep holding it straight down like that, your tip is either gonna get stuck or break off."

Tyler nodded nervously. "Got it, boss." He angled the jackhammer and looked down at the white and red branding sticker that read KING'S CONSTRUCTION.

Vinny could see how green Tyler was the moment he'd stepped into his office, but he still liked the kid. There was a drive inside Tyler that he respected. He was polite—a rarity in their business—and willing to learn. The latter was all

Vinny asked of his guys.

To Vinny's surprise, Curtis had actually allowed him to hire someone outside of Len's halfway house. Apparently, after much thought, Curtis had reconsidered their dinner discussion and decided to give Vinny a chance to prove himself in a more administrative sense.

But with Tyler not really seeming to acclimate as quickly as Vinny hoped, it left him something to worry about.

Hopefully he's not the reason I never get to hire men outside of Len's pool again, he thought.

Vinny slapped him on the shoulder, stirring a cloud of dust and dirt. "Hey, relax. This is your first time on the hammer. I'm not gonna break your balls too bad. Just remember what I said. Otherwise, you'll be out here all night and into the morning. These corporate cocksuckers have us on a stiff deadline."

"I'll definitely get it done right," Tyler said.

Vinny nodded. "That's what I like to hear."

"Well, that's not what I like to *see*," a gruff voice said from behind them.

Vinny turned around to face Curtis King.

Curtis pointed to the metal skeleton of the building that had been partially erected already. "We've got exactly five months to get this thing off the ground. I can't have a retard that doesn't know how to work a jackhammer slowing my operation down."

Tyler's jaw slacked. "But it's my first—"

"Hit the bricks," Curtis said, shooing him off the site.

Vinny's eyes scrunched with concern. "Hold on—Curt—he's just a little green. I can work with him, I promise. I'll have him up to speed in no time."

"You wanna go with him?!" Curtis yelled. He looked back at Tyler. "Now get the fuck out of here or I'll bounce your scrawny ass myself."

Wrinkles of frustration and fear accompanied the look of heartbreak on Tyler's face. It mirrored the expression on Vinny's. He watched Tyler huff, drop the jackhammer, and toss his hard hat as he turned, heading for the gloomy parking lot.

Shaking his head, Vinny glared at Curtis. "I could've trained him."

Curtis scoffed. "Bullshit. He's been here for three god-damn days now. I've seen enough. That kid's a piece of driftwood, and that's all he's ever gonna be. The sooner you open your eyes and stop giving people so much credit, the sooner you'll get to make the big decisions. Potential ain't tangible. You already know we're on a killer schedule, and if we're gonna cash in then we need people who already got this business in their blood."

"Oh, c'mon, you didn't learn all this overnight," Vinny said. "We gotta teach people first, give 'em a chance."

Curtis lit up a cigarette. "I didn't become the *King* of construction because someone gave me a chance. You know as well as I do, they got our fuckin' nuts in a vise grip on this job. We're about a month short on time, and it's a miracle we're somehow on schedule. But that's only because we're going day and night."

Vinny threw his hands up in the air. "Then why fire the fuckin' guy and make more work for us?"

"Because we need pros! People who've done it and know how to do it! Not some soft, pimple-faced nerd that hasn't been laid yet. And I'm afraid it's not more work for *us*, it's more work for *you*. I tried to give your way a shot. I went against my instincts and allowed you to hire a guy that you saw potential in for some reason. But after this little failed experiment, it's Len's guys and Len's guys *only*. Find me someone who's capable this time. Don't disappoint me again."

"All right," Vinny said solemnly.

Part of him wondered if Curtis had just allowed him to pick the guy so he could manifest a failure and shitcan him. Then there would be no more discussion, and the conclusion would feed Curtis' already massive ego.

Vinny looked down at his watch. "I'll start lookin' after the weekend. I've gotta get going. I need to catch at least a few hours of sleep tonight."

"No, you'll be working tonight."

Vinny furrowed his brow. "But I—"

"You're gonna have to be here for a while." Curtis bent over and lifted the jackhammer, handing it to Vinny. "There's no way around it. We're a man short now, and it's gonna have to be your hands that keep us on track."

Vinny shook his head in disbelief. "N-*no*, you already know this weekend is Ashley's birthday. Kelly and I are takin' her up to Capron Pond early tomorrow morning."

Curtis took another deep drag of his smoke. "When are you gonna learn to look at the *big* picture? Everything's about timing, and if you'd wake up and smell the fuckin' Folgers, you'd realize that your time can be now. You do remember our conversation at the steakhouse, right?"

Vinny bit his lip and nodded.

"Well, mark my words, 1997 is *my* year—the Year of the King. It's gonna be when the rocket ship is strapped to my ass and takes off. Now, if you're smart, you'll come along for the ride. Even though you're thickheaded, you're still a damn good supervisor. And I think you'd make an even better manager."

Vinny wanted to interrupt him, but when he started talking about the promotion, his ears perked up. He'd been wondering since their steak dinner if what Curtis had said back in the restaurant was just lip service to keep him motivated. But now he was bringing it up on the job. It made the opportunity feel more realistic.

"But if you want *that* job," Curtis continued, "then you're gonna need to show your worth *before* you go on your little trip. We can't afford to have any more setbacks. This Halpert project needs to be finished on time—no excuses."

"C'mon, Curtis. You know I'm a family-first kinda guy. It's the kid's birthday—"

"Listen, if you really want to put your family first, you'll do everything in your power to get that job. Because I think, oh, I don't know, an extra fifteen, twenty grand each year would probably help your little girl out more than a couple of candles and a cake, don't you?"

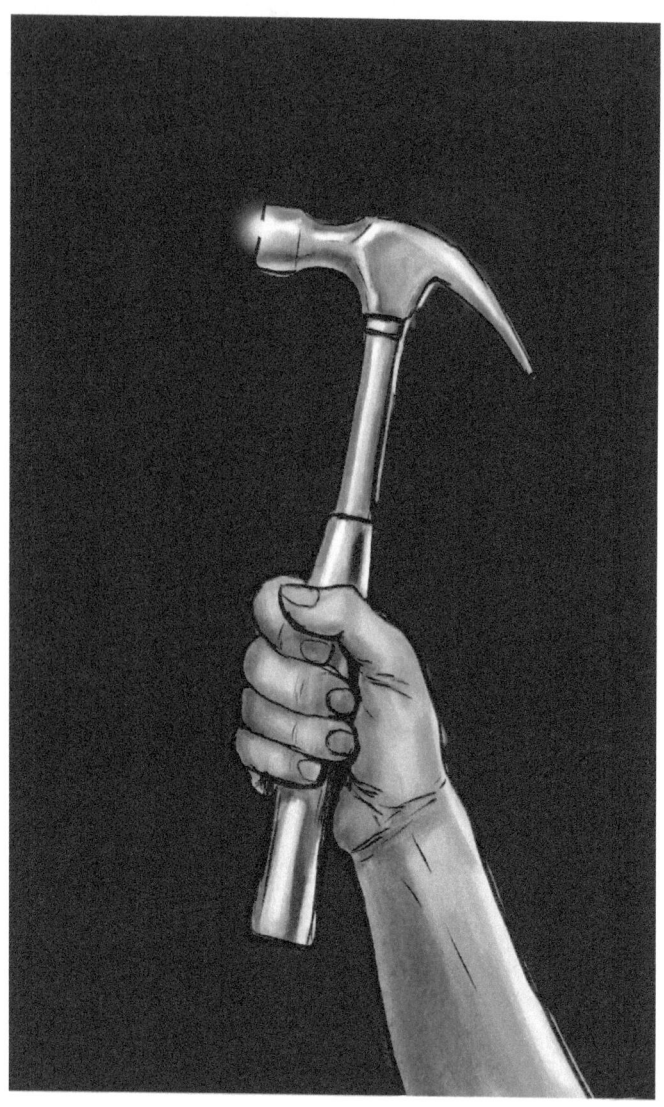

Vinny looked down at his watch again.

"There just ain't enough hours in the day, is there?" Curtis snickered. "Follow me."

Vinny sighed, lingering behind Curtis as he approached his truck. He watched his boss open the door and lift a brown paper bag from behind the seat. He gave it to Vinny.

Vinny squinted at the offering. "The fuck is this?"

"See for yourself."

Vinny stuck his hand into the bag and couldn't believe what he was retrieving. The weight felt magical, and she sparkled like a diamond. The golden hammer was a true show tool—so gaudy and spectacular that it would be difficult to drive a nail with it. He didn't know what to say.

"A little token of my appreciation," Curtis continued. "I know what you're capable of. And now, when everyone else sees that hanging from your toolbelt, they will too."

"You . . . you got me a Madison?" Vinny stammered.

"I'm not blowin' smoke up your ass," Curtis said, taking another big drag from his cigarette. "I want you to run my second team. You're my top guy. All you've gotta do is keep your foot on the gas."

"These cost like—"

"I'm aware of the cost," Curtis interrupted, flicking his cigarette butt into the dirt. "That's a lotta overtime I just handed you, so I'm sure you're gonna crush this concrete, then get on the horn over the weekend and figure out how to replace that fuckstick. Did you talk to Len Anderson about the other men already?"

"Yeah . . ." Vinny paused, feeling an internal shudder at the mention of the creep's name. The gatekeeper of cheap labor wasn't someone he ever wanted to think about. Just recalling their meeting made his skin crawl. "I talked to him in person before our meeting and met some of the guys, and again on the phone after we had dinner. I've got a crew organized. Even found a guy that I think has the potential to lead a little on some of these more compartmentalized gigs you were thinking of expanding on."

"That's good," Curtis said. "Leadership is quality you can never have enough of. What's his name?"

"Who?"

"The guy you said seems like a leader."

"Oh. I think it was Ryan Clemson . . . no, Clements— Ryan Clements. But as far as finding a replacement, Len said he's got more waiting already. I'm sure it'd be easy enough. I'll just have him send one more our way."

Curtis slapped his hand against Vinny's shoulder and grinned. "I knew you'd figure this out."

While Vinny smiled and acted outwardly appreciative, inside he was molested by a deep feeling of shame. He hated having to make deals with scumbags to cut corners. But for his family's sake, that would have to be another secret he kept to himself.

"You can count on me, boss," he said.

Curtis pointed in the direction of the ground that still needed to be demoed. "Then don't just tell me. Get on the hammer and show me."

LONG NIGHT

When the hot water from the showerhead hit Vinny, he could hear the sandman whispering to him. Sleep was a commodity that had been particularly difficult to come by since King's Construction had taken on the Halpert project. Like most phases in life, the build was a sprint. But once they reached the finish line, Vinny was hoping to catch a break.

His palms throbbed, still pestered by the phantom vibrations of the jackhammer. The several extra hours of staring at the computer browser and pulling résumés and conviction highlights from the files Len Anderson had sent him didn't help much either. Vinny had gathered what he considered to be a big enough list to review on the trip before calling Len with a decision.

After setting aside the new files he planned to assess, he went back to one of the older ones. Ryan Clements seemed like the obvious choice. He had an impressive work history, and it also helped that Vinny had already gotten a chance to meet him in person. For a creep, Ryan seemed pretty stable. And after the whole screwup with Tyler, a plug-and-play worker with stability was what he needed.

Can't fuck up two hirings in a row, Vinny thought. *Curtis is only so forgiving.*

Ryan had previously managed a small team of independent contractors for nearly a decade before his career was derailed for several years. The first time Vinny reviewed the file it had made him nauseous. But now, it just made him angry. It wasn't difficult to locate a more detailed article on Ryan's dark history. The nasty incident he'd been involved in that led to his incarceration had been front-page news at the time. Despite the shower's warm water caressing his skin, Vinny felt a chill as he recalled the headline.

LOCAL CONTRACTOR IMPLICATED IN ABUSE OF YOUNG GIRL BUT NOT DEATH.

The details were burned into Vinny's memory. How Ryan had been contracted to build an addition to a newly purchased home for a family several towns over. The article explained how Mark and Laurie Nelson needed more space for their daughter Eden, who was on the cusp of being a teenager. And how Ryan's company promised to make it happen for the middle-class family without breaking the bank.

But he'd broken something else instead.

Over the course of several months, Ryan had become extra friendly with twelve-year-old Eden—so close that she saw it fit to log the abuse he'd inflicted in her diary. She talked about how every time she saw the contractor's van pull up, she panicked. How Ryan had threatened her, saying that if she told anyone about the things he'd done to her, no one would believe her and her entire family would pay dearly for it and it would be all her fault.

In the end, Eden believed the only way out of the sick, abusive situation was to stop Ryan from coming to the house—in other words, to halt the addition to their home. Based on Eden's diary entries, it didn't seem like she was trying to kill herself when she lit the house on fire. She was only trying to burn the addition to the ground. But, sadly, she became part of the ashes.

Sick fuck. What if that was Ashley . . .

Mark and Laurie Nelson survived, and firefighters were able to stop the fire from spreading to the entire house, but Eden was swallowed up by the inferno.

Eden's diary was not able to be entered as evidence in Ryan's trial due to a technicality. The defense noted that there were several fictional stories at the beginning of the diary that included monsters, magic, and dragons, and they further argued that it was impossible to rule out the possibility that the latter parts of Eden's writings—which included the accusations against Ryan—could be fictional literature too.

With only the witness testimony of Eden's parents to go on, Ryan couldn't be convicted. He would go on to be released with time served and have a suspended sentence of five years.

Vinny shook his head, disgusted as he thought about the article, and he washed the soap out of his overgrown beard.

She was just a little older than Ashley. . .

His ire shifted to his boss and how he was okay being around these vile men.

What the fuck is wrong with Curtis?

The sound of the bathroom door opening interrupted his thoughts.

"Vin?" Kelly's sweet voice whispered. "Are you just getting in now?"

"Ah—*nooo*," Vinny lied, "I just wanted to be up early for the trip is all. Oh, and I hit the pharmacy and grabbed your 'script before work last night—the bag is on the table. Along with a little something extra for you."

Kelly slid the shower door open and looked at Vinny. "When are you gonna realize that I can tell when you're lying?"

"Huh?"

She rolled her eyes and exhaled. "Your side of the bed was perfect—not even a ruffle."

Vinny wiped the water off his face and started to rinse his body off. "Okay, you got me. Curtis fired the new guy I hired and made me pick up the slack. He . . . he said he's considering me for manager after the expansion, so I didn't have much of a choice. Guess he's gonna make me kiss his ass before I can get a shot at it. I didn't wanna take away from Ashley's birthday this weekend, so I did my best to get as much done as I could last night."

Kelly smiled at him lovingly.

He grinned. "What?"

"You're lucky that your lies are always so sweet." She moved in and kissed him on his wet, bristly cheek, twirling part of his hair before she whispered in his ear, "I married a good one."

"You married the *best* one," Vinny corrected, turning and planting his lips on hers. She felt soft and heavenly—a texture he never wanted to be separated from. As they drifted apart, his gaze fell upon the modest glimmer of her wedding band. While the sight of the stone would always be a symbol of their love, its size made him uncomfortable.

"Once I get this raise, you and Ashley aren't gonna have to worry about another thing—not ever. And that rock on your finger's gonna multiply times three."

"I was never worried, babe. I love my ring just the way it is. I'm glad you've got an opportunity and all, but that's not the world. *You're* my world. If you get the job, great. Just don't burn yourself out. That's all I care about."

Vinny turned off the faucet and reached for a towel. "That's all well and good, but to me it *is* everything. I don't want to hear any more comments from your parents about the size of your ring." His face crinkled.

"Babe—"

He put his finger up in the air as he continued. "But even more than that, I definitely don't want our daughter having to break her back for decades and claw her way up like I did. I want her to have an education. I wanna get us out of this fleabag city. She deserves better, right?"

Kelly nodded. She couldn't dispute that part, and he knew she felt exactly the same.

"You know who else deserves better?"

Vinny smirked. "Who?"

She reached behind his towel and put her hand on his cock and squeezed. She let out a little moan and kissed his neck before stroking it. As his thickness inflated, she dropped to her knees. But just when she was about to spit on the head, there was a pounding on the door.

"Mommy?" Ashley's groggy voice asked. "Are . . . are you in there?"

Kelly rolled her eyes in annoyance. It was sexy to Vinny when she got frustrated with not being able to have him.

"I've gotta use the toilet," Ashley called out.

Vinny looked down at his wife with sadness in his belly. He shook his head. "And we'll need a big house too. One with *multiple* bathrooms."

THE BLACK BOX

As Vinny finished stuffing the last piece of clothing into his suitcase, the bedroom door opened.

"First of all, thank you for my flower," Kelly said, sounding smitten. "Second, breakfast is ready."

"You're welcome," Vinny said. "I'll be right there."

"One other thing . . . My folks got tickets for us at McCoy Stadium in a few months for the Fourth of July. Haven't been since I was a kid, but it's the *best* fireworks show I've ever seen. I just know Ashley would love it, not to mention seeing her grandma and grandpa again."

The series of words scraped into his brain like the back of a clawhammer being dragged over concrete. Suddenly, Vinny heard the intense explosions of the firecrackers popping off in his head, accompanied by a flashing memory of a marsh. The eerie glow of taillights submerging into the swampy waters and the buzz of blood-thirsty mosquitoes around his ears. The sickness infected his soul, and a hollow feeling rumbled in his heart like he was back there again.

"Vin?"

Snapping out of the vision, Vinny turned his attention back to his wife. "Yeah?"

"You all right?"

"I'm fine, just a little tired. Nothing a few cups of coffee can't fix."

"What do you think about the Fourth?" Kelly bit her lip, almost like she was expecting him to say no.

"Let's just focus on surviving this weekend first."

Vinny instantly noticed his wife's body language. Her shoulders drooped as the excitement deflated out of her. Unable to see her in such a way, he decided to add a caveat to his response.

"But . . . if we get through Ashley's birthday without any issues, then I don't see why not."

Kelly rushed toward him and threw her arms around him, and they kissed. When she pulled away, her eyes stayed fixed on his.

"I just want you—and Ashley—to be happy," he said. "So we can completely move on from everything that happened before."

"That decision you just made is a huge step in the right direction. Now we better eat breakfast and get moving!"

She pecked him once more on the lips.

Smiling, Vinny gently squeezed her hand. "Okay, just give me another minute. I'll be right in."

As the door closed behind her, the beam disappeared from Vinny's face. The last words he'd said still resonated in his mind.

It's hard to move on, Vinny thought.

Another flash of the submerged taillights flickered in his head as he turned to the closet. He opened the door and grabbed an oversized bin buried under several others. Prying the lid open, he sifted through the contents until he felt the cold metal against his fingers. Slowly, he extracted a black metal box that was partially rusted. The tension and anxiety spiked inside him.

Maybe it's finally time.

Reaching into his pocket, he extracted his keyring and located a tiny silver key. He stared at the keyhole, trying to muster the willpower to do what he knew he needed to.

As the grooves of the key sank into the lock and turned, his mind was peppered with more images. The collection of empty whiskey bottles under the workbench, the mechanical growl of the cutting machine activating, the can of oil draining, the steel scraping against enamel as the sounds of choking grew louder.

Twisting the key in the reverse direction, Vinny locked the black box and quickly slipped it back into the bin.

No. It's not time. It'll never be time.

FAMILY FIRST

"You've gotta eat up now," Kelly said as she dropped the scrambled eggs onto Ashley's plate. "We're gonna be on the road a while before we get to the lake, and probably won't stop for lunch until we need gas."

Ashley stuck her tongue out childishly. "Yes, Moth-er," she said in her best robot voice before devouring a piece of bacon like a savage.

"What are you . . . a robot again?" Vinny asked.

Ashley stared at her father, nodding stiffly. "Mr. Graham says that, in a few years, there's gonna be way more robots, and probably, in the future, people might even be part robot."

Vinny shook his head, wrinkling his face in disgust. "Yeah, well, Mr. Graham might be jumpin' the gun on some things. Daddy says that you've got some time before you turn into a cyborg."

Sipping his third cup of coffee, Vinny watched his wife unroll the white paper bag on the table. Her beauty was something that never failed to captivate him. But as Kelly retrieved her medication, the beauty that he so often admired was replaced. Kelly was no longer young and attractive—the perfect skin and glowing eyes that he always got lost in vanished.

The flesh on Kelly's face suddenly glistened with a translucent slime and was blackened by decay. Many of her teeth were rotten or absent, and a pus-like fluid oozed from one of her gum pockets as she tried to pull her cracked lips back. She gagged on the filthy tube stuck deep down her esophagus as an off-white mush got pumped inside her. The flies, maggots, and worms writhing beneath her skin and peppering her destroyed tissue forced her distorted face to move. Her bloodshot eyes pleaded with him.

"Vin?" Kelly asked.

Shaking his head, Vinny forced himself up from his chair and over to the coffeepot. He didn't respond to his wife's question and instead focused his mind on trying to suppress the erection inflating in his pants.

Not now, he thought. *Keep your head on straight. Stop this goddamn madness.*

Catching a glimpse of his reflection in the stainless steel, Vinny could see the puffy bags under his eyes. He widened them, doing his best not to look like a zombie. But as he heard Kelly's footsteps approaching him, more than anything, he hoped she no longer looked like the undead.

Clutching her bottle of gabapentin, the look on her face was one of profound concern.

"Sweetie," Kelly said. "I think I'm just gonna push out my morning dose a few hours so I can drive. You need to get a little sleep. We'll still get there in time to give Ashley her surprise."

"I'm fine," Vinny said.

He dumped a couple spoonfuls of sugar into his cup before finally summoning the courage to peek back at her. He was relieved to see that her face was once again the beautiful version he'd devoted his life to.

Thank God.

Kelly shook her head. "No, I think you're—"

"It's okay. I just need my coffee is all."

"You worked all night and you look exhausted. I'm fine to drive—a couple of hours isn't gonna matter much."

Vinny looked at Ashley—she remained distracted by her breakfast. Returning his gaze to his wife, he lowered his voice. "Babe, when you had that seizure, it was the scariest moment of my life. I don't know what I'd do if I . . ."

The mere thought of Kelly's permanent absence made Vinny emotional. He paused to compose himself.

"Since you've started this new 'script schedule," he continued, "we haven't had an issue. I don't wanna mess with it. Let's just keep your dose on track. I'll be fine, okay?"

Kelly took a moment to reflect. "Okay."

"What are you whispering about?" Ashley asked.

"Umm, nothing really," Vinny replied. "Just some boring grown-up stuff.

They each took their seats at the table and started eating.

Kelly looked at Vinny. "Oh, I forgot to tell you. That, ah, that guy called again."

Vinny squinted. "What guy?"

"Alan—no, Alfred, I think his name was. He said he had another job for you."

"If he only knew I could barely do my first one."

"You do it perfectly," Kelly said with a smile.

"Hmmm."

"What?"

"It's weird," Vinny said, shoveling another forkful of eggs into his mouth.

Kelly furrowed her brow. "He's just offering you work. Is that really so strange?"

"Yeah, is that strange?" Ashley mimicked.

"Well, a few months back, Curtis took a contract to remodel some rooms in this old mansion upstate. It was for this old, ritzy brother and sister."

"Wait, so it wasn't a commercial job?" Kelly asked. "I thought you guys only did commercial work."

"That used to be true, but I guess it was the kind of gig Curtis couldn't refuse. So profitable that it changed his whole philosophy on residentials. A lot of my new responsibilities have been prepping for more of these side projects."

"Interesting," Kelly said.

"You could say that," Vinny said. "This brother and sister are both elderly and have boatloads of money laying around, I guess, because they paid us a pretty penny for what ended up being very little work. But the strange part is, the rooms they wanted redone were perfectly fine in the first place. Better than fine—they were beautiful."

Kelly shook her head. "Ugh, people with money drive me crazy."

"Crazy like the king in *Dragonheart*?" Ashley asked.

"Crazier."

Nodding in agreement, Vinny sipped his coffee. "Yeah, maybe I read them wrong, but they seemed a little on the nutty side to me. The whole time there I got weird vibes. They were always lurking around, and at times it was almost like they were more interested in talking to me and the crew than the actual job we were doing."

"What's 'ritzy' mean?" Ashley asked.

"It means not us," Vinny said.

He grinned as the confusion manifested on his daughter's face. But when he turned back to his wife, his cadence grew serious again.

"Anyway, when we were wrapping things up, the two of them approached me and tried to offer me another gig on the low. So, I told 'em I'm under contract and that if they wanted me to do any kinda work, they'd have to go through King's Construction again."

Kelly shrugged. "And?"

"And the old creep didn't wanna do all that." Vinny took another sip from his mug. "He just wanted me."

"I guess my baby's just that good."

"Maybe. He sure is persistent. How'd he even get our number?"

Kelly raised her eyebrows. "Um, phone book? I guess those rich types just can't handle being told no. It's some kind of ego thing."

"I want a phone book," Ashley said.

Kelly smirked. "We already have one, but you can only see it *after* you finish eating." She returned her attention to Vinny. "What is it?"

"I don't know, exactly. There was just something off about those two. What brother and sister do you know that live together in their sixties?"

Ashley finished the last bite of food on her plate.

"I don't know," Kelly said. "But I think that's a question for the car ride." She winked at him. "We need to get moving if we're gonna stay on schedule."

SUPREME SIN

Blanche sat on the couch staring at her brother as he positioned the dried lump of excrement in the center of the symbol. The charcoal circle was outlined in chalk, as was the etching of the tuning fork overlaid atop it. Holding the phone to her ear, she listened intently to each ring, until they were interrupted by a female voice.

"You've reached the Fowlers," she said. "Sorry we can't come to the phone right now, but—"

Slamming the phone in annoyance, Blanche shook her head and sighed.

"Still no answer?" Alfred asked.

She shook her head.

"Well . . ." He looked at the arcane insignia on the floor. "This is the only way, then."

"But suppose something goes wrong. Then what?"

"Damnit, Blanche!" Alfred jumped to his feet. "You know as well as I do, we don't have any more time to waste! Not that it even matters, because my decision is final, but we agreed on this before already. Whether you believe it or not, the time is now."

Blanche clenched her jaw. There were so many things she wanted to say to him, but she restrained herself.

"Keep calm . . . We agreed on other things before too," she growled, thinking back to the pact they'd made when they were children. "Like governing ourselves as equals . . . but thing's change, don't they?"

"That promise came before we read Oswald's journal in its entirety," Alfred said. "There can only be one and you know as well as I do . . . I'm the one."

Blanche picked up on the anger, malice, and frustration in her brother's eyes and decided not to press him.

"And I'm not getting any younger." Alfred scratched the side of his face in frustration, not realizing some of the fecal matter rubbed off on his cheek. "It's an embarrassment that it's taken me this long. I need to finish this."

Blanche glared at him, shaking her head. She could hear the animalistic growls and rattles of the cage coming from outside of the study.

"An embarrassment to whom?" she asked.

"Uncle Rooney, for one," Alfred said.

A chuckle escaped her.

Alfred furrowed his brow. "What's so funny?"

"You murdered the man, yet you still seek his blessing?"

"This ridiculous society would have you believe that killing is the worst thing, but it's not. Killing *in vain* is the worst thing."

Blanche rolled her eyes.

Alfred turned and looked down at the feces within the symbol and sighed. "If I don't finish this, Uncle Rooney's demise will be for naught." He turned back to his sister. "Don't you still want this as bad as I do?"

"Of course I do. Don't be foolish." Blanche shook her head dejectedly, perturbed that he would suggest otherwise and wishing he could understand her position. "For you to even ask such a question . . . it can only be motivated by insult or ignorance."

"Well, sometimes the way you act begs to differ . . ."

"What do you mean? I've been here every step of the way. Don't forget, *I* was the one who found Willis."

"Will there ever be a day that you don't throw that in my face? Who acquired our wealth and this property? Who sniffed out our most recent candidate? Furthermore, who had the stones to dethrone Uncle Rooney and capture the metronome and Hitchens' journal?"

"Brother, I'm not trying to argue with you." Blanche bit her lip for a moment. "I love you. I live only to generate the gateway to what we *both* have always desired."

Alfred still had an aura of angst about him. The tension in his body kept him rigid.

"We've survived the Great Depression," he said, "we've scraped and clawed our way to fortune, and most importantly, we've captured opportunity. Yet, despite our countless accomplishments, death still stalks us. He inches closer with each day that passes, eager to eradicate everything we've worked for."

"All the more reason we need to be cautious," Blanche said. "If we bungle this opportunity, then who knows if we'll even get another chance? This might be it."

Alfred scoffed. "What good's a chance if you don't take it?"

Blanche didn't have an answer.

"I'm opening Herman's cage," Alfred said.

"You never listen to anything I say!" She smashed her bony fist into the nightstand.

Smoothing out his brow, Alfred sat down beside his sister. "You told me to keep calm just a few moments ago, and now I must ask the same of you."

Blanche craned her neck away from Alfred, but he pinched her chin with his smelly fingers and turned her face back toward his. When Alfred kissed her, he did so deeply, slipping his tongue into her mouth and massaging her gums. As their faces separated, a thin thread of drool dissipated between them.

"Do what thou wilt," Blanche whispered, a massive grin manifesting.

"Now that's the spirit," Alfred replied.

"I'm sorry, but it's like torture." Blanche gazed back down at the symbol on the floor. "We've been close to laying the final foundation for so long, but now we're old and our bodies have failed us."

Alfred looked to the doorway, toward the grunting and rattling of the metal cage. "I don't prefer to be dependent on others either. But what choice do we have?"

THE DARKEST DRIVE

When Vinny pulled off the highway, it was just starting to get dark. The bricks, steel beams, and concrete sidewalks had transitioned to insects, dirt, and forest. The little natural light that remained beyond the gloomy tree line had all but dissipated, allowing darkness to ensue.

His eyes were getting heavier, and the faint hum of the radio was no longer enough to keep him awake. Vinny gently slapped himself in the face a few times, then took a big sip of his lukewarm coffee.

Stay awake, he thought. *Only about another hour.*

He looked back through the rearview mirror at his darling—Ashley's tiny, seven-year-old body was motionless, strapped into the car seat. She could be a ball of energy while driving, which sometimes could be a nuisance. But in that moment, Vinny would've much rather preferred her zany antics to her current calm. The quiet only made his mind creep closer to slumber.

"Honey," Kelly whispered, opening her eyes. "I'm sorry I fell asleep. Whenever I take my second dose it always makes me wanna nap."

Vinny chuckled. "It's okay, babe. I'm sure the long car ride doesn't help either."

She looked at the digital clock on the dash. "You still think we're gonna make it by eight-thirty?"

"Of course. I wouldn't want your parents to have to wait." Vinny's tone carried more than a touch of sarcasm. "Might get crucified if I do that."

"C'mon," Kelly pleaded. "I wasn't saying it like that, I was just curious. They're only gonna be there for the first day, and you know Ashley doesn't get to see them much."

"I just don't wanna give them an excuse to hate me more than they already do."

"Vin, they don't hate you. They just weren't a fan of how you were before." Kelly swallowed. "Neither was I . . ."

An awkward silence filled the car.

It seemed Kelly didn't want to end on that note. She turned her head. "But that's not you anymore. You haven't had a drink in ten months, and I'm so damn proud of you."

"That makes one person, at least," Vinny grumbled.

"You can't expect them to just forget about everything right away. Healing takes time. Trust needs to be earned and nurtured. They'll come back around, I promise."

Vinny's forehead creased and his grimace faded. Flashes of his screaming fits, broken furniture, and chaos erupted in his head. Tears trickled out of Ashley's eyes while fear filled Kelly's as she clenched a duffel bag stuffed full of clothing. The lonesomeness of his weeks spent isolated in their apartment while his wife and daughter stayed with his in-laws were recent recalls, but ones he'd locked away. Whenever he chose to go into that range of memories, it was like a punch in the gut.

She was right.

She was *always* right.

It was hard for Vinny to tell how much time he'd spent in thought, but his response was finally ready. "I'm—I'm sorry, babe. You're right. They're right. That whole stretch was awful, and sometimes I'm just anxious to get past it— to be who I am now—that I overlook what I put everyone through."

Kelly yawned, her voice dropping. "It's okay, sweetie. I know that wasn't you. I know what you've been through."

No, you don't, he thought.

"We all deal with our demons in different ways," she continued. "But as long as you're not dealing with them *that* way, I'm always gonna be here for you."

Vinny's eyes widened. He pictured the metal black box he'd stuck his key in that morning. The profound terror he'd felt when he unlocked it, despite still not having the guts to pry it open. The shameful memories with Ashley, Kelly, and her parents were nothing compared to what he was hiding.

She only knows what I've told her.

Vinny shook his head. "That means everything," he whispered, still trying to distract himself from his shadowy thoughts. "Another year, or even a *lifetime* of dirty looks from your parents is a small price to pay."

He turned to look at his wife, but her pretty eyes had already shut. Vinny's thoughtful words remained true, and he hoped Kelly heard them in her dreams. But even more than that, just like he'd locked away the black box that morning, he wished the thought of it would go away. But it wouldn't. Until he figured out a way to face them, his memories were there to stay.

1976

THE FLAT

"How long will it take?" Beverly asked.

Vinny held open the door to the main garage as the woman dropped her keys into his father's greasy hand.

"I think we can get you outta here in about an hour and a half," Dennis said.

"An hour and a half?" she said, incredulous. "I can't wait here an hour and a half!" When she yelled, her perfectly curled hair bounced, green eyes ablaze with anger.

"That's about the best I can do," Dennis said.

Beverly sucked her teeth in disbelief. "It's just a flat, for Christ's sake. What kind of backwoods operation is this? You might be able to just sit around in your little shop all day and twiddle your thumbs, but I've got news for you. Outside the walls of your little ghost town—you know, in the real world—things are different. I'm an important part of the meeting that you're about to make me late for."

Vinny looked over the woman's business attire. The manner in which she was dressed did in fact project an image of importance, at least in his fifteen-year-old brain. Her fingernails were perfectly manicured, her makeup was layered strategically, and her teeth were far whiter than anyone he'd ever been around.

The rage in the woman's face was much different than what his father projected. Dennis' expression wasn't dominated so much by rage as it was by darkness.

"Ma'am, your car isn't the only one we're working—"

But Beverly wouldn't allow him a word. "This is how you treat out-of-towners? It's a wonder anyone passes through this shithole at all!"

A shiver ran down Vinny's back. He didn't like it when people yelled. When one person yelled, it made him think of all the others he'd heard yell. The cryptic chorus played in his head as he watched his father ball his fist around the keyring in his palm.

He soon noticed that his father's flatlined expression had warped into a grin. Why he would be happy during such an exchange was beyond Vinny. Such bizarre behavior made him nervous. He prayed that it was just his father's usual manner—numb to emotion, numb to reality. But his instincts screamed that it was something else. Something Vinny was continuously haunted by and feared.

Please, God, don't let that be it, Vinny thought.

"It's fine," Beverly said. She exhaled and shook her head. "I wouldn't expect a grease monkey to get it, anyhow."

As Dennis turned his back on Beverly, absorbing her final insult without flinching, he passed Vinny and entered the garage.

After the door closed, Dennis looked at Vinny and tossed the keys his way. "I'm opening up bay two. Pull her in."

"Yes, sir," Vinny said.

As he walked out to the dusty lot, it felt like his heart was trying to rip out of his torso.

Please, not again.

Vinny quickly started and pulled the white Pontiac convertible into the garage. It wasn't uncommon that his father had him drive the cars into the bays—he'd started him behind the wheel young—but it was uncommon for Dennis to rifle through the gloveboxes of the cars. It was something he hadn't done in a long time.

More importantly, it was something Vinny's dad had promised him that he'd never do again.

"Dad, I thought—"

"Shut up," Dennis snarled, his façade suddenly falling.

After shuffling through the various paperwork, he'd found what he was looking for. He pulled a small pad and pen out of his pocket and jotted down the address listed on the paperwork.

After slamming the glovebox shut, Dennis turned off the car and yanked the keys from the ignition. He dangled the ring in front of Vinny, eyes darting over to the door near the workbench in the far corner of the garage.

"Make copies of all of them," Dennis said.

"But . . . but why?" Vinny asked, trying to control his fear. A tear welled up and slid down his cheek. "You said we weren't ever gonna do that again."

"I don't have to explain myself to you. Just make the fucking keys and make 'em right. Understood?"

"Yes, sir."

Vinny took the keys and exited the car. Moving along past the bench, he opened the door to the small backroom. He zeroed in on the key-cutting machine camouflaged among various other equipment and tools. It wasn't a standard device that every auto shop kept, but for Vinny's dad it had been a critical piece of equipment.

As he removed the first key from the ring and held it up, his hand shook. He eyed a small bottle of whiskey amid several other bottles on the ground. After unscrewing the cap, Vinny took a sip and tried to calm himself. He knew if he didn't keep his head on straight, things would only get worse.

But when Vinny activated the key cutter, the sinking feeling in his stomach only deepened.

FATHER'S WISDOM

As they drove down the dark highway a stagnant silence filled the car. Just getting in the car had made Vinny want to retch. They'd been on the road for hours, and with each second that ticked away, he was that much closer to horror. The terror paralyzing him wouldn't let up.

I can't just stay quiet, Vinny thought.

His father may have never physically harmed him, but he didn't have to. After all the things he'd seen over the past several years, he knew what the man was capable of. Things had grown far darker than dropping stones on frogs. The disturbing memories flared in his brain.

"You promised me," Vinny finally said.

"Son," Dennis said, "a lotta things'll be said to you in this life. Sometimes they're true and sometimes they're not. And sometimes, they're said with the intention of sincerity, until the surrounding circumstances distort 'em."

Vinny tried to control his trembling. "W-what do you mean?"

"Well, for example, take your mother and me. Now, when we got hitched, she told me until death do us part she'd be by my side. She said no matter what this life threw at us I'd always be able to rely on her."

Don't say it.

Vinny winced like he was about to get punched.

"But then you came around, and the circumstances changed," Dennis continued. "As a baby, you wouldn't stop crying. Doctor couldn't really say why—you were just needy, I suppose. And slowly, over time, you just sucked the life right out of her. She couldn't sleep. She couldn't eat. She couldn't even really think about anything. Your mother started leaving for many hours each day. She couldn't bear to be around your crying. She just kinda lost her mind. Then, one morning, I woke up and she just wasn't there."

He couldn't hold the sadness inside any longer. Vinny burst into tears, sobbing as quietly as he could manage while holding his head in his hands.

Dennis patted him on the back. "Hey, I wasn't saying that to make you feel bad. Just because you're the reason she left us . . ." He let the notion linger in the air several seconds before picking back up. "Well, that doesn't mean it's your fault, necessarily."

It wasn't the first time Vinny had heard this backstory, but it didn't make it hurt any less. His father seemed to take a subtle joy in the act. It usually happened whenever Vinny questioned him. Each time his dad explained it, he made it a little different. Adding some extra detail or something he'd left out from the previous version. It was as if his father was trying to stab a bit deeper into his heart each time.

Dennis flicked his turn signal as they approached the highway exit. "Is it your mother's fault? Sure. But is it *just* hers? No. *Females* are the problem. They aren't strong. They aren't to be trusted. They have no loyalty. And there's only one goddamn thing they're good for."

Vinny didn't have to ask what that was. The ghoulish, sexually charged images in his father's magazines came to mind.

"That's why it's important that you come with me on these missions," Dennis said. "It's important that you learn and pay close attention. I wouldn't want you to have to go through what I did."

"I-I-I don't want you to hurt anyone," Vinny cried. "Please, Dad, *please*."

The car turned two more times before Dennis checked his notebook and matched the street name. A twisted grin appeared on his face. He killed the headlights as they approached the house and parked discreetly near some trees.

"Always far enough away to avoid attention, but just close enough for a quick exit," Dennis said.

Looking off into the distance, Vinny spied the white Pontiac droptop in the driveway. The property was as nice as he would've imagined based on the game Beverly had talked back at the shop. Plenty of land separated it from the nearest neighbor.

"Please, Dad," Vinny wailed.

"You think I wanted this?" Dennis pointed toward the house. "She chose this, not us. I tried minding my business, but these fuckin' whores, they just won't let up. They keep calling me back, again and again."

Another uncomfortable silence crept up, but it didn't last long.

"Besides, it only hurts for a little," Dennis explained. "But after that pain, you've done something beautiful— you've set them free. Because God knows, cunts like your mother and the bitch inside that house, they aren't meant for this world."

EFFORTLESS ENTRY

Having the key gave them an unfair advantage. The drive was far enough that they'd arrived at such an hour when very few people weren't sound asleep. The bedroom door was another story, but when Dennis turned the handle, Vinny was disappointed to learn it was unlocked.

He now stood silently at the foot of the bed while his father loomed over the sleeping Beverly. Vinny was grateful that she lived alone, but he was still terrified by the thought of what came next. The moment of horror was growing closer—there was no turning back.

Watching her massive breasts rise and fall as Beverly slept peacefully made Vinny uncomfortable. He'd seen that natural human motion stop before, and no matter how many times, each one hurt him in a different way.

Suddenly, Beverly twitched in the sheets, as though her subconscious told her she was in danger. Confusion and terror dominated her expression as she gasped.

"What the—?" A look of recognition set in as Beverly gawked up at Dennis. "What the hell are you doing here?!"

Dennis' lips twisted into a sinful grin as he slowly held up the uncapped can of motor oil. "I forgot to check your fluids."

Her scream didn't have time to escape. When Beverly shot up from her bed, her mouth was met with the tip of the motor oil can. Dennis slammed her back down onto the mattress.

"Hold her fuckin' legs!" he commanded.

Vinny pressed down on her ankles, pinning them in place, while he watched his father mount the woman. Kneeling on each of Beverly's arms, Dennis used one hand to keep the can upright and pouring while the other tightened against her jaw to keep her from spitting out the liquid.

He didn't like watching his father make women go to sleep, but Vinny's wide eyes were glued in place. Beverly's feet tried to flail, but he held them in place. The amber oil leaked out of her nose as she choked and gagged on its thickness, teeth scraping against the metal can like nails on a chalkboard. The look of horror and helplessness was one he would never forget. The moments of malice felt like they'd never end, but eventually Beverly's eyes rolled up inside her head and her body no longer resisted. Her legs were still. Vinny had felt and watched every hint of life flee her flesh.

Removing the bedding, Dennis quickly wrapped up the dead woman, roping the comforter around her head several times over. As he carried her lifeless body out the door, Vinny opened the trunk of Beverly's car.

Seeing his dad kill women used to make him feel sick—he'd even puked a few times before and had had to clean it up. But now, despite the fear and horror stewing inside, the feeling of sickness had strayed.

What's wrong with me? Vinny wondered. *I feel okay . . . but should I?*

After Dennis dropped her limp body inside, he closed the trunk and hopped in the driver's seat of the convertible. He started the car and activated the mechanism for the top.

"The less they can see of you the better," Dennis said. "I'll drive behind you, that way if anyone's getting pulled over it's me. Just keep an eye on me in the rearview. I'll flick my turn signal ahead of time so you know where to go."

"Y-you want me to drive?" Vinny asked.

"You earned it. I'm proud of you, Son. I know you don't enjoy this, but I'm glad you understand it. I said last time was the last time, so I imagine this was hard for you. But you came through for me anyway. You always do."

Vinny's bottom lip quivered, but he forced himself to control it. He wasn't sure what his dad might say if he broke down for a second time.

Dennis scratched the side of his face. "Because of the way you conducted yourself tonight, this will actually be the last time. For you, anyway."

"What do you mean?" Vinny asked.

"I mean I'll never involve you in this kind of stuff again. When the summer's over, you'll be sixteen. You'll be old enough and will have earned the right to make your own decisions. I know I didn't keep my word with you last time, but this is a promise I'll never break."

Dennis extended his hand toward Vinny, and the boy quickly took hold of it.

"Thanks, Dad," he whispered, doing everything to keep his emotions bottled.

"Seeing as this is your first time driving outside of the garage lot, just make sure you follow the lines and abide by the signs. You're a smart boy, I know you've watched me enough already to do it blindfolded."

Vinny nodded as his dad ushered him into the driver's seat. Dennis closed the door and turned back to his own car.

"Hey, Dad," Vinny said.

Dennis turned around. "Yeah?"

"Where are we going?"

The old man's mustache rose as he brandished his yellow teeth. "Where we always go."

THE SWAMP

Beverly's body had been seat-belted into the front passenger seat, which Dennis had removed the headrest from. He sat in the backseat behind her, the teeth of the collapsable handsaw blade biting at her neck.

"Hope it was worth it, bitch," Dennis whispered, grabbing hold of her hair and positioning her throat.

Vinny watched from the side of the Pontiac as the saw burrowed through her flesh with ease. Heart pounding, he felt the sweat on his palms as the mixture of blood and the motor oil Beverly had choked on oozed from the gaping wound in her neck. As he focused on the ruby and amber colors, Vinny realized not only was his body telling him something, so was his mind. He'd had an epiphany that he was afraid to admit.

No, it's not right, he thought. *That's sick.*

He was changing. It wasn't by choice. Most changes weren't as sudden as the flip of a switch. Most changes were gradual and incremental, occurring over an extended period of time. While the sickness that accompanied the murders and acts of depravity he'd witnessed his father commit had left him, it hadn't left a void—that feeling had been replaced with something.

Excitement.

The vibrations he was getting in his chest were the kind he'd gotten on Christmas morning, and the blood rushing into his penis felt like it had the first time he'd spent time with his father's nudie magazines alone.

Every instinct and observation about how the real world worked told him such things were forbidden. School and observing his peers had made him aware that the things his father did weren't normal. If such acts ever came to light, not only would he be shamed for his association, but he might also be jailed if it was discovered that he'd participated.

As the gristly decapitation continued, Vinny recalled the times when he'd watched his father rip his prior victims apart—callously cutting, pulling, and trimming various parts off the female carcasses. He seemed to take different pieces from different people without rhyme or reason. Skin, bones, organs, teeth, and more. But Vinny had never seen him just take someone's head.

He used to sit there in a state of pure horror and sadness, grieving for these women he'd never known. But they undoubtedly had families—there were people somewhere who were going to miss them. Maybe the same way he missed his own mother. Or maybe worse. Unlike Vinny, the family members of these women had probably had a chance to bond with them before his father ripped them to shreds. Lives would undoubtedly be impacted. Promising futures would be stunted and left decomposing at the bottom of the massive swamp before them.

What's wrong with me?

It was a question that Vinny never expected to be able to answer, yet he still felt compelled to ask it. It bothered him deeply that his mind was occupied more with curious thought than with revulsion. He'd chosen to ponder what his father did with the body parts of the women he'd killed rather than express his grief for the loss of life as he'd done many times before. And his own bodily reaction repulsed him. How could he be more excited than disturbed by Beverly's bodily desecration?

Vinny's eyes darted to his father as he exited the car and closed the door behind him. Dennis held Beverly's head by the hair at his side. He set it in a plastic bag spread open on the ground.

Am I becoming like . . . him?

"Vinny, put it in neutral and let's send her packin'."

Nodding, he didn't say a word and did as he was told. When he half sat down beside the headless body, he did his best to stay clear of the blood. He made sure to roll his window down before shifting gears and racing out of and behind the car.

Dennis helped him push the rear of the car forward. The Pontiac went rushing down the small embankment and crashed into the green water. Vinny watched with his father as the vehicle vanished into the murky pool. The evidence of their heinous deed was now hidden, all but for the bag in Dennis' hand. And Vinny couldn't help but wonder why.

UNDER LOCK AND KEY

Vinny glared out the window, eyes sifting through the darkness and zeroing in on the storage container. The bottle of whiskey on his windowsill and the glass beside it were mostly full. As he sipped the alcohol, he felt a bit calmer. His dad never seemed to have any problem with him drinking—the old man was often too busy exploring the vice himself to keep track of it or care. The last thing Vinny wanted was to be like his dad, but he understood why his father drank. The numbness was something special.

He looked at the wallet-size picture in his other hand. The snapshot couldn't be displayed openly—his father didn't allow pictures of his mother in the house. Vinny kept it well hidden, in a shoebox with other random items under his bed, only taking it out when he wanted to look at it.

The fact that he'd found the photo in the attic at all was a bit of a miracle, considering his father had burned every other trace of his mother after she'd left them. But as he looked at the smile on her face, it helped him find comfort. She wore a beautiful red dress, and baby Vinny smiled giddily on her lap. Holding one of his little hands up, she forced him to wave at the camera. On the underside of her wrist were three letters inked in black: *VIN*.

Why'd you have to go? Vinny wondered.

He'd asked himself the question countless times before, but could only imagine her answer. Flipping the photo over, he saw the writing:

My little munchkin, Fall of '62.

Staring at her cursive handwriting, at the sweet words she'd inscribed on the back, helped him find a smidge of comfort. Maybe his dad had been lying about why she'd left. After all, she seemed pretty enamored with him in the photograph and inscription. Why get his nickname tattooed on her wrist if she despised him that much?

Maybe it was just to remember me by . . .

He liked to fantasize that to be the case, but deep down, as much as he didn't want to, he believed what his dad told him. His old man was a lot of things, but he wasn't a bull-shitter. And for all his horrible faults, he was still the only person in his life taking care of Vinny. He'd given him food and shelter, brought him to school, helped him with home-work, taught him a skillset he could use in the real world, and given him a job. That didn't excuse his old man's dark side—nothing did. But at least he'd looked after him, which was more than he could say for his mother.

I know things would be different if you were here. Vinny raised the glass and took another mouthful. *I wouldn't be thinking the way I think. I wouldn't be so messed up.*

The booze usually helped, and hopefully it would start doing its job soon. Vinny couldn't wait to forget about the terrible things he'd seen—or, maybe even worse, the things he'd thought. Drowning all his fears and questions in the forgetfulness brought on by a stupor was all he wanted. But as he sipped his drink eagerly, he thought about that evening and what lay beyond it.

The storage container had been on the back of their prop-erty for as long as Vinny could remember. And for just as long, he'd wondered about its contents. It was no longer at-tached to his father's old big rig, it sat on the ground wheel-less, but the truck remained nearby. Driving the rig was how his father had originally saved enough money to open the garage in town.

But, like most things, the old machine eventually decayed—truck's tires gone flat, much of the body covered in rot. The overgrown weeds around the rig and container camouflaged them in with the rest of the junk and scrap that filled the several acres of land behind and surrounding their house.

Vinny had seen his father disappear into the box at some point after each time they'd visited the swamp. And just like before, the same was true again. Even before he'd been made aware of the killing, for as long as he could remember, his father seemed to spend a lot of time in the old truck.

His curiosity had swelled before, enough to take a look at the big lock that kept the container inaccessible. The lock was rarely taken off, but Vinny had witnessed it from afar on several occasions. One time he'd heard the roar of an engine inside the box. He imagined there was some kind of machine inside, but what exactly remained a mystery.

Without failure, whenever the doors opened, they closed almost immediately. But even after just being opened for seconds or minutes, a horrible smell emerged in the yard.

While the vile stench was always brief, it was also quite memorable. Vinny knew it had to be the pieces of the women his father had kept. The aroma of a rotten human wasn't anything he'd ever enjoyed smelling, but this time was different—a lot of things were. He needed to see the source of the smell with his own eyes. He needed to know what his father was doing inside that storage container.

Another sip of the harsh whiskey assaulted his tastebuds as he slowly pieced together the plan in his head. What he needed to do was obvious, but he'd just never had the guts or the morbid motivation.

But things were different now.

Vinny was different.

A NIGHT TO REMEMBER

It had taken a few weeks for all the circumstances to fall into place, but as moonlight shone down on the back of the storage container, Vinny knew all the work would be worth it. For better or worse, he would find out what his dad was hiding in there.

He held up the bottle of whiskey and took a big gulp. Looking down at the key in his hand, he felt his chest pound. Vinny's father had instilled in him the skill to copy keys long ago but probably never imagined that he might use that ability against him. It was the fastest copy he'd ever made. His father typically took short breaks, so when he'd snagged the old man's keyring off the door in the shop, he knew he only had as long as he took to eat a ham sandwich, a bag of chips, and drink a soda.

Even after he'd successfully crafted the key, he couldn't just stroll out back anytime and have a look. During summer vacation Vinny and his dad were practically joined at the hip. They worked the same hours and then went home together. The only window for him to sneak a peek without his father knowing would be late-night. But even that wouldn't be easy. His father was a notoriously light sleeper, which was why he'd had to wait several weeks.

Vinny had taken his time and waited for just the right moment—when his father had put away enough whiskey to keep him asleep through a thunderstorm.

As Vinny's trembling hand inserted the key into the lock, he readied himself. Still, as he maneuvered the doors open, he wasn't prepared for the vicious scent that violated his nasal cavity. Sure, he'd had a whiff in the distance on several prior occasions, but nothing as concentrated as the stomach-churning aroma wafting its way out of the darkness.

As the buzz of the flies hummed, Vinny threw up into the weeds as quietly as he could. With every heave he felt the strangeness swell, his cock hardening a bit more with each vibration of his ribcage. After the initial wave, the smell was no longer as dreadful. An odd adoration manifested inside as he stepped into the pitch-black container.

Thought of everything except a flashlight, he thought.

The moonlight cast into the entrance of the container revealed part of an orange extension cord sitting near the wall and roped in a circular fashion. The area he couldn't see disappeared along with the cord into the darkness.

It's too risky to go back. Maybe there's a light in here. If not, I'll just have to wait for my eyes to adjust to the dark.

Vinny suddenly found himself salivating as he breathed in the scent of human rot like it was his favorite perfume. The stray flies patted against his face in the darkness, but he paid them no mind. Being a country boy, he was already accustomed to the countless variety of bugs that roamed their property. Flies were the least annoying insects he'd had to deal with.

As he scaled the wall, lurching deeper into the darkness, he noticed something else. Despite it being a particularly humid evening, the inside of the storage box was nowhere near as hot as it was outside. He listened, trying to weed out the deafening chirp of the crickets, until he heard the faint hum of machinery. To achieve such a temperature, there had to be some kind of cooling system inside.

It's nicer in here than inside the house!

As he moved onward into the obscurity, he continued to follow the cord until he was at least a dozen steps inside. The orange extension cord's path went no farther. Vinny felt it ride up the wall beside him, and hanging from the steel ceiling was a single-bulb droplight. Vinny's pulse thudded as he felt around the darkness for the switch.

Here we go . . .

His finger had found the button, but he hesitated.

You wanted to know. It's time to find out.

There was a part of Vinny that feared light. He'd been running from confronting the atrocities, doing his best to stay functional after being exposed to such perversion. Oftentimes he'd envisioned the day he was old enough to sever ties with his father altogether. He tried to focus on such fantasies, the hope of evading the smear of his familial skeletons, but his adolescent imagination continued to run wild. While Vinny was fearful of his father and the lasting reverberations of the murderous lifestyle he'd forced him to be a part of, there was another horrible thought stewing inside his head.

Could it get worse?

What if turning on that light snuffed out any hope of him slyly detaching himself from his dad? What if whatever it revealed left him with no exit plan?

I have to know.

Still, all of Vinny's worries were outweighed by his curiosity. He couldn't be a coward forever. Everything was on the line, and whatever lay in the darkness was a part of his history.

Vinny pressed down and flipped the switch.

RANCID

The car resembled the shape of a Dodge Charger, but its outside was mostly obscured. Bonded to a ghastly shell, the true make and model were unidentifiable. The paint that most vehicles sported was absent. In its place, adhered to the entire body of the vehicle, was a gray, stringy tissue. The outside of the car looked like it was covered in decaying slabs of beef jerky. He was looking at a literal muscle car.

That's why he stripped their muscles, Vinny thought.

The macabre traits of the murder car didn't stop there. Overlayed on the front grille was a series of rib bones. But that was just the first area with skeletal elements. Various bones were fixed around the edges of the car—from the hood to the roof and back to the trunk, the blend of red and white humanity outlined the entire frame.

That's why he took their bones.

Vinny's eyes drifted back to the dual headlights at the front of the car. The larger bulbs on the outside were each covered in facial skin. The smaller fog lights on the inside were covered in breast skin, a nipple blackened by decay at each of their centers.

The twins . . .

A shudder ravaged Vinny's body.

He thought back to the only time he could recall his father killing two at once. This was before he'd even taken him on any ride-alongs—back when he'd only seen his dad return at odd hours of the night with bags.

But the old man still bragged about what he'd done over breakfast.

"Got me a pair," he'd said. "Two dumb cunts for the price of one."

At the time, Vinny hoped such vile statements were just part of his father's sick sense of humor. That kind of wishful thinking had died long ago, and Vinny had since forgotten about the twins.

He was telling the truth.

His father always talked about how it was too risky to take on more than one person at a time. Vinny had even witnessed him pull the plug on a couple jobs they'd attempted in the past for that very reason. But apparently the gamble had been necessary—at least once, anyway, if he wanted to keep the look of his meat mobile balanced.

He's even crazier than—

Vinny's thoughts were interrupted by a noise coming from the rear of the car. As he took a step closer, he realized it was coming from the trunk. His heart started to race even faster, but he couldn't tell if he was more nervous or thrilled at the prospect of something being alive in there.

The reservoir of deep red blood and motor oil vomiting from Beverly's throat flashed in his mind. His cock started to solidify again. He pictured his father's porno magazines. Only the faces of the women pictured inside were altered, some mutilated beyond recognition, others aged and rotten.

They were kept in their sexual poses. One was fucking herself with a dildo, the blood raining down her tits as her head hung on sideways by a thread. Another sat on a chair, her thick backside popping off the page, the burrows where her eyes should've been instead filled with darkness and insects. The model's skin was glistening with the slime of decomposition fluid oozing down her perfect body.

115

Vinny jerked off regularly, but never to the thoughts that were infesting his imagination. Inside, he knew such things were perverse. He fought that desire tooth and nail, but as he gazed upon the feminine meat that encompassed the car, he'd never wanted to blow a load so badly. With the temptation right before him, he wasn't sure if he'd be able to control himself this time around.

He adjusted the erection in his pants.

I have to know what that noise is.

Pulling the door handle, he felt the rough bone touch his flesh. His loins only tingled with more intensity.

It was unlocked.

Stylistically, inside the car was very much like the outside except there were far more insects. The buzz of their wings rumbled in his head as he peered around the interior.

The seats, steering wheel, dashboard, and console looked like they were made of leather. But upon closer inspection, it became clear the skin was human. It was particularly obvious in the areas where the skin tones of various victims intersected.

The headrests were both adorned with a patchwork of crusty scalps—several hair colors, styles, and lengths coming together to create a bizarre visual. The buttons on the radio had molars and incisors affixed to them. The knobs had eyeballs slid over, and a tongue sat in the ashtray. Atop the stick shift rested a tiny head. The lower jaw was missing entirely and the cranium of what appeared to be a fetus was slid over. The gums were toothless and somehow still glistened. Many things ran through Vinny's mind, but at the forefront he wondered how fresh it was.

One of them must've been pregnant.

Some areas inside the car squirmed as larvae pulsated within the decaying flesh. The overfed grubs were almost hypnotic as they danced in the decadence.

"Uuuuuuuugghhhhhhh!"

The sickening moan, coming from the trunk, sent a cold shiver down Vinny's spine.

Someone's definitely in there . . .

Vinny took a deep breath and felt around below the seat for the trunk release. When his fingers felt the crusty flesh that adorned the lever, he knew he'd found it. Vinny didn't hesitate. As he heard the mechanism unlock, he could hardly contain his anticipation.

STARING HORROR
IN THE FACE

The woman in the trunk barely looked human. Each of her legs had been severed above the kneecap. The raw ends seemed to have been scraping around, most likely trying to find a way to free herself. But from the looks of it, she'd been in there for a while.

Her skin was pruned and drooped. Patches of severe infection could be seen on her sagging stomach, torso, arms, and face. Her breasts appeared to have many scars. The jagged lacerations of old were mixed with some that were more recent. Several rows of chain were wrapped around her, both horizontally and vertically. The unforgiving, rusted metal was undoubtedly aggravating and rough on her infected wounds, appearing to have either religiously reopened them or never allowed them to close. The messy, white and red irritated tissue hurt to look at, but the moist and greasy nature of the wounds also excited Vinny.

Despite the trunk being roomy, the woman's legless body wasn't able to move very far. A massive lock weighed down the center of her chest, holding the many rows of chain together. The other, much shorter end of the shackle was attached to a lone steel bolt screwed into the rear of the vehicle's framework.

But the chain wasn't the only thing attached to her.

A thick, white tube that was somewhat transparent was smeared and partially clogged with her fecal matter. One end disappeared inside her rectum while the other was angled into an oil pan on the side of her. The crude colostomy bag substitute had ushered several soft logs and clumps of excrement from her asshole. The fresh and aged fecal matter intermingled, piled up in a massive puddle of piss. The urine came from a catheter inserted into her urethral opening. By the looks of the red flesh and pus that oozed out a little each time she squirmed, the catheter had been shoved inside her some time ago.

And those weren't the only tubes connected to her.

There was another single tube that was about the size of her windpipe and had been shoved halfway down it. The other end left her mouth and forked in two different directions. Attached to the underside of the trunk that hung in front of Vinny's face, were two jugs. One was filled with dingy water, the other with an unknown white mush. The specks of black within the purée made it look like moldy grits. While each of her arms was tied to the rear of the trunk, her right arm was positioned close enough to the fork in her feeding tubes to reach the knob. If she turned it once, water would come out. Turning it a second time, Vinny assumed, would trigger the mush. But if she left it where it was, it stopped anything from going down her throat.

As the woman's bloodshot eyes connected with Vinny's, her desperation was plainly visible. He could hear the depressing message almost like it was being relayed to him telepathically:

Kill me.

But Vinny didn't have the heart to consider such things at that moment. He was still studying the horrifying details of her face. Her rotten teeth rounding the outside of the filthy tube she was gagging on. The enflamed gum sockets, absent of enamel, discharging a thick, pea-soup-like pus that smeared down the side of her jaw.

The defeated expression of the sickly woman looked like it'd been pulverized by a boxer. The tissue was so swollen and distended that it was difficult for him to decide if she was beautiful or not.

But with Vinny's new way of thinking starting to take hold of him, she most certainly was—he couldn't keep his eyes off her.

The woman's sexy cheeks were so puffed out that it looked like she was hiding a plum inside each of them. The wounds on her face seemed to be ripping, based on the intensity of the inflammation. If she was in any way religious, she wouldn't have to wait for Hell on Earth—for her, it had already arrived.

Vinny's erection had nearly stabbed a hole through his pants. When he looked down at his jeans, he saw past the throbbing bulge to the trunk floor nearest him. A collection of condoms—some used, some sealed—was spread around a shit-smeared dildo and a small bottle of lubrication.

That's the stuff from the magazine . . .

Vinny looked at the bottle of Smooth Lube as he slowly unzipped his pants. He didn't even have the internal debate that he'd battled himself over on so many other occasions. The temptation was too much. Before he knew it, his dick was out, and he was squeezing the bottle all over his shaft.

As he tugged at his rod, he stared into the watery eyes of the destroyed woman. Each stroke brought him closer as he examined every forbidden anomaly on her body. He bit his lower lip hard.

Should I put it inside her? Wait . . . looks like Dad already did.

Disgust, terror, and shock all battled each other on the woman's face. But there was something else there too. As the teardrops beaded off her bulbous cheeks, he saw a hurt that was deep. A hurt that, despite the pure carnage his father had put those other women through, Vinny had never seen.

A strange tingling sensation drummed inside Vinny's ribcage. A feeling that he wasn't sure he was capable of any longer manifested.

The absent sickening sensation had returned, mingling with his dread as his mind started to wander. He felt his jaw slack as he put together a hypothesis, one he hoped and prayed wouldn't be proven true.

His masturbation had slowed to a stop as his gaze drifted to the length of chain around the woman's wrist. Reaching out with his shimmering hand, he slid the metal down to reveal the tattooed letters:

VIN.

HIT THE ROAD

"Mom . . . ?" Vinny whispered, stupefied by the revelation.

He quickly pulled his pants up, mortified beyond words. But as he zipped his fly, another light, unbeknownst to Vinny, came on. As the fixture sitting above the car of death illuminated, fear struck him. Instinctively, Vinny closed the trunk as quietly as possible and made his way around the vehicle in the direction he'd came in.

Dennis stood to the right of the doorway, guzzling more of the whiskey that had put him on his ass just a short time ago. As the remaining liquor disappeared, he dropped the bottle on the ground.

"I had a dream," Dennis said, slurring his words and staggering forward. His eyes were locked onto Vinny's. "I had a dream about you, Son. I dreamt that, after I'd passed on, you continued this for me. And, well, now here you are. Ain't that something?"

"I-I'm sorry, Dad," Vinny mumbled, doing his best to discreetly wipe the lube off on the back of his pants.

"Nothing for you to be sorry about. You came in here because you were drawn to it. You came here 'cuz you're like me. And guess what?"

Vinny didn't want to guess. "What?"

Dennis pulled his hand out of his pocket and dangled a keyring. "I'm gonna take you for a ride." A sinister grin crinkled his father's face as he jingled the keys.

As his father stumbled toward the meat mobile, Vinny took notice of another area inside the storage container that the main light source had uncovered.

The wall before the car was plastered with black-and-white newspaper clippings. Some had the faces of women while others were small articles of text. Beside each clipping dangled a lone key.

The most recent was closest to him—the key he'd made to get inside Beverly's apartment several weeks prior. Her local newspaper had already put out a full-page story on her strange disappearance. Apparently she wasn't just bragging about being important—people had already noticed her sudden absence.

"C'mon, hop in," Dennis said.

When he plopped down into the seat, Vinny could hear the maggots imbedded in the fleshy leather popping. He tried to avoid contact with the vile insects, but there was little he could do.

Dennis jammed the key into the ignition and fired the car up. The roar he'd heard from time to time coming from the storage container was no longer a mystery. But knowing that his father had crafted such a cadaverous car terrified him. The old man's blood-alcohol level must've been through the roof.

Driving around in this . . . murder mobile, how the hell does he not expect to get caught?! The thing has body parts all over it! And—as if that's not enough, Mom's in the trunk!

The terror was crushing him; it felt like a new level of anxiety that made it hard to breathe. But Vinny had to say something. If he didn't talk some sense into his dad, the night could end even worse.

"Dad . . ." Vinny begged.

Dennis revved the engine, ignoring him, eyes glued to the darkness ahead.

"Dad, a-are you sure we should be going out in this? Won't the—"

The car peeled out. Smoke from the burned rubber filled the storage container, stirring up the insects as the car shot out the opening. Cutting through the weeds, his father whipped it around the house, slamming on the brakes just before the front door.

"Fetch us a six-pack," Dennis said.

"But, Dad—"

"Just go fuckin' get it!"

Vinny did as he was told and returned with the beers. He twisted the cap off a bottle for his dad, then opened one for himself.

Gonna need *this.*

Just as he finished the thought, his father peeled out again. The country roads were dark and vacant. With the way his father was driving, Vinny was thankful.

"This is what it's all about," Dennis said, chugging his beer. "Just 'cuz everyone else don't think it's right, don't mean it ain't right for you." As he finished off the bottle, Dennis tossed it into the backseat. He raised his hand, looking for a high five. "Am I right?!"

Vinny had no choice but to appease him. As their hands slapped together, the car started to veer off the road.

"Dad!" Vinny screamed.

Dennis quickly jerked the wheel to the left, causing the car to skid side to side before regaining control.

"Don't you be afraid, Son. Don't let them run your goddamn life."

Vinny wanted to settle his father down but had no idea what to tell him.

Just then, a mixture of blue and red lights exploded behind them, reflecting off the rearview and sideview mirrors.

"The police!" Vinny yelled.

For the first time, he felt like it was going to happen. All the horrible things he'd seen his father do, all the times he'd helped him. The world was about to find out.

Vinny wasn't stupid; he was a sponge that absorbed everything around him—to a fault sometimes. He'd seen how people talked about killers, creeps, and weirdos. Each member of his family could be classified as at least one, if not multiple. The fact that he was born into perversion and baptized in blood wouldn't give him a pass. Vinny knew that if they were caught, his life would be over. Still, the way his father was driving, his life might very well be over anyhow.

"Fuck 'em," Dennis said. "I give a shit about a cop. Open the glovebox."

"What?" Vinny asked.

"I said open the glovebox!"

Vinny did as he was told, and when the glovebox popped open, he saw a familiar face. Beverly's glistening, gore-caked expression was the picture of dread. One of her eyeballs was missing—it looked like the socket had been drilled out with a steel bit. Her mouth was agape, a family of larvae throbbing like she had a white, bumpy tongue.

"Gimme that cunt's head," Dennis said, unzipping himself. He maneuvered his cock through the hole of his pants and licked his lips.

"But what about the—"

"Just listen!"

Vinny grabbed the oily cranium and handed it to his father while various bugs rained down on his lap. He desperately wanted to brush them off but was promptly given an alternate task.

"Take the wheel," Dennis said.

"What?!"

"You heard me."

Vinny grabbed onto the leathery wheel, grateful that they were still on Maple Valley Road for a bit longer, which he knew to be a straightaway. But in the darkness, his steering was anything but certain.

"I don't know if they deserved to die," Dennis said, holding Beverly's head in front of his own. "But I like 'em better that way."

Dennis drunkenly rammed his wet tongue into the horde of maggots nesting in Beverly's mouth. As he kissed her wildly, the insects overflowed, and he eagerly slurped at them. Biting down on the rubbery lip, Dennis bellowed out a moan of pleasure.

"I want that fucking mouth on my pecker," Dennis wailed.

Pressing down harder on the gas, he leaned back. The head slammed into his lap as he thrust his cock into the necrotic entry.

Vinny was sobbing hysterically, his arms starting to hurt. The squad car lights flickered as he did his best to keep them straight. But inside, he felt the end was near. He didn't believe there was a way for the situation to solve itself, and his old man was certainly in no shape to fix it.

His father let out a guttural howl, and Vinny could only assume that he'd blown his load in the decapitated woman's mouth. When Dennis tossed the head onto the floor near Vinny's feet, a puddle of cum and maggots lay on his throbbing cock and lap.

"Gimme this fuckin' thing," Dennis said, taking hold of the wheel again. "You put that bitch away." He adjusted the rearview mirror, looked at the flashing lights, and then beat on the steering wheel. "And I'll put this one away."

As Vinny stuffed Beverly's head back into the glovebox, he saw his father push down on a molar in the car's console. The button opened a panel of muscle that lay behind the stick shift. Inside looked to be a human pinky with orange nail polish that had been skewered, resting atop a switch.

Dennis grinned, the beer streaks on his cheeks glistening. In a single motion he cranked the wheel sideways and slammed on the brakes. He fanned out onto the dirt breakdown lane on the other side of the road, suddenly facing the opposite direction. The cop behind them slowed, trying to follow their erratic U-turn.

"Let's see if this fucker has nitro," Dennis said with a chuckle.

He peeled out again, and once he'd recouped a little speed, Dennis bent the finger back like he was trying to break it off. A wailing, mad laugh filled the car.

They accelerated so quickly that Vinny was forced back against the seat. He could feel the hair of the dried scalps against his own, looking in the mirror as the blue and red lights got smaller. It wasn't long before they were able to hit one of the backroads and lose the cops altogether.

1996

DEAD TIRED

The last ten minutes had been agonizing. Not because Vinny's eyelids had grown heavier, but because the dark memories of his father were the last thing he was hoping to rehash. The thoughts were heavy and laced with issues he'd never figured out how to cope with, let alone address.

There was a piece of him that had truly believed he'd beaten the curse. Despite the sinister feelings he occasionally fought and the morbid things he sometimes saw—like at the breakfast table or in the bedroom when he watched Kelly's face and body transform—he'd found the path to a relatively normal life. But there was always still the fear that one day it would all come apart. The deliberate façade he'd crafted, the control he believed he harbored, the box of uncertain doom sitting in his closet.

Will all those recurring dreams—nightmares, Vinny thought, correcting himself. *Will all those recurring nightmares about making love to Kelly's corpse come true?*

Vinny pictured his father's face. He hated the son-of-a-bitch. He'd passed the curse down to him. But he couldn't be sure if it was genetic, psychological, or both. Regardless, there was something inside Vinny that he'd been holding in for a while.

The feeling scared him—especially now that he actually had something to lose. All the darkness inside him was just begging to get out. Still, there was more to his situation, but he wasn't prepared to analyze the rest of it yet. He might never be. Just going through those thoughts drained and disturbed him.

Just stand firm. Thinking about him or the nightmares doesn't help. Focus on the good.

The sense of isolation grew as he tried to detach himself from it, driving his family deeper into the brush. It didn't help that the area they were traveling through looked more like the countryside he'd grown up in than the metropolis he'd escaped to.

The streetlightless road remained dim, and as the car's headlights cut into the night, the path ahead bordered on hallucinogenic. The wavy streaks of light intermingled with the trees and tar.

Almost there . . .

Vinny reached for the coffee cup, only to find it empty. *Shit.*

When he turned his eyes back toward the dark road, he couldn't believe them. What was just seconds ago a lonely straightaway was now occupied by a most unexpected and alarming sight.

The pale woman's figure was topped with brown, greasy hair—a white streak of lightning gave the follicles contrast. The tips of her large breasts were dominated by hockey-puck-size nipples. Her gut was strangely littered with hair that led all the way down to her overgrown pubic area.

While the woman's complexion was ghostly, the smattering of a muddy-colored substance that was caked on her hands, nose, and mouth wasn't. Flaring out from between her lips was a pair of glittering fangs. But amid all her shocking features, Vinny was drawn to her eyes. They were black and beady—too beady to be human, and blacker than the darkest water well.

"What the fuck?!" Vinny cried.

With an instinctual jerk of the wheel, the car careened off the road.

"Shit! Hold on!" Vinny screamed.

Feeling the velocity of his head whipping, a sharp pain shot up Vinny's neck as the car flipped several times over, tumbling down the hill. When the passenger side of the vehicle connected with the ground, it instantly dented inward.

The glass beside Kelly's head blew out and the pieces showered the interior of the vehicle. His wife let out a blood-curdling scream, adding a new layer of horror to the soundtrack of violence.

Then, just as the car smashed into a massive tree trunk, everything went black.

THE WORST NIGHTMARE

It was the pain that woke Vinny.

The crushing sensation of the steering wheel column on top of his leg lit his nerves on fire. Fighting through the excruciating agony, he reached up to the throbbing wetness that coated the top part of his skull and pressed down. The massive gash stretching deep past his hairline, over the top of his cranium, was leaking blood everywhere. After a crash of such magnitude, Vinny expected to be injured, but he didn't expect the smell.

Some elements of the odor were familiar; others weren't as easy to pin down. The mangled interior stank of wet dog, skunk spray, fecal matter, and garbage juice. The nauseating aroma made Vinny gag, but as he raised his hand to his mouth and coughed, speckles of blood sprayed all over the steering wheel and windshield.

He was still in shock, but as his eyes started to focus, it suddenly dawned on him—he would never recover from the horror that confronted him.

There were some things in life that couldn't be unseen.

The face he loved to pieces—the one that had dragged him from the depths of despair and showed him he had a place in the world—wasn't there anymore.

Kelly's smashed head was crumpled beyond repair. The bloody hunk was an impossible jigsaw puzzle—a ghastly jumble of flesh, bone, and ribbons of hanging skin. Red rained out of the many gaping wounds in her face.

No, Vinny thought, trying to shake it off.

He was waiting for the forced fantasy to dissipate—for the love of his life to somehow return as she was. The muddles of meat remained, looking like wads of bubble gum that had been chewed up and spat out. The destruction visited upon her almost seemed illogical, based on the type of accident. But when Vinny started to focus on the animated gnawing noises coming from behind him, it suddenly made sense. His eyes found the distorted rearview and the glimpse of hell that came with it.

Ashley was gone.

But she was a different kind of limp than what he'd witnessed earlier when she was sleeping so peacefully. The veiny, pink globs mushroomed where her throat was ripped open, staring back at him. Blood rained down her entire body in such a generous volume that it had changed the color of the car seat.

Part of Vinny expected to see the strange woman he'd seen in the road, and while she wasn't there, some of her unsettling features were. The white and brown mass of fur blanketed the backseat beside Ashley's remains. The black eyes of the beast squinted, causing a golden gleam to flash in the reflection of the lunar light. The razor fangs of the strange creature transitioned from the countless gaping wounds that covered Ashley's adolescent throat and torso to gnawing aggressively on her lifeless face.

In addition to the ones he'd already spotted, the wild animal harbored other weasel-like features. Vinny watched helplessly as the beast thrust the off-white nails on its paw deep into her mutilated neck tissue. As the claw tore deeper, its jaws excitedly clamped down on Ashley's cheek. The skin extended to its ripping point, and the animal pulled away a chewy wad of gleaming flesh.

Vinny was already screaming, but it was in a windless way. He was so injured and exhausted that his moans and pleas were muffled. He wanted to protect his daughter—or what was left of her—but he was barely capable of staying conscious. Rescuing his child from the creature's clutches seemed out of the question with the severity of the head trauma he'd sustained. His skull pounded. He could feel himself starting to fade.

"Get the fuck off her . . ." he managed to mumble.

The hungry fangs snapped, sinking deep into the tissue around her tiny nose. It yanked violently, whipping the little girl's head back and forth. The beast twisted its neck and pressed both of its paws into her chest as it pulled back. The rubbery cartilage was no match for the thing's strength. After a loud rip, the hunk detached from Ashley's face.

Vinny's eyes widened as the animal pulled away. His little girl's cavernous nasal passages were unveiled—two foul pits of darkness staring back at him. The blood married to Ashley's clumpy snot discharged slowly but surely, oozing out of the holes, glistening in the moonlight.

"No . . ." Vinny whispered.

He couldn't believe it was real. The creature's eyes were black, but they glowed as he watched it finish chewing and swallowing another clump of his daughter's face. When Vinny's traumatized gaze locked on to the creature, its snarl and bloodstained teeth were the last thing he saw.

ALONE

Everything felt like a dream. The audio around him sounded like it was distorted and being slowly turned up in unison with the lighting. The blurry blob of colors smoothed out, and a face came into focus.

"K-Kelly . . . ?" Vinny asked. When his ears reprocessed the words, what he'd just said sounded like it was being spoken underwater. "Is that you?"

The facial tissues started to wrinkle before smoothing out, and finally, the glob looked more human.

"Can you hear me?" the woman asked.

Vinny nodded but felt a severe ache upon moving his head. Gradually his eyes glanced upon the golden nametag that read: *Sara St. James, Registered Nurse.*

"That's good, just take it easy," Sara whispered gently, checking the machinery around him.

"S-Sara?" Vinny groaned. "Why are you here?"

"Well, I'm here because I'm a nurse, which means you're at the hospital," Sara said with a profound expression of sadness. "You were in a car accident, Vinny."

"Car accident?"

"Yes . . . but it looks like you're gonna be okay. Your injuries are non-life-threatening."

"Where's Kelly and . . . and Ashley?" Vinny asked, an instinctual dread elevating his tone.

Sara looked uncomfortable with the question. As the silence lingered, flashes of his hand jerking the steering wheel and their car careening off the road entered his head. A dim light shone eerily, illuminating his wife's pulpy face. Vinny's grimace continued to further exaggerate as the mental imagery transitioned to the creature's gore-caked fangs plunging into Ashley's garbled flesh.

In his struggles with the darkness and with alcohol, he'd often unintentionally intermingled sex and death. His psyche did it instinctually after surviving his adolescent trauma. While that remained a battle he continued to fight daily, not even in his darkest nightmares or most disturbing daydreams had he imagined anything happening to his daughter. Even in his own fucked-up head that was off-limits. Instantly he knew the answer to the question he'd asked the nurse—the memories of mutilation explained that much—but he still couldn't believe it.

He *wouldn't* believe it.

"No! This—it can't be real," he said.

A life-changing nervousness blossomed in his belly as the sadness in Sara's eyes seemed on the verge of dribbling out.

"I'm terribly sorry that I have to—"

"We'll take it from here," a firm but tremoring male voice said.

Sara looked back at the seated pair and nodded before stepping aside. "Of course."

Walking past Vinny's in-laws and slipping around the curtain, the nurse made her way outside the room, leaving the door open just a crack.

Still confused and disoriented, Vinny found himself confronted by the last people in the world he would've hoped to see. If the morbid memories in his mind were as real as his gut indicated, Kelly's mother and father—Jessica and Clark Gibson—weren't there to check on his well-being.

139

"How could you?" Jessica asked, tears streaming down her wrinkly face.

Vinny's eyes widened—what could he possibly say to them? They'd hated him even before the accident.

But his mind wasn't able to focus on his in-laws. Sobbing uncontrollably, Vinny realized the only people he loved in his life were gone. The two people who he'd never imagined he'd have. After his vile past, he'd always believed he was doomed to be alone. But Kelly had changed all that. There were so many things he envisioned doing with his family. But sharing holidays, milestones, and growing old with them was no longer an option.

They were gone.

The visions of the future that Vinny projected whenever he thought about Ashley becoming an adult were suddenly obsolete. The void in his heart ached for them. They were the only family he'd ever known. Vinny would've given anything to hold them close once more. But such an idea wasn't possible any longer.

He was alone.

Clark was every bit as upset as his wife but more aggressive. "You're fucking drinking again, aren't you?" he asked through clenched teeth.

Vinny tried to control his sobs enough to respond. "No, there was something—a woman ran out into the road. She was naked and had—"

"Look at this," Clark said, shaking his head. He turned to his wife and gestured to Vinny. "He's still wasted!"

Jessica's eyes remained burning into Vinny's. "You killed them. You killed our babies . . ."

"You drunk piece of shit!" Clark yelled. "We tried to tell her that you were no good. She moved up here to get away from you! But you followed her! You clung to her like a leech until you sucked her dry!"

"I-I love her," Vinny spluttered.

Clark's rage continued to boil as spittle flew from his mouth, and there was no end in sight.

"Of course you did, Vin, you're a fuck-up! Why wouldn't you?! You have nothing else in life! You drag everyone else around you down! Then, when the girls needed you most, you just fucking sat there and watched them get torn to shreds! You let an animal eat their goddamn faces off! Fucking coward!"

"I—I'm sorry!" Vinny cried. "I don't know what—what happened. I didn't want any of this to happen." As he spoke through his crying, ropes of drool leaked out of his mouth.

Sara's footsteps made their way back into the room. "Mr. and Mrs. Gibson, maybe it's best for you to take a few moments apart—"

"A few moments?!" Jessica yelled, glaring at Sara. "No, thank you." Her gaze drifted back to Vinny as she grew uncomfortably calm, the tears on her cheeks rolling down, then she looked at the nurse. "Outside of a courtroom, this'll be the last time I ever see this bastard again." She turned back to face Vinny again. "You're dead to me. Always were."

Jessica headed for the door and Clark followed. When he passed Sara, through gritted teeth he said, "Contact us immediately when that blood-alcohol test comes back. We wanna press charges as soon as humanly possible. Understood?"

Sara nodded. "Yes, sir."

As the Gibsons exited the room, Clark slammed the door as hard as he could behind him.

NO WINNERS

Sara couldn't believe it was him.

Peeking inside the room, she could see the emotional agony that Vinny was going through—a type of agony that was quite recognizable. While she didn't know him well, there was something about him that made her care—something inside that Sara couldn't quite put her finger on.

During her drives to the hospital, she'd daydreamed about Vinny a bit. After meeting him, there was a certain energy stirring inside Sara, triggering her mind playing out a scenario where their paths crossed again. She imagined bumping into him at the drug store once more, but this time the ring that was around his finger would be missing. They'd get to talking a little more and share a few laughs together.

The daydream didn't go beyond that. Sara wasn't truly entertaining the idea that she'd ever see Vinny again. It was just a thought that made her feel warm inside. Even so, as much as she'd wanted to see him again, she didn't want to see him the way he was now.

There are no winners at a time like this, Sara thought.

Her brow furrowed, the hurt stabbing inside her all too familiar. The picture on her dashboard of her, Eric, and Michael flashed in her head.

As nasty as the Gibsons had treated Vinny, she could understand their outrage. Even if he hadn't been drinking, they had a right to be upset. They'd not only lost their daughter, but their young granddaughter as well. While she prayed that their anger toward Vinny was misplaced, it still resonated with her. Right or wrong, she understood all too well how such devastation had the ability to transform people—she'd gone through it herself.

"I-I . . . didn't mean to," Vinny whimpered, holding his trembling hands over his face. "That woman . . . that woman appeared out of nowhere."

As Sara snapped out of her memory and back to Vinny, she felt terrible for him.

He doesn't seem drunk.

She'd had plenty of experience with drunk drivers in the ER. While she couldn't be positive until the test results came back, Sara's gut told her that Vinny was clean. Usually, if a driver had been drinking, she could smell at least a hint of alcohol in the air or on their breath. While Vinny was stuttering some, that was different than slurring his words. There was nothing about how he was acting that led her to believe that the Gibsons were correct in their assumption.

What if the entire thing was just an accident?

That word, *accident*, echoed in her head.

If they'd said such horrible things to Vinny during his most vulnerable time without justification, Sara knew the kind of damage it could do firsthand.

As she watched him continue to cry and moan, she felt like she was being forced to relive her own trauma. The suffering in his inflection was so intense that what came out of him sounded inhuman. She didn't want to lie to him, but he could clearly use some hope. She leaned over and gently placed her hand on Vinny's shoulder, rubbing it.

"Don't worry," Sara whispered. "Things'll get better."

HELLO, OLD FRIEND

Vinny sat in bed staring at the wall. His eyes were bloodshot as he lifted the bottle of Jim Beam up to his lips. After a life-changing stretch of sobriety, he'd found himself addicted to the stinging shock of alcohol ever since he'd left the hospital. It had helped him through the horrors of his adolescence and thereafter, and for the last few weeks, it was all he had to fall back on.

He yearned for sleep, but the sandman only teased him. Each time he lay his head to rest, Vinny recalled the warmth that he'd taken for granted. The warmth that had rested beside him every night without fail for nearly a decade. Since the accident, when he tried to close his eyes, all he saw were their faces—or what was left of them, anyway.

The guilt in his gut was the root cause of his nagging insomnia. As the restless nights piled up, it seemed he could only achieve slumber when he finally passed out—only when his body had nothing to keep him activated with any longer.

And even then, there were the nightmares.

While he struggled to deal with the dawn of another day he had no desire to be a part of, Vinny tried to suppress the haunting images.

The flashes of muddled gore.

The moist mouth of the creature.

The deep gashes below Ashley's face.

The lipless monstrosity in the passenger seat that was now incapable of receiving Vinny's morning peck.

While his physical injuries no longer caused him pain, those stomach-churning memories were there to stay.

On what had proved to be Ashley's final birthday, she'd never gotten her cake filled with candles burning bright. Never got to make a wish. Instead, the fire inside her had been snuffed out, spawning a profound guilt that Vinny would be forced to live with for the rest of his miserable life.

He felt exposed and empty every waking moment. But even as he tipped the bottle back again, the bourbon didn't make him feel any better. It did do one thing, though.

It helped him forget.

Vinny got up, putting on the same dirty clothes from the day prior again, just as he did every morning. He didn't bother showering. What was the point? Who was he trying to smell good for?

Once dressed, Vinny entered the kitchen. He stumbled past the forlorn seats where his daughter would playfully eat pancakes beside his wife on the weekends. His blurry vision gazed upon the cluster of childish drawings magnetized to the fridge, then moved to the several boxes of cereal sitting atop it that he'd bought special for Ashley.

Everything around him was a stinging reminder of all he'd lost.

Vinny was sick to his stomach, but it still rumbled with hunger. Feeling weak from not eating often, he knew if he was going to get through the day he'd need to force something down. When he opened the fridge, his eyes scanned for something quick and easy to take along with him. But instead of a fast snack, he was confronted with an item he'd purchased weeks prior.

The alcohol rushed through his system, making Vinny's shaky vision blur as it fixed upon the raw, bloody pound of ground beef. The meat had been sitting there so long that it had gone gray. Ground beef was one of his favorite foods, but since the accident, things were different.

Even just buying the beef these days made Vinny feel nauseous. Considering the human slaughter he'd seen on a regular basis as a child, the new repulsion didn't make sense to him. Maybe it was because he was detached emotionally from the women his father had killed. Or maybe it was the primal way Kelly and Ashley had been mauled in front of him.

His father was a lot of things, but he'd never watched him devour a face.

At first, Vinny figured it would pass, but that wasn't the case. Each day, when he pulled the handle of his refrigerator open, those pulverized rows of flesh sat waiting. This morning was no different. This time, his pounding headache and distorted vision seemed to only intensify the feeling. Suddenly, over the neglected meat, the flashes came. Ashley's face chewed to a gummy jumble, the gaping holes that exposed her nasal cavity puckered with blood and snot—her last appalling moments imbedded in the rancid meat.

"No," he whispered, slamming the door shut.

Vinny staggered to the side, bumping into a smaller table that rested against the wall. He looked down at the trashcan below and started to vomit.

Due to the lack of nourishment in his body, the watery regurgitation was mostly partially digested alcohol that burned his esophagus and nostrils en route to the overfilled wastebasket. Tears streaked down his eyes as the slimy discharge coated the garbage.

I'm . . . I'm sorry . . .

He tried to calm himself and used his sleeve to wipe the dribbles of puke from his face. Atop the small table, the red light on the answering machine flickered, catching his eye. Many neglected messages awaited his review, but he no longer had the will to communicate with anyone.

He'd already decided there was only one thing that was going to help him.

Vinny staggered over to the dishrack and retrieved his Thermos. He filled it with a mixture of day-old coffee and whiskey. As he lifted the drink to his lips and took several gulps, he couldn't push the thought of Ashley's mutilated face out of his mind.

I just . . . I need another drink.

Shaking his head, Vinny looked back at the answering machine and thought about the interactions he'd been steadily ignoring. But the sight of the device also made him consider the ones he was about to be forced into.

Vinny shook his head dejectedly, lifted his keys off the table, and left his apartment.

PROFESSIONAL SUICIDE

When Vinny entered the mobile trailer and approached his desk, there was another man sitting behind it. The swirls of confusion that the alcohol fostered in his brain were only amplified by the unexpected sight. The man looked up at Vinny with amusement in his eyes.

"Hey, Vinny," Ryan Clements said softly.

The tension in Ryan's jaw and his smirk stirred Vinny's nerves and rage. His confusion was now dwarfed by his irritation.

"Why the fuck are you at my desk?"

"It's *my* desk now," Ryan said, lifting a photo off the shelf behind him and setting it on the desk. "That's a beautiful family you've got—sorry, *had*."

Vinny's heart sank as he looked down at the picture of him hugging Kelly and Ashley.

"Especially the little one," Ryan whispered. "What a cute little darling she was."

Vinny pointed his finger an inch away from Ryan's nose. "You don't say a word about my fuckin' daughter, freak! Wh-who the hell do you think you—"

"Vinny!" Curtis interjected from his office at the other end of the trailer. "Get in here, *now*."

Curtis' glare was deathly serious. He wasn't speaking in his normal, pushy-prick tone. His cadence was stone-cold.

Closing the door behind Vinny, Curtis walked around his desk. "Take a seat," he said before taking his own.

"What's this all about?" Vinny asked.

Curtis took a slurp of coffee from his mug with the King's Construction logo. "You're done here. Ryan's taking over your position and that's effective immediately and indefinitely."

The shock nipping at Vinny shouldn't have been a surprise, but he was so far gone that nothing made sense to him any longer.

"What the fuck are you talking about?!"

Curtis gave an almost annoyed laugh. "What fuckin' planet are you on these days? Listen . . ." He paused, seeming to choose his words carefully. "I know since the accident things have been . . . difficult. But—"

"Difficult?" Vinny scoffed. "I lost everything!"

"I know, damnit! But since you did, the fact of the matter is you're a liability! A liability to us finishing this project and to every man on this site. You're half in the bag every morning, and you're giving overlapping orders. You told Martinez to start on the walls yesterday and the goddamn electrical wasn't even finished! If he went over there and touched the wrong wire, he'd be looking like KFC right now! If I didn't stop him, he could be dead—or even worse, lawyered up. And then"—he snapped his fingers—"just like that, it's the end of King's Construction."

"That's right, I forgot! This is all about you. It's always about *the King*. Never mind the guy with the dead fuckin' family!"

"Oh, don't give me that shit," Curtis said, slamming his hand on the desk in frustration. "You act like we haven't been through this before. I've been telling you for weeks— *weeks!*—no drinkin' when you clock in, but you just can't do it. I got too much shit on my plate to be a safety net for you, especially when that's one of *your* fuckin' responsibilities!"

Curtis forced himself to cool down and took a deep breath. Calming his tone, he straightened up and looked Vinny in the eye.

"Listen, this is the biggest year of my life. I can't afford to lose you, but you've given me no choice. I've gotta cut you loose."

Vinny hurled his full Thermos at Curtis' head, but his aim wasn't even close. It went crashing into the wall and the cap exploded off the top.

"You crazy son-of-a-bitch," Curtis grumbled, bolting around his desk.

Spit flew from Vinny's mouth. "You bastard! Y-you made me stay up all night! I was tired 'cuz of you!"

Vinny thought back to the late hours and how groggy he'd been that fateful night of the drive. Despite knowing the nude woman who appeared in the middle of the road was at the crux of the tragedy, it wasn't the first time he'd wanted to place blame on Curtis for what happened. Maybe he could've reacted quicker and not flipped the car if he'd had a little more rest. Maybe he wouldn't be waking up to his own personal hell every day.

"They're dead because of you!" Vinny wailed.

Vinny lunged like a spear tossed by a gladiator, trying to tackle Curtis, but his inebriation made his attempt easy to dodge. His boss sidestepped him, and Vinny went crashing headfirst into the steel filing cabinet before sliding to the floor.

"You're a grown man," Curtis said, opening his office door. He returned back to Vinny's woozy frame and started dragging him by the shirt. "You made your bed, now you've gotta sleep in it."

Ryan looked startled as he rose from his desk, but not startled enough to wipe the smirk off his face. "Jesus, Curtis, you need any help?"

"I'll handle it," Curtis replied firmly. "Nothing for you to worry about, just keep reviewing those blueprints."

As they neared the trailer exit, Vinny tried to regain his footing, but Curtis sent a swift kick into his ribs.

"Stay down. If you know what's good for you, you won't make it any worse on yourself."

Vinny went flying out of the trailer and landed face down in the dirt lot. As the door whipped open and his body thudded onto the ground, the commotion attracted the attention of all the workers scattered around.

"You can leave now and I won't press charges," Curtis said, "or you can stay and get the shit kicked out of you."

Curtis sent his steel-toed boot blasting into Vinny's ribcage again, and he let out a hiss of air. He moaned, rolling over, pain stinging his side.

"I should've never given you this," Curtis said, reaching down and snatching the golden Madison hammer from Vinny's toolbelt. He held it up like it was a tool bestowed to him by God. "This was a symbol for my next leader. One that you're too damn weak to carry."

Curtis cocked his boot back and blasted one additional parting shot into Vinny's gut.

He wheezed, trying to catch his breath, as he struggled to drag himself toward his van. The harsh beating left Vinny scatterbrained, the confusion and fear overwhelming his senses.

As he closed in on the van door, he caught a glimpse of the judgmental faces of his former coworkers. They looked at him like he was just some scum at the bottom of a dumpster. Like he was a homeless stranger causing trouble. It was as if they'd all suddenly forgotten that Vinny had been their guide and had their backs. He'd stuck up for them when the King wanted his pawns to feel his wrath.

Even after Vinny had lost his family, there was no understanding.

Their loyalty was nonexistent.

But the anger he had for Curtis and the workers was fleeting. The embarrassment, hot on his face, was the most dominant emotion.

Vinny needed to get away from them—to get away from *everyone.*

He picked himself up, pulled open the door to his van, and hopped inside. Vinny's vision was blurry, but he managed to stick the key in the ignition. As he backed out sloppily, over the rumble of the engine he could hear something that made his stomach ache, coming from the vicinity of Curtis and the rest of his former coworkers.

Laughter.

TREADS OF TRAUMA

The air was warm and comforting—aside from the scent of manure that tainted it, but that was a smell Sara had become familiar with and hardly even noticed anymore. She washed the bits of food off the dish in the sink and looked out the open window—the beautiful orangey sun continued to ascend over the barn out back.

I'm so damn lucky, Sara thought.

A big grin spread across her face as she dunked a sudsy plate into the sink of rinse water. But as she removed it, there came a hideous wail, and a dreadful feeling instantly filled her guts.

"Ahhhhhhhhhhh!"

The cutting howl shattered Sara's morning serenity. The horror embedded in the sound was so profound that it was hard to determine if the shriek was male or female. She dropped the dish into the water.

"Eric?!" Sara yelled, bolting out the back door. "What's wrong?!"

The wetness from the sink still coated her hands as she ran closer to the wailing. When she turned the corner, the surplus of blood, bone, and brains was unavoidable. Michael continued to cry out as he switched the tractor's gears.

"Oh my God! Eric!" Sara shrieked.

Her little boy's body remained motionless as the massive tractor tire rolled forward. Eric's head—or what remained of it—had lost its natural shape. The face she'd stared into and caressed to sleep so many nights had lost all familiarity. It looked like a grenade had been set off inside the child's mouth. Above his blood-drenched overalls was only a neck nub—a permanent stump surrounded by an explosion of rosy filling and fragments. It looked like a crimson pumpkin had been smashed and pulled apart.

Eyes darting to the man seated on the tractor, her horrified howls joined Michael's. The barrage of shrieks ripped deep throughout the farmland. Despite the shock, an unsettling feeling crept up inside her when Sara suddenly realized she was screaming alone.

"What about me?!" Michael yelled, eyes looking like they might bulge out of their sockets.

Sara's horrified gawk transitioned from the headless body of her baby to her husband. Michael still sat upon the running tractor, but suddenly his face looked different than before—he looked older and tired. She watched as he retrieved the handgun from behind his back and put it to his temple.

Tears leaked from Michael's eyes. "What about me?! I'm still fucking here, Sara!"

She watched helplessly, knowing what was about to happen. Her husband pulled the trigger, and the bullet tore its way into his temple, exiting the left side of his skull. The path of violence caused Michael's cranial tissue to blow out like carnal confetti, leaving his body slumped over sideways, leaning against the wheel of the tractor.

"Noooooo!" Sara cried.

Suddenly, the drying wetness the dishes had left upon Sara's hands began to intensify. She looked down at her palms and fingers to see that they were no longer covered in water. As she noticed the change in pigment, her crying became more unhinged.

It was blood.

"My blood's on *your* hands," Michael whispered, brains and gore spilling out of his mouth.

Sara looked at her husband, who was no longer slumped over, and her jaw dropped.

Michael's face was now rotten. Decomposition fluid poured from his nostrils and mouth while clumps of blackened gore and brain tissue fell from the massive hole in his head like shit from a cow's backside. His dead eyes were clouded with milky-white slime.

"It's on *your* fucking hands!" he yelled.

***

"Michael!" Sara screamed.

When Sara awoke her heart was pounding. The terror on her face wasn't new, but it wasn't expected either. After wiping the sweat from her brow, she sat up. It wasn't the first time she'd had such a nightmare, but it was the first time in a while.

She rolled out of her bed and walked into the kitchen. Approaching the refrigerator, she looked at the piece of paper with the name *Vincent Fowler* in the clutches of a magnetic clip. Her eyes drifted to the phone number scribbled below it. She recalled the night that Vinny was rushed into the emergency room after his horrific wreck.

Sara had tried to talk to Vinny more in the hours after he'd awoken, but he'd retreated into himself. The severe trauma had taken hold of him, and he had no words to offer her or the world around him. He was a broken man.

Observing him in such a state made Sara understand just how much Vinny needed someone. She'd jotted down his number, and for a week she'd thought about calling him—especially after his blood-alcohol test results came back negative. But even once she'd mustered the willpower to reach out, Vinny wasn't willing to talk. The ensuing messages she'd left on his answering machine had never been returned.

After her short stint at Lakeland Hospital, Sara had returned home. Part of her just wanted to stick her head in the sand and forget the entire ordeal.

But she couldn't. If there was one thing Sara had learned about herself through all the tragedy she'd witnessed, it was that she always cared.

Every time she thought about Vinny, it reopened her own wounds. And with Eric's and Michael's anniversaries still fresh on her mind, it was becoming impossible to forget. When she wondered about Vinny, she couldn't help but think about the eerie similarities of their struggles. She credited the totality of the anniversaries and Vinny's situation with the recent return of the gruesome nightmares.

I can't fail like that again, Sara thought, pulling the phone number off the fridge. *I won't. Eventually, you're gonna answer.*

COLD STONES

The soil in front of Kelly's grave somehow still seemed fresh. Vinny gently pressed his fingertips against the slab of stone and then looked at Ashley's. He hated the stones. They put forth an uncomfortable truth—outside of the handful of pictures at home and the images rooted in their resting places, Vinny would never see them again.

On that particularly dreary afternoon, the sky above Grayfield Cemetery was surrounded by a cluster of ominous clouds. As Vinny sat sniffling, he lifted the steel flask to his lips and guzzled. It was the first time he'd seen his family since the funeral. The first time he'd had the guts to return to their plots. Tears dribbled from his eyelids. He wanted to control his emotions, but he was falling apart.

You failed them, Vinny thought. *And what do you have now?*

He knew the answer, and it wasn't anything he cared to remind himself of, but still, he seemed to do it all the time. Losing his job had also made him lose the only other distraction in front of him besides the drink. All he had now was time to think. And the one thing he couldn't stop thinking about was the night of the accident. More specifically, he couldn't stop wondering about the strangest part—the part that no one seemed to believe.

Who the fuck was that woman in the road?

It was possible that she was just another twisted vision that his sick, wandering mind had projected—a repercussion of his violent childhood—but there was no way for him to know for sure. The enigma that was the strange, dirty woman would most likely haunt him for the rest of his days. And as things stood, his final stretch wasn't looking so robust any longer.

And that animal . . .

He didn't want to relive the violent acts perpetrated against his family. As he forced the image of the gore-caked animal out of his mind, his gaze fell back on the headstones. The sharp cut of the alcohol in his flask entering his mouth made him wince.

"Maybe I'll see you sooner than later," he whispered.

DARK DAZE

As Vinny lurched into his apartment, he sucked down the last of the liquor in the bottle. Staggering, he threw the empty container on top of the table, currently blanketed by piles of bills, junk mail, and a few overdue notices.

Vinny's eyes shifted and stopped on the length of rope dangling from the ceiling fan. He'd fashioned the noose weeks prior but hadn't had the gall to approach it. But the visit to their plots had given him the strength he needed to make his exit.

It was time to say goodbye.

In his heart, Vinny hoped that goodbye meant saying hello to Kelly and Ashley again, elsewhere. While he couldn't be sure, anything was better than being so alone.

They'd moved into the apartment to be closer to Kelly's family. The change of location didn't matter to Vinny—he didn't have anyone he'd grown close to besides Kelly, anyway. The only people he'd thought were his friends had laughed him off the construction site. Their laughter still echoed in his head.

Some friends they were, Vinny thought. *I've got no one left, no reason to keep going.*

He pushed the table aside, knocking a pile of mail onto the floor, and grabbed one of the wooden chairs. Sliding it underneath the noose, Vinny took a deep breath.

"Things will be different soon," he whispered to himself as the tears trickled down his face.

Just as he set his boot atop the seat, the phone rang. The answering machine beside it still flickered with a load of ignored messages. He couldn't imagine who might be calling him—collectors maybe, since he'd been neglecting the bills, but something told him it wasn't.

Vinny stared at the phone while deeply contemplating and feeling the roughness of the rope against his fingers. As he slid the loop around his neck, the phone gave a final ring before the answering machine activated. When the tape rolled, the room filled with a kind, female voice.

"Ah, hello . . . My name is Sara St. James, and I'm calling on behalf of Lakeland Hospital with a message for a Mr. Vincent Fowler."

Vinny remained hesitant as he stared at the machine, footing secure as he listened.

"Some of your test results have come back, and . . . if you have a few minutes, I'd like to discuss them."

Heart pounding, Vinny suddenly recognized the voice: the kind woman from the pharmacy who he'd never expected to see again. She was the first person he'd seen when he'd awoken in the hospital and was introduced to his new nightmare universe.

He recalled how when Kelly's parents had berated him, she'd stepped in. Their words had been like daggers in his heart. Vinny was grateful that she'd given him the benefit of the doubt and stopped their onslaught.

As he listened to her caring tone, his instincts triggered. Vinny didn't know if he was just desperate for some human contact or wholly enchanted by the woman's sweetness. As much as he wanted to finally end the cycle of constant agony, Vinny wanted to speak with her just a little more. He stepped down, staggered over to the phone, and lifted it off the receiver.

"Yeah?" Vinny said.

"Oh, um . . . hello. Is there a Vincent Fowler there?"

"Yeah, I'm here."

"This is Sara St. James. I—I tended to you in the hospital after your accident. You were obviously going through a lot, so I wouldn't blame you if you didn't remember—"

"I remember you. I remember you at the pharmacy too. Thank you for being there for me . . ."

His words were as hollow as the liquor bottles on his counter. While the injuries he'd sustained weren't life-threatening, dying in the hospital would've been a dream come true when he reflected on what his life had devolved into.

"It's no problem. That's my job, and I . . . I just wanted to say that I'm so sorry about your family. But I also wanted to reach out to you because . . . well, I heard what your in-laws said to you when you woke up."

The salty, hate-filled faces of Vinny's in-laws appeared in his head. The disgust and hurt in their eyes were like nothing he'd seen before. They yearned for him to be tortured and encompassed by misery. And while they might not know it, they'd gotten their wish.

"I'm sure you obviously know this already," Sara continued, "but your blood test came back negative for both drugs and alcohol. I've tried calling you a few times since the results came in. I left you a few messages, but I . . . I really wanted to tell you myself."

Vinny's bottom lip began to quiver. "Why?"

Sara paused. "I don't know. I guess I just figured you deserved a word of encouragement after all you've been through. They shouldn't have blamed you. You're a victim, too, whether they want to acknowledge it or not."

"But I failed them," Vinny cried. "I-I failed everyone. Nothing's ever gonna change that. And when I'm gone, that's all that my legacy will be."

"Hey! Don't talk like that," Sara said sternly.

The sharpness of her words awakened Vinny.

"You think *I* haven't failed?" she asked.

Vinny wiped tears from his eyes.

"Just because you fail once doesn't mean you can't make amends for your mistakes," Sara went on. "I didn't just call you because I feel bad for you, I called you because I know what you're going through. I can help you."

Vinny's hysterical sobs rattled through the phoneline. He was trying to bottle his emotions, but it wasn't easy. Sara's words made him feel a way that he hadn't felt since the accident—distracted.

"Why don't the two of us meet for coffee?" Sara asked.

Keeping the phone to his ear, Vinny looked back at the noose hanging from his ceiling and did his best to compose himself.

"C'mon, just one cup of coffee," Sara persisted. "It's not gonna kill you. What do you say?"

Vinny straightened up, trying his best to hold it together. He couldn't help but feel like there was a reason she'd called right when he'd reached for that noose.

"All right," he whispered.

WAKING UP

After a short nap—interrupted countless times by images of his dead loved ones, of course—the intensity of Vinny's drunkenness had finally dulled. He stepped into the warm shower, shocked that he'd found the motivation to wash himself. He hadn't yet found a reason to be inspired outside of a couple of occasions when he'd become overly appalled by his own musk.

As he washed his body, his ribs still ached from Curtis' steel toes. Even more painful than the bruised areas of his flesh was his stinging pride. The public belittling he'd been through at work and the hurtful comments and blame his in-laws had hurled at him he'd surely never forget. It was like the entire world was against him.

But the instant Vinny awoke from his slumber, there was another sensation stirring inside him too. A dull feeling festering in his gut—one that had seemed so alien to him since the accident.

Hope.

He didn't know where the hope had come from, but the way Sara spoke to him on the phone spawned an aimless motivation inside him. While he didn't know exactly why, it seemed they really did relate to each other.

She had no reason to reach out to him and spout lies. Unexpectedly having someone who cared for his well-being had helped him keep the suicidal thoughts at bay. He finally had something to focus on besides his inner turmoil.

Once he'd dried off, Vinny shaved his face. He even applied deodorant and a few dabs of cologne. There was still a buzz in his brain from the booze, but he believed he'd be able to drive without killing someone. He wouldn't have even had the wherewithal to consider his own safety earlier that day, let alone someone else's. As he slipped on a decent pair of jeans and a shirt, he thought about what Sara had said to him.

You *know what* I'm *going through?* he wondered.

Vinny approached the mirror to give himself one final look over and leaned in. As he examined the scar tissue on his scalp where the doctors had stitched his head shut, he hoped Sara was embellishing.

A NEW BEGINNING

The all-night diner was bustling just enough that, with the heavy rain pattering outside, their conversation blended in with the rest of the chatter. They sat stoically, tucked into a booth in the back corner, as the waitress topped off each of their coffees.

"I'm glad you decided to come," Sara said, twirling her blond lock in her fingers.

"Me too. Me too."

The privacy gave Vinny a certain comfort in speaking to her, yet he couldn't help but feel a little awkward. The woman had seen him berated by his dead wife's parents, and just a short time ago heard him whimpering like a lost child on the telephone. He'd never shared so much darkness and despair with a total stranger.

"I needed this," he added.

"I figured." She dumped some sugar into her coffee. "You know, I wasn't just saying I can relate to you to make you feel less alone. I wouldn't lie to you."

Vinny thought about the inference as he sipped his coffee. "I'm afraid to ask."

"It's terrible." The hurt in her eyes flared. "But I'd tell you . . . if you think it'll help."

"I'm not going to make you relive something so painful just for me. I wouldn't feel—"

"I relive it every day of my life," she interrupted. "Whether I want to or not. I'll never get past it. But what I have been able to do is learn to live with it. You were in a bad way on the phone. It sounded like you needed to know that."

Vinny hung his head and looked down at his coffee. If he said anything else, he'd risk breaking down on the spot. Instead, he nodded and said, "Thank you."

Sara looked at the downpour outside the restaurant. "I wasn't always a nurse. A little over just eight years ago I lived on a farm with my husband, Michael, and our son, Eric. Eric was a little over seven years old. I imagine you've probably got some idea of what farm life's like—everyone pitches in to keep things running. There's always work to be done, and Eric was always wanting to help us."

Vinny could see Sara beginning to struggle as she conjured the memory—clearly recounting it was torture.

"Anyway, that morning . . ." she continued. "That morning started out like any other. Eric had been helping Michael clear out some junk from behind one of the barns. I was inside the house when I heard it. I don't know how it went down exactly, but when Michael's screams started, I imagined he'd been hurt pretty bad—I had this immediate instinct. I'd never heard anything like it. The wails were so guttural that it hurt to listen to them. My heart dropped into my stomach, and I took off running. When I got to where they were, I realized that Michael wasn't screaming because he was injured. He was screaming because of Eric. It didn't even look like my baby anymore . . . he was a mess. I guess Eric dropped something under the machine and Michael didn't see him. He didn't mean to back over his head with the tractor."

Vinny's jaw dropped. He didn't know what to say. Biting his lip, he decided to just listen.

"The tractor tire . . . it . . . Eric's little head was just . . . flattened. Like a fresh piece of roadkill on the highway. And that's the last memory I have of my baby."

Sara quickly wiped a tear out of the corner of her eye.

"Jesus, I'm so sorry," Vinny whispered, trying to hold himself together. "I know that look."

She glanced at him. "What look?"

"I see it in the mirror every day. You can't blame yourself. It was a freak accident."

"I don't blame myself for *that*," Sara said. "It's what happened afterward that I blame myself for."

Vinny's eyes widened, as if to say, *There's more?*

"Even though it was an accident, Michael and I were never the same. I told him I forgave him, but the divorce papers said otherwise. I left him at his lowest point." The tears were now welling again. "And exactly one year later, on the anniversary of Eric's death, while he was in his darkest hour, Michael put that gun to his head . . . I should've been there to tell him it wasn't his fault. Excuse me a moment."

Sara got up from the table and disappeared into the restroom.

Vinny sat waiting, dumbstruck by his emotion. He was having difficulty digesting the conversation.

When Sara returned, she'd composed herself. There were no longer tears trickling from her eyes. Showing her hurt and weakness clearly wasn't what she'd intended, but to Vinny, in a strange way, it helped.

"Sorry," she said. "As you know, dealing with all this is . . . it's very much a process. But I think now you probably realize why I had to reach out to you. When I saw your in-laws saying those awful things to you, saying that you're dead to them, I thought about the mistake I made with Michael. Your exact situation"—she gestured to Vinny with her fingers and back to herself—"it's why I became a nurse. This is how I deal with my guilt. I'll never *truly* be able to make things right, but I can acknowledge the error of my ways. I can still have an impact. *You* can get past this. And you will, even if I have to drag you there myself."

Vinny sat there, taking in the powerful statement. The woman sitting across from him was far tougher than he was.

While her character gave him hope, he was anything but confident that he could pull himself out of his slump.

Vinny dropped his gaze to his lap. "I'm not sure I'm as strong as you. Everything . . ." He tried to muster some composure. "Everything's falling apart."

"I know it may feel that way, but—"

"Not feels, *is*," Vinny interrupted. "My old demons have found me again. There's no way for me to hold them back without Kelly and Ashley."

Thoughts of his morbid fantasies flashed in his head. Dead female anatomy, rotten and waiting. He saw Kelly's deformed face—a twitching garble of muscle and gore—in the passenger seat. And then naked and fingering her cunt vigorously. She smeared the blood from her facial wound all over her digits as she rammed them in and out of her hole.

Vinny closed his eyes.

Stop it! he thought.

The perverse imagery ceased, and he was able to focus again. Those weren't even the demons he'd been referring to—that was a whole different can of worms that only he could deal with himself.

One step at a time.

"Are you all right?" Sara asked.

Refocusing on the task at hand, he nodded. "Yeah . . . it's just hard to find the right words sometimes."

"It's okay, Mr. Fowler. Speak however and whenever you're comfortable. I'm not here to judge you."

"Call me Vinny."

"Okay, Vinny."

He scratched the side of his face, still piecing his partial confession together. "It's just . . . I've been wasted almost every day since the accident. And as a result, I got my ass handed to me at work and fired from my job. Now the bills are piling up. I can't fuckin' sleep unless I pass out from exhaustion. I just keep seeing their faces—or what was left of them. When you called me, I was . . ." The emotion stopped him for a moment. "I'll just say thank God you called."

"I'm glad I did," Sara whispered.

Vinny nodded, hand over his mouth. "Me too."

"You just need help," she assured him. "You think I got this far on my own? There are places that can get you on the right track, evaluate you and—"

"No," he said firmly. "I ain't going to a fuckin' shrink or—or some loony bin."

"Okay, I understand," she conceded. "But will you at least let *me* try and help you?"

Vinny's face scrunched with skepticism, but he had no one else who cared. Still, the hesitancy to take the help right in front of him remained.

What's the worst that could happen?

"What did you have in mind?" he asked.

"It's a process," Sara said again. "And the process is all based on acknowledging your progress and looking to the next step. For example, you said you've been drinking non-stop, but you don't seem drunk now."

"So?"

Sara sipped her coffee again. "So, that's progress. The fact that you were able to dry out enough to meet me tonight is a *huge* step in the right direction."

The waitress approached their table and dropped a plate with a burger on it in front of Sara.

"You need anything else?" the waitress asked.

"No, thank you," Sara said, returning back to their conversation as the waitress left. She looked Vinny in the eyes. "So now that you know you're strong enough to control yourself, that unlocks more ways for you to get back on your feet. If you did it once, you can do it again. If you can do that, you can get a job. If you can get a job, you can pay the bills, and if you can pay the bills, you don't have to think about what you were thinking about when I called. Right?"

Vinny's eyes gravitated toward the burger. The shiny beef was cooked, but it still made his stomach rumble. Poor little Ashley's destroyed face and the ribbons of meat and skin hanging off it manifested in his mind again.

"Is everything all right?" Sara asked.

Vinny forced his eyes to connect with hers again. Not looking at the meat seemed to help. He considered her plan. It actually sounded somewhat feasible.

"What about sleep?" he asked. "Drinkin' is the only way I get any rest. Otherwise . . ." Visions of the familial mutilation appeared in his mind again. "Otherwise I just keep picturing the aftermath of the accident."

"You'd think sleep would be the hardest one to figure out, but it's actually the easiest. I started taking sleeping pills a while back, and they've really helped me. I lay down, fall asleep, and in the morning I don't remember a thing. The days are still challenging, but when you're rested, at least you have the energy to confront the demons."

He couldn't believe it. It was like she had an answer for everything. Furthermore, her responses were well thought out and seemed realistic. Vinny nodded in agreement.

Sara pulled a small bottle of pills with the label ripped off out of her purse. She carefully slid her hand across the table, finding his.

When their skin touched, Vinny felt a strange electricity. A connection with her—a tingle ravaging his body. As she pulled away from him slowly, she left the medication in his palm. He didn't quite know why, but part of him hoped she'd felt the same energy he did.

"It worked so well for me that after about a year I didn't even need them anymore," Sara said. "But I still kept filling the prescription, just in case I did . . . or in case I met someone else who did."

Vinny slipped the bottle into his jacket and smiled—something he hadn't done since before the accident. There was a different vibe surging through his body now. He felt lucky to have encountered someone like Sara. Going from beckoning death to a civil conversation in such a short time gave him hope. Having Sara around was like having a guardian angel.

"I can't even . . . I don't know how to thank you," he whispered.

"You can thank me by getting your shit together," Sara said, returning his smile.

"I'm . . . I'm going to try my best."

"There's a few weeks' worth in there. That should get you the rest you've been missing. After that, you can build back up. And what was it you did for work?"

The idea of thinking about his professional downfall irked him.

"Construction," he grumbled.

"Well, that's a plus." Sara lifted her coffee cup and finished it. "There's almost always construction jobs that're available."

The annoyance on Vinny's face must've been obvious.

"What?" Sara asked.

"I kind of blacklisted myself from the biggest company in these parts. And I'm also not sure how good I'd work around other people right now."

Sara's mind seemed like it was computing the details, until suddenly, her eyes popped with excitement.

"Then why don't you work for yourself?" she asked.

"What do you mean?" Vinny asked.

"You know, like a handyman. I'm sure you can roll all your experience from the big projects you worked on over to smaller jobs. You can start slow and go at your own pace, be your own boss. Take whatever gigs you're comfortable with and build your way up from there. Joyce—this nurse I worked with—said her husband does something similar. Takes out ads in the paper to complete odd jobs, and apparently he makes a killing."

Sara was a miracle worker. Every problem he had, she seemed to have an answer to. Not just an answer, but she made it sound exciting. She could've been a used car salesman. Her pitch seemed ideal. It was *exactly* what Vinny was looking for.

"Okay," he said.

"Okay . . . ?"

"I mean I'll look into it."

Sara grinned but then flattened out her expression. "Just promise me one thing though?"

He bobbed his head and raised an eyebrow, awaiting the ask.

She squirmed in the booth. "If I try to call you again—you know, to see how you're doing—promise me you'll answer the phone or at least return my call. Okay?"

A slight grin now buckled one corner of Vinny's face. "I think I can do that."

A moment of awkward silence arose.

He saw the hotness flare on Sara's face as she started to blush. While Vinny didn't think her request was meant to sound flirtatious or in any way romantic, it still kind of came off that way.

"You never know," Vinny added, "maybe I'll call you first."

He didn't know why he said it, but he was glad he did. There was something about Sara—she was able to comfort him in a comfortless time. He didn't realize it in the moment, but that caretaker quality and overall sweetness she spouted was magnetic.

She gave him hope.

Sara's eyes widened as Vinny's heart started to race. She looked like she wasn't expecting to hear that.

"I think I'd like that," she said. Before the awkward silence could return, she finally looked down at her plate. "I'm starving. Are you sure you're not hungry? I don't think I can eat all of this myself."

Vinny watched as she sank her teeth into the soggy bread and greasy patty, ripping away a sizable mouthful. He'd been able to keep the flashbacks at bay—distracted by her guidance and their flirtatious exchange—but as Sara held the shiny beef in her hand, he saw a flurry of visions.

The disgusting woman in the road.

The glistening teeth of the beast.

The dark bloodshed.

The mauled faces.

His cheeks puffed out. "Excuse me, I'll be right back," he blubbered, stumbling toward the restroom in the back of the diner.

Sara's eyes widened. "What's wrong?"

"I'll be fine," he said, promptly disappearing into the bathroom.

Quickly locking the door behind him, Vinny fell face-first into the toilet.

Vomit plopped into the water and spewed into the seat. As Vinny recalled the horrific sights from the accident, he heaved even harder. When he looked at the chunky porridge continuing to pile up inside the yellowed bowl, Vinny knew that it wasn't going to get any easier from there.

ODD JOBS

Sara was right. When Vinny awoke the next morning, he felt rested, and his mind was a blank slate. The pills had done the trick, and with his head clear, he was even able to start the day off with a shower.

As he used the soap to create a lather on his body, he thought about what Sara had suggested to him. About answering her calls or at the very least returning them. She had done so much for him, the least he could do was keep his word.

After he dried off and got dressed, Vinny made his way to the kitchen. He looked at the collection of empty liquor bottles and crusty food dishes near the sink and sighed.

I'll get to you later, he thought.

Diverting his attention to the side table with the phone and answering machine, Vinny examined the red digital readout. It read: *FULL.*

I suppose I've gotta clear these out if I'm gonna stay true to my agreement with Sara.

He pressed the play button and listened intently. There was a message from a bill collector first, followed by one from the funeral director that had helped with the services for Kelly and Ashley. Just hearing the man's voice again made him cringe.

That dreary yet caring tone reminded him of the awful looks he'd gotten—not only from Kelly's family, but from essentially everyone in the funeral parlor. Their judging eyes and frowning mouths. He could practically hear them wishing aloud that it was him inside a box instead of his wife and daughter. He didn't blame them—on the contrary, he agreed with them. If Vinny could've made the switch he most definitely would've, but instead he was stuck with their hatred and spite.

He was thankful when Sara's voice hit and dragged him out of the memory. Her messages were short and sweet. He wished he'd heard them before the fallout at King's Construction. Maybe things would've been different. Maybe he wouldn't be looking for a job.

Vinny's eyebrows elevated when the topic of jobs was raised in the very next message. The velvety voice perked his ears—the man spoke with a pompous tone, but still one that demanded attention.

"Mr. Fowler, this is Alfred Edwards," he huffed. "I assume you'll recall the excellent work you did at my estate some months ago—work I was highly pleased with. I've called you several times now and even spoken with your *wife*, and, I must confess, I'm growing tired of leaving messages that receive no follow-up. Do you not like money? Because I can offer you a handsome reward, one that's *beyond* generous, simply for your assistance with a minor residential matter. If it's your employer that worries you, they needn't know of our agreement. I'm happy to be discreet. Call me."

The strange man rattled off his phone number before abruptly ending the message.

It had been so long that he'd forgotten about what Kelly had mentioned to him just before the accident. Apparently there was a high-paying job already waiting for him. He didn't need to take out an ad in the paper, after all. The man seemed eager. Vinny used the pen and paper on the table to jot down the number.

Maybe things are looking up, he thought.

Without hesitation, Vinny punched the numbers into the dial pad and lifted the phone to his ear.

"I was wondering when you were going to call," Alfred Edwards answered snidely.

Vinny furrowed his brow. "How did you—"

"It certainly took you long enough, Mr. Fowler," Alfred interjected. "Since I've been waiting many weeks now, what do you say that we just cut to the chase?"

"Ah—all right," Vinny said. He wasn't prepared for just how pushy the man was. Still, he was hungry to hear what he would say next.

"I have a project in mind. A project that only someone of your . . . *experience* would be suitable for. I want nothing more than to go over the specs with you this evening. In fact, my sister, Blanche, and I would love to have you over for dinner to discuss all the pertinent details—and, of course, your compensation. What do you say?"

"Tonight?" Vinny asked, unsure if he was stable enough to meet with a potential client. He hadn't had a drink all day and was feeling a little jittery.

"Yes, of course, tonight," Alfred barked. "We need to start this project sooner than later. Due to the extended period of time it's taken me to get ahold of you, we are already far behind schedule. Now, can you, or can't you?"

He could always take a little drink to settle his nerves before he left. Chances like the one being dumped on his jobless lap weren't going to come often. Vinny knew he'd be a fool to pass it up.

It's not what Sara would want, but I need a job. Just one more time to get through this. Then I'm done for good.

"Well?" Alfred persisted.

"Um . . . where is it?"

"Mr. Fowler, have you forgotten us already?"

"I'm sorry, I don't mean to be rude . . . it's just . . ." Vinny looked at the empty bottle of booze on the counter, thirsty for a swig. "I've been having some issues with my memory lately."

"Not to worry. At my age my mind isn't exactly what it used to be. I can't say it's going to get any better. Do you have a piece of paper and pen handy?"

"Um . . ." Vinny reached for the sticky notes by the answering machine and snagged a pen out of a cup. He slapped the adhesive side of the paper beside a picture of Ashley on the fridge. As he stared into his dead daughter's eyes, his mind went blank.

"Mr. Fowler, are you still there?"

"Yeah."

Vinny lifted the pen and scribbled *First Job Back* on the sticky note.

Alfred sighed. "Are you ready?"

"Shoot."

"1 Bovine Drive, Wickford, Rhode—"

Vinny jotted it down but stopped to cut him off. "Say no more, I remember you now. I didn't even need to write it down. That's the biggest house in Wickford—maybe the state."

"That it is. We are certainly blessed to have the property and land. And rest assured, your contribution to it will be greatly appreciated."

Vinny turned away from the fridge and dropped the pen beside the machine. "Well, I'm certainly looking forward to discussing the job."

"I can promise you two things, Mr. Fowler," Alfred said. "You'll be enamored with the compensation . . . and you absolutely won't forget us this time around."

DINNER OF DEPRAVITY

Just enough to take the edge off, Vinny thought.

He took the last swig from the flask and winced. While he wasn't totally shitfaced, he certainly felt nice. Once he got in the house and put a little food inside him, he figured he'd be at a perfect balance to talk business—or that's what he'd convinced himself, at least.

As Vinny exited the van, he swished a shot of Listerine around his mouth and spit it on the ground. He'd gone out of his way to do his best to mask his buzz, not planning to let his drinking blow another opportunity.

The property looked as incredible as he recalled. He admired the sharp, gothic architecture just as much as the first time he'd seen it. But, while he'd enjoyed the style of the manor, working on it had been another story. He could never quite put his finger on what caused his discomfort. Alfred and Blanche were odd and snooty enough, but even when they weren't in the picture there was something about the home that kept him on edge.

When Vinny entered the walkway, the dim glow of the vintage post lanterns illuminated the path to the black door and front steps of the property. But before he could even reach the entrance, the knob was already twisting and Alfred's pale, haggard face was soon revealed.

"Good evening, Mr. Fowler," Alfred said with a smirk. "Such a pleasure to see you."

Vinny tried to keep his pace and footing as normal as possible. If he came staggering in, that wouldn't make a good impression just before the gig.

"Call me Vinny, if you want." It was Vinny's goal to make things between them as comfortable and casual as possible.

Alfred's grin faded. There was nothing comfortable or casual about him. "I prefer the former, thank you."

As Vinny broke the threshold of the manor, he extended his hand.

Alfred ignored the gesture and closed the door. "Follow me, please. Dinner is right this way."

As the old man breezed past him, Vinny looked down at his palm, unsure if Alfred had even seen it. He followed the scrawny elder past the dual staircase in silence, until they entered a magnificent study. The well-preserved wood of the built-in bookshelves, the vintage leather couches, and the Tiffany lamps somehow even further highlighted their status.

"Wow," Vinny said. "This place is even nicer than I remember."

Alfred craned his liver-spotted neck sideways, aiming his wrinkly face at Vinny. "Everything gets old eventually. Even what's priceless. But I suppose someone who hasn't been granted the opportunity to experience such sophistication would have no way of knowing."

Vinny had already figured a few cocky comments were bound to occur. While he didn't enjoy being spoken to like a peasant, he was prepared to let the little digs roll off him to secure the job.

The next room seemed to be dedicated to billiards. It consisted of an oak bar, a pool table, a pair of aged-leather chairs, and a fireplace. This room was part of the remodel that Vinny had participated in, but all the furnishings inside were new to him. As he took it all in, eventually his eyes found the painting.

It was an oil, hung above the mantle, of much younger versions of Alfred and Blanche. They were wrapped in each other's arms—a little more lovingly, Vinny thought, than expected for a set of siblings. The faux version of Alfred and Blanche somehow managed to evoke the same emotions in him as the flesh-and-blood ones: uneasiness.

"Here we are," Alfred said, finally ushering Vinny into the dining room.

The space was just as garish as the rest of the house. At both ends of an unnecessarily long dining table hung stunning chandeliers. They cast a spooky glow that made their shadows appear oversized on the crimson wallpaper. There were two silver candelabras at each end of the table adorned with freshly lit candles, and behind the runny wax sat the lanky and gaunt body of Blanche Edwards.

"Herman!" Blanche called, clapping her hands together twice. "Come, come!"

As Alfred led Vinny to his seat, another man dressed in a chef's uniform entered through the door at the other side of the room, approaching with a large, steaming pot in his oven-mitted hands.

Herman set down the pot in the center of the table between three bowls. Removing the top, the man used a ladle to drop a few spoonfuls into each bowl. Once they were filled with a hearty, brownish stew, the chef nodded.

Within the thick fluid Vinny could see several girthy slices of meat. Glasses had already been filled halfway with red wine and placed beside the sparkling silverware and impeccable china.

"Thank you, Herman," Alfred said, glaring at the help. "Now please, leave us."

Vinny studied the quiet and calculated chef. There was something about the man's face that looked familiar. But he pushed through the door and exited the dining room before Vinny had a chance to figure it out.

"I certainly hope you brought your appetite," Blanche said, "because this meat is quite succulent."

Vinny's appetite went on life support the moment he saw the huge hunks of meat. His mind was peppered with images of the creature's bloody fangs pulling clumps of garbled flesh from Ashley's dead face.

"This is . . . unbelievable," Vinny said, finally finding the word. He was able to control the rumbling sensation in his gut by forcing his eyes away from the plate. "Thank you so much for having me."

He could feel his internal discomfort pushing outward. As the sweat pissed from his pores, his stomach wanted to retch, but he put his game face on. Despite the disastrous dinner choice, he refused to let his lone chance at getting back on his feet be derailed by his newfound phobia.

Vinny thought about Sara and how strong she'd been throughout her own ordeal. Considering how far she'd come after witnessing a sickening, double dose of tragedy, she inspired him to be tougher.

You can get past this—no you're gonna get past this. Just . . . eat around the meat if you have to.

"But of course," Blanche replied. "We're very excited that you decided to join us."

"*Very* excited," Alfred agreed.

Blanche's crooked grin offered Vinny another look at her unsettling enamel. Considering how well-off they were, it struck him as odd that her mouth would be ravaged by such decay. There was much attention to detail elsewhere, but not to her own hygiene.

"You can take this one," Alfred offered, pulling out the chair across from Blanche for Vinny.

Vinny nodded before taking a step closer and plopping down. "Thanks."

"We're beyond grateful to *finally* have you here with us to discuss the work we require," Alfred said.

The man walked around Vinny's back and took the final seat, between him and Blanche, at the end of the table.

"Well, I'm grateful to be here," Vinny said. "And I've been wanting to ask you. Why me—"

"Shhh," Alfred whispered, holding his long finger to his lips. "All that can wait. While the rest of the world may operate in a business-before-pleasure chronology, we prefer our pleasure up front." He raised his glass in the air. "To new beginnings and finishing old missions."

Vinny joined in, clanging his glass against the others'. While they all drank during the toast, Vinny might've gulped down a little more than either of them. He was going to need more gas in the tank to make it through this bizarre dynamic.

Blanche stared across the table at Vinny, adjusting the white locks that hung in front of one eye. That eerie grin returned to her face.

"Now, let us eat," she said.

Vinny reached for his fork but paused when Blanche suddenly spoke again.

"But before we do . . ." She raised her finger in the air. "You wouldn't mind if I say a few words first, would you, Mr. Fowler?"

"Of course not."

Blanche smiled and reached toward the seat of the empty chair beside her. She elevated a triangular box with a black, wooden exterior.

Vinny watched as the old woman set the slim pyramid down on the tablecloth, taking notice of the unfamiliar symbol painted on the face of the object. A black circle—even blacker than the wood—with a thin white trim. Within the circle of darkness sat an elongated, gray tuning fork, the handle of which overlapped outside of the circle. The upside-down, U-shaped depiction looked like a long doorway.

Strange . . .

"What . . . what is that?" Vinny asked.

The words left his lips slower than he'd expected and seemed to echo against his eardrums, as if each syllable were a stone being cast into water. He registered the ripple of audio over and over. Confusion swelled in his brain as he watched the old woman respond.

"Oh, it's nothing, dear," she whispered. "Nothing at all. It just helps me remember how to . . . find all my words. Keeping pace is important. Otherwise, nothing would ever get done. We all need something to help keep us on track . . ."

Vinny's eyelids stretched as Blanche's grin suddenly grew far more maniacal—a blackness that made him think of used motor oil evacuating her mouth and raining into her bowl. An image of Beverly, struggling and gagging with his father's can of oil shoved inside her mouth, manifested in Vinny's mind. He shook it off, looking from Blanche to his glass of wine. The liquid inside appeared far thicker than before.

"What . . . what the fuck is happening?" Vinny slurred.

"Everything that's supposed to," Alfred calmly replied.

Blanche popped off the front panel of the obsidian artifact to reveal a metronome needle. But instead of the typical metal weight that might be attached to the top, there hung a black eyeball with a red pupil.

Vinny wanted to move, but it now felt like he weighed a thousand pounds. Glued to his seat, he could only shift his gaze to Alfred, who, like his twisted sister, looked much different than when he'd first answered the door. His shining, orangey eyes were wide, and the wrinkles upon his pale skin had multiplied many times over.

The siblings looked like well-aged coffin cargo.

When Vinny's eyes shifted back to Blanche, her pruned fingers pinched the metallic hoop around the lone piece of steel that was inserted into the side of the metronome. She cranked the winding key counterclockwise several times, until it would move no more.

The runny hallucinations kept the atmosphere around Vinny surreal. The once ordinary, regal wallpaper pattern now looked like thousands of tiny cunts lined up against each other. They puckered and bounced excitedly, leaking a heavy flow in rivulets. Red oozed from every inch in abundance. The overwhelming visuals left him stupefied, until another sound cut into his melting mind.

Click . . .
Click . . .
Click . . .
Click . . .
Click . . .
Click . . .

Blanche's finger hovered over the black eye atop the metronome as it swayed left to right. The peculiar, pulsating clicking remained consistent as she arose from her chair.

Vinny tried with every fiber of his being to run away from the madness, but something had changed inside him. Fear blossomed inside as he realized that his bodily autonomy had somehow been compromised.

When Blanche spoke, her dead eyes stared deep into his soul, and the tarry drool continued to leak from her mouth. Her delivery was demonically poetic. Somehow, Vinny not only heard Blanche's voice aloud, but also in his head.

> *To drag you down, remove your love.*
> *Let the largest weasel sniff your mud.*
> *Torn away from what you be,*
> *I wind you up, I set you free,*
> *Provide a piece, a joyous morsel,*
> *So inside your gut blossoms the portal.*
> *Tune the darkness, pointed mouth,*
> *Then* you *shall build our crimson house.*

Vinny's body started to violently tremble. The wicked vibrations of the incantation traveled from the airwaves through his pores. There was a power in the words Blanche spoke that made the table rumble.

"Feel it! Embrace it!" Alfred screamed.

The old man's wicked, orangey eyes flickered chaotically in unison with the room's lighting. Vinny felt his heart pumping along with them.

"That he shall," Blanche said, squirming in her chair. "But first, we eat."

Both Blanche and Alfred picked up handfuls of the stew and pushed it into their mouths. They chomped on the softened herbs and moist meat hungrily, slurping up the clumps of fatty tissue.

Vinny watched as his hand reached into the steaming bowl and lifted out a wad of the slimy meat. Even without the trauma of his accident, the meat before him was the opposite of mouthwatering. The exterior displayed a pale, gray complexion—like a soul trapped in purgatory.

While he had no craving to devour it, Vinny's actions were no longer predicated on his own desires. He sank his fangs into the dead flesh, tearing side to side like a ravenous wolverine—emulating the actions of the animal that had dined upon the faces of his family. The action, and the feeling of the meat in his mouth, sickened him deeply, but he was unable to fight the urge.

"It's been stewing for days," Blanche said. "By now it should melt in your mouth. It's nice and rehydrated."

Ripping into the tissue uncovered bulbous maggots trapped within. Drowned by the briny broth that forced Vinny's tongue to tremble, the obese insect larvae rolled onto his palate. They erupted like rotten grapes, releasing a gelatinous sludge of deadness inside his mouth.

"Isn't that delicious?" Alfred asked.

Vinny nodded involuntarily as he unleashed gagging noises. Then he picked up the bowl and put it between his lips. As he slurped and swallowed massive gulps, he felt like his body was doing something besides consuming. He felt himself . . . sifting. For what he wasn't sure, until there was a metallic clanging against his teeth.

"But don't thank us . . ." Alfred said. "Thank Herman."

Vinny paused his ingestion, holding the hard piece in his mouth as he watched Alfred point at the doorway to the kitchen. Herman's face could be seen in the circular glass window.

Reaching into his mouth, Vinny was horrified by the trinket he retrieved. Even in the dim light, when he held the ring out, the glimmer of the modest diamond was unmistakable.

It was a diamond that some had said was too small for his wife's beautiful finger. Their criticisms mattered little now as he stared at the forlorn digit peeking out of what remained of the broth in his dish.

An image of Kelly's unrecognizable face exploded in his head, followed by his memory of the oddly upturned dirt from the day he was drinking at her gravestone.

WHAT HAVE I DONE?! NO! KELLY!

Vinny's horrified emotions wailed inside his head. But he was unable to speak; thought was his lone outlet. He looked up from the dead finger at the madness sitting across from him.

Click . . .

Click . . .

Click . . .

The metronome stared back at him, along with Blanche's wicked, glowing eyes. As Vinny's wet tongue flailed, attempting to pick the shreds of his deceased wife from between his teeth, he wished the evening wasn't real. But as his gaze hung on the other side of the table, he knew the nightmare had only just begun.

DARK METAMORPHOSIS

As Vinny followed Alfred down the steps into the bowels of the manor, he wanted nothing more than to push the old man forward. To watch his head crack on the stone, like an egg against the side of a counter. But Blanche—and the pulsating clicks rippling from the metronome she carried behind him—controlled his stride.

You . . . you ate her, Vinny thought. *That's more fucked up than anything Dad ever did. This whole time I was worried about becoming him . . . but I'm worse than him.*

Ensnared by dread, Vinny remained dumbfounded by his conundrum. There was little he could do. He was now merely a passenger, watching and waiting to see what his body would do next.

As they slowly descended the staircase, Vinny felt like he was inside a tunnel that led to a different dimension. When they reached the bottom, a grim feeling found him. The darkness felt and looked like it was . . . *alive.* His eyes finally came upon the tools in the basement. Arranged along the wall and strewn about several tables, they ranged from draconian to modern. There were already two lanterns glowing—as if the plan had been to make it down into the chamber all along.

Vinny took a seat on a weathered stool in front of a pedal-operated grinding wheel. Beside the chipped slab of stone sat a box of nails, a hammer, and a single pair of grease-caked pliers. He reached down and opened the box.

"There you are," Blanche whispered. "Settle in."

She set the metronome down carefully on the shelf beside her, excitement radiating from her being like the orange glow did from her eyes.

"Embrace him," Alfred commanded, pulling out Oswald Hitchens' journal as Vinny picked up a nail. "Become him."

Vinny grabbed hold of the pliers and pinched the flat head of the nail. He applied tight pressure and then stepped on the pedal to activate the grinding wheel, pushing the malformed metal into the spinning stone. Sparks flared when the steel was struck.

As the wheel wore down the metal, Vinny wondered what he was crafting. He spun the metal around evenly. Vinny finally pulled the nail away, revealing a sharp tip that was nearly identical to the pointy, factory-manufactured end. He set the double-sided spike on the table and repeated the process over and over, until the pile grew.

Vinny then took the pliers back into his hand, but this time he didn't return to the box for another nail. This time, he opened his mouth and moved in with the tool.

No! What are you doing?!

Blanche looked on approvingly while the metronome swayed side to side while Alfred pointed into Hitchens' journal.

Please! This is insanity! Fuckin' insanity!

He didn't even know who he was pleading with, but Vinny wished for someone to hear him—for his body to hear him.

Obediently, his body followed the tempo, turning on itself. The jaws of the pliers clamped around his front tooth with such intensity that the rigid metal scraped into his enamel. He tasted the scrapings from his tooth as he listened to the metronome bob side to side.

Click . . .

Click . . .

YANK!

Hands in a death grip, Vinny jerked both of his arms downward in unison. He felt a firm tug and a piercing pain erupt at the nerve, but his tooth didn't come out. Vinny's body prepared for the next revolution, ignoring his internal wails of agony.

Click . . .

Click . . .

YANK!

Vinny felt like a maniac going in on himself—like a disturbed dog chasing his own tail and trying to chew it off. After a couple more of the sequenced pulls, the tooth finally popped free. The deep red root glistened under the glow of the lantern as Vinny set his front tooth onto the table. The blood poured, filling his mouth partially before leaking out over his lips.

AHHHHHHHHH!

The pain was so intense. He couldn't believe his body hadn't so much as twitched. Vinny wanted to jump out of his skin. But in the face of self-mutilation, he could do nothing except remain helplessly along for the ride.

"One down," Blanche said, gently patting her leathery hands together.

No! Not again!

Vinny brought the gunky pliers up to the next tooth and took hold of it.

Stop it! Please, stop!

The dark energy throbbing inside him pulled each of the teeth that remained in his mouth, and just as steadily as the pile of dual-sided nails had manifested on the table, so did a blood-drenched pile of choppers. His crimson fingers reached for a nail and the hammer. As he aligned the custom tip with his gory gum hole, he stuck it in a half inch. A squishing sound wormed around in his ears, the blood spattering out around the steel as he hammered it into the tissue.

Vinny was emotionally exhausted by the unconveyable suffering, his spirit and mouth numb. As he smashed the dual-sided spike deep into his gumline, a piece of the puzzle had been placed. One by one the nails on the table disappeared, until none remained.

As Blanche scooped up the pile of bloody teeth on the table, she marveled at their creation. The nails replacing Vinny's teeth were hammered in at a slight angle so that the two-inch spikes ran past each other. Her eyes drifted from Vinny's new, nefarious leer to the table behind him.

"Just one more step now," she whispered.

Vinny turned and activated the stationary belt sander. The coarse paper cycled the conveyer rapidly, and without hesitation, he pushed his fingertips against the strip. The meat where his fingerprints had resided opened, scrubbing his identity down to the bone. The bloody bits and biological dust flew, dissipating as he pressed his other digits into the unforgiving paper. His fingers rained, same as the countless holes in his mouth.

Once each had been whittled down to satisfaction, Vinny joined Blanche and Alfred at the final table. Since he'd drank their concoction at dinner, his vision had been wavy. He felt like he was trapped inside of an absurdist painting produced by a serial killer.

Laid out in front of him sat a pair of weathered gloves. Vinny slid them over his leaky hands before his eyes drifted to the blue-collared worker's shirt laid beside them. The shirt was covered in grease stains, sawdust, and dried blood. The embroidered nametag simply read:

HANDYMAN.

A GRIM REALITY

When Vinny awoke, he felt nothing. The anguish from his countless wounds had dulled, and the hellish hallucinations from the siblings' serum had subsided. The first thing that came into focus was Blanche. She was standing over him, but her exaggerated features had flattened out. Her eyes no longer looked like those of a jack-o'-lantern. The hag still brandished that rotten smile, but not of the otherworldly nature that he seemed to recall.

There was a horrible smell in the room. He couldn't be sure if it originated from the ghastly old woman or not. But when Vinny tried to turn his head, nothing happened.

What is this? he wondered. *Is this . . . real?*

As he focused on the black necklace wrapped around Blanche's throat, his questions were answered. The teeth that he'd hand-extracted the prior evening were roped and knotted around the necklace every few inches or so.

"Evening, Mr. Fowler," Blanche said. "You nearly slept all day. It's fine—I didn't want to wake you, seeing as you'll need every bit of rest since you start work tonight."

"And it's going to be a *long* night," Alfred interjected, stepping into the bedroom. "Maybe the longest you've ever had . . ."

In his hands, Alfred held the sinister metronome. It continued to bob side to side with that creepy black and red peeper atop it.

Vinny tried to talk—he had so many questions to ask them—but he couldn't. No matter what idea or action his brain tried to entertain, he remained piloted by an unknown perversion. The frustration filled him as he lay immobilized on the mattress.

"I'm sure you've probably reached the peak of your confusion," Alfred said. "Not to worry. That is completely normal."

There's nothing fuckin' normal about any of this!

Blanche took a seat on the bed beside Vinny and laid her hand on his leg.

"For that tiny speck of who you were that still remains, my dear sister is going to address a few of the questions I know you must have. It's the least I can have her do for you, considering what you're going to do for me."

"For *us*," Blanche said.

Alfred didn't acknowledge the correction.

Blanche turned back to Vinny, apparently deciding to obey her brother's command. "Forget about fear. The pain you felt yesterday was the worst of it—at least from a physical perspective. No matter what happens to your body moving forward, you're numb now. Forget about free will." She grabbed the enamel necklace. "This charm will ensure you don't partake in any unwarranted conversations while fulfilling our contract. You will not be able to speak about our manor, nor our mission, when you leave this property."

"We require your full attention," Alfred said. "As I said yesterday, we've been waiting for you longer than we'd have preferred. And since we're now behind schedule, you're going to need to work *extra* efficiently."

"Precisely," Blanche said. "And furthermore, forget about your life. Not that you had much of one anyway. I'm sure you've noticed by now that your actions have been automated. You shall follow the beat of our drum. You're *our* Handyman."

Vinny couldn't help but focus on the sound of the metronome as it clicked side to side.

Click . . .

Click . . .

Click . . .

"But don't forget about your darkness," Alfred added. "That's why we waited for you. We know you understand. That side of yourself that plays quietly in the shadows, that you've been trying so diligently to keep the rest of the world from seeing—the side that attracted us to you in the first place. It's time for that side to blossom."

"Precisely," Blanche said. "But you must also remember, you are now a cog in a much larger machine. You finally have a purpose. Disobedience isn't an option within your crafted destiny. So, it would serve you well to purge any thoughts of revolt from your mind immediately. Otherwise, you'll end up like him."

Blanche pointed behind the bed at the corner of the room. Vinny's head turned where she wanted it to, revealing the source of the mystery smell. In a rocking chair sat the deteriorating body of a shirtless, middle-aged black man.

"Willis tried to hold on to his life," Alfred grumbled.

"And you see how that worked out for him." Blanche snickered. "With such a rancid example staring you down, I doubt you'll try to be so foolish."

Willis' chest cavity had been cracked open, offering a window into some of his insect-riddled anatomy. His toothless, rusty-nailed frown was coated in crusted blood. Besides the gory grimace, Vinny could see that Willis' fingertips were also just like his—torn to hell.

As Blanche walked up to the corpse, she snorted deeply, gathering as much phlegm from her throat as possible, and then spat on the dead man's horrified face. "He put our project on hold. He didn't live up to his end of the contract . . . and for that, his punishment shall be eternal."

"We removed his heart, and very soon we shall hold his soul," Alfred said. "A traitorous twit he was."

Blanche turned back toward Vinny. "But let's not be so negative. If you perform properly, you don't have to end up like him. Simply finish the tasks we set forth, and after the project is complete, we'll ensure you're rewarded in ways you could never imagine."

Vinny remained static.

What the fuck is wrong with these people?!

Looking at her brother, Blanche grinned. "I'm sure he must be wondering what comes next."

Alfred's face was stiff as the dead. "Quite frankly, I don't give a good fuck what he's thinking anymore, dear." He pointed at Willis' body. "What do you say we just have Mr. Fowler bring this old chap out back?"

Blanche nodded and looked back at Vinny. "Why, I'd say that's a marvelous idea."

THE NEXUS

Vinny followed the siblings, helplessly dragging Willis' rotten corpse behind him. Blanche and Alfred moved into the woods behind the manor, each holding an oil lantern in front of them, illuminating the bare trees and dead leaves while casting creepy shadows. As the elders pushed through the pathless nature, they drifted farther into the heart of darkness.

Blanche looked back at Vinny. "Just a little farther. We're almost there."

As the moonlight cast down from the sky, it revealed an outline that seemed out of place. Surrounded by dying nature, a crescent-shaped structure—the exterior of which looked to Vinny like a greenhouse—stood ominously. But unlike a typical conservatory, the glass and supporting beams of the structure were a strange, midnight black. And sitting atop the half-circle building was a stone antenna in the shape of a tuning fork.

What in God's name . . . ? Vinny thought.

Alfred held the glowing lantern up to his haggard face. "And here we are."

He removed a key from his coat and stuck it into the lone hole at the front of the structure. Grabbing hold of the onyx door, Alfred pulled it open.

The flies buzzed.

The ants chewed.

The worms wiggled.

The maggots pulsated.

The rodents plundered.

The warm, putrid air flowed into their faces as the three of them, along with Willis' corpse, made their way inside.

When the potent scent of decay invaded Vinny's nostrils, it reminded him of how he'd felt entering his father's trailer. He wanted to puke, but his jaw remained stiff, and his body carried on dragging Willis. The aroma was as if spoiled eggs, sickly feces, moldy garlic, and mothballs had an orgy inside an oven set to broil. Wanting to throw up but not being able to felt about as comfortable as holding in explosive diarrhea at a dance hall.

While the rancid smell was ghastly, the morbid visuals that accompanied it were on a plane of existence all their own. Within the house of sable glass stood another house, far fouler and unsettling. The pink and slimy exterior of the two-story structure was comprised of decaying meat, cartilage, skin, bone, teeth, and most any other bodily tissues imaginable. A literal skeleton house of rotten humanity stood before him.

While there was one wall with a wide gap plaguing the perimeter, everything else seemed relatively symmetrical. The house of human decomposition was a sight to behold.

As Vinny dragged Willis inside behind the siblings, he noticed that much of the interior house's building materials were gray with decay. The enamored insects and rodents feeding upon the abhorrent structure seemed to make way for them, scrambling and sticking to spots away from the area they occupied.

"So," Blanche said, "here you have it. Here lies your grand project."

Alfred kicked Willis' rotten chest cavity. "Seeing as our last Handyman didn't get the job done, it's now up to you, Mr. Fowler."

"And as we explained earlier," Blanche said, "insubordination is unacceptable. And it is with that sentiment in mind that you will use Willis' sad excuse for a husk to craft the commode. It is only fitting that such failure becomes a canvas for excretion. But you needn't start just yet. You'll be going out first."

It was difficult for Vinny to digest everything that was being thrown at him. While his feet remained firmly planted, he felt like his head was spinning.

"And unless you want to achieve a similar fate, you shall do exactly as we say," Alfred said.

Blanche moved toward a wall of decaying flesh that had a long patch of back and thigh skin, along with various parts of several faces, crudely stapled together. She tapped the graying, unlively gore and looked to Vinny.

"As you can see, due to our friend Willis' incompetence, this material is no longer vivacious. But not to worry—the rot, the nibbles of these vile pests, even the tone and texture, is all reversible."

"With your support, we are mere days away from laying the final foundation," Alfred said.

"Precisely," Blanche said. "Our lost progress can—no, *will*—be regained. Building upon the base with fresh, warm material shall alleviate the necrosis. And bone by bone, brick by brick, you shall compile a house of anguish. We have but one remaining patch inside to remediate." She pointed at Willis, then at the rotten bathroom. "Drop him in there for now, then come with us."

Vinny dropped the dead Handyman in the small room and followed Blanche and Alfred over to a pair of thick, black curtains.

"Inside lies The Nexus," Blanche explained. "And—"

Alfred stepped in front of her and opened the curtain a crack. "And while it's not necessary for you to go inside just yet, look there."

Vinny noticed the annoyance on Blanche's face after Alfred seemed to overshadow her explanation. But his eyes soon fixed on the gap between the curtains—the patch of damaged wall missing the bone and flesh that solidified the rest of the structure.

"Once you've gone out and harvested the materials required to apply the patch to The Nexus, this place shall liven right up." Alfred turned to his sister and winked. "Isn't that right, dear?"

"Of course it will," she snapped back.

Alfred nodded. "But before you go out, you'll need to make a few modifications on your van."

A sinister grin curled Blanche's cheeks. "Since it's your first time, we're going to do you a favor. We're going to allow you to harvest materials that we believe you'll take enjoyment in."

"We've been watching you very closely," Alfred said. "We want you to unearth that darkness you buried so long ago. You mustn't be afraid to be who you are. You must embrace your true nature. It will fuel your hammer. Speaking of which, that golden beauty that was so unfairly stripped from you should be the first thing you collect. Don't let cracking a few heads distract you—their bodies can wait."

How do they know so much?

Vinny felt like his soul was trembling. As he looked up at the house of gore, pictures of his father's meat car forced their way into his head.

You've always been sick . . . sick like him. Maybe it's finally time to follow the visions. Maybe they found you for a reason . . .

Maybe they're right.

"And these are heads that deserve cracking," Blanche said. "These are the ones who turned their backs on you. When you were at your weakest, they left you to drown in your misery. This evening will serve as the gauge for your potential. For tonight, you shall dethrone the King of construction."

THE PRECURSOR TO DECAY

As Vinny barreled down the road, he expected his foot to hit the brake any moment. He envisioned pulling to the side of the road and turning the van around and retreating to his apartment to figure out what the fuck was going on.

None of those desires came to fruition.

He continued down the stretch of highway, on a path he'd been down so many times before. His body was rigid and unresponsive to his commands.

Click . . .

Click . . .

Click . . .

The all-consuming sound of the metronome continued echoing between his ears. He remained enslaved to the unsettling tempo.

This is happening, he thought, dread filling his abdomen. *This is actually fucking happening.*

Vinny wasn't in disbelief any longer. He'd been tricked into eating Kelly's rotten remains and hypnotized into horrifically maiming himself. He'd visited The Nexus and been shown his future. He'd accepted all this. The part he was struggling to wrap his head around was how eerily in tune his future was with his past.

He'd worked so hard to distance himself from his father and his inhuman methods—only to be drawn back into an equally twisted world of depravity and extreme violence. Vinny had deliberately ignored many opportunities to work as a mechanic. He'd ignored the masterclass in automotives his old man had given him, specifically so he didn't have to confront his past. If he didn't dwell on those dark times, there would be no way for his demons to seduce him again.

So much for that logic.

As his van pulled up to the outskirts of the construction site, Vinny's mind sputtered through more visions of the violence he'd witnessed over the years. An overwhelming montage of mayhem controlled his brain, as if it was preparing him for what came next.

He felt an uncomfortable energy surging inside his body—the same one he'd felt when he'd witnessed his father cut Beverly's head off, only worse. Before, Vinny had only been aroused by the sight of the decayed or damaged female form. But the feeling bubbling within now lusted to do the damage, to be the precursor to decay.

If Vinny could've shook his head, he would've. He'd done everything he could to subdue his desires. But the perversion he'd once pondered was now amplified. He had stayed clear of a murderous mechanic, only to become a homicidal handyman.

In the distance he could see a crew of men inside the building, hard at work on the night shift. Vinny didn't want to go inside—he knew what would happen if he did. But as he turned off the van and opened the door, he also knew the decision was no longer his.

A WINDOW TO BRUTALITY

Alfred sat on the bed in his briefs, the metronome on the nightstand beside him aimed at a standing mirror. The reflection staring back at him was not his own.

The image inside the oval frame displayed Vinny's first-person view. The familiar, weathered gloves reached outward, grabbing hold of a Hispanic man's throat. As Vinny slammed the man's head into the wet paint on the wall, one hand held him in place while the other pushed the point of a box cutter blade deep into his neck. The razor made short work of his windpipe. As the terrified man squirmed, half of his face was smeared in a mixture of blood and the baby-blue paint spilled on the surface he'd been dragged over.

Alfred continued watching the onslaught eagerly. As tears streaked down the man's face, he tried his best to hold together and protect his bleeding neck. The brown glove slashed at his fingers, some strikes slicing the flesh while others cut down to the bone. As the gloved fingers made their way into the man's neck, they grabbed hold of his thyroid cartilage and esophagus and yanked.

"Marvelous," Alfred whispered.

"What did I miss?" Blanche asked, exiting the bathroom in her negligee, leash in hand.

"He just ripped his throat out."

As Blanche led Herman, a growl and begging whimper mixed, echoing through the spacious bedroom. The creature's animalistic panting resembled that of a dog.

Alfred turned his attention to the salivating beast. "Not to worry, my fair weasel. We haven't forgotten about you."

"Is Herman jealous?" Blanche asked. "That's so sweet."

The wolverine snarled, seemingly still upset, brandishing its glistening fangs and pink tongue.

"While you don't hold enough darkness to be capable of completing The Nexus, that doesn't make you any less important," Blanche said.

Looking down at Herman, Blanche watched as the face transitioned from weasely wolverine to masculine man. The sharp teeth of the beast looked oversized in Jack's mouth as his eyes blackened even deeper.

"We'd prefer if you had more holes this evening, dear," Blanche said.

Jack's face melted from the manly one with massive teeth back to the hairy wolverine before finally transitioning to Jill—the same woman who'd stood in the path of Vinny's car the night of his crash.

"That's better," Blanche said, seductively stroking the creature.

"While you may not see it, you are equally as big a part of our preparation," Alfred said, watching Blanche lead the creature toward the massive bed.

"Of course, of course," Blanche whispered.

"You see, for man to become the beast, he must first lay with it," Alfred said. He licked his pruned lips, gawking at the long hairs around the creature's genitalia. "He must *intimately* understand it. He must become one with it."

"Only then shall *they* be prepared," Blanche said.

Alfred looked at Blanche and furrowed his brow. "Your inclusion isn't required."

As Herman crawled onto the bed, Blanche let her robe drop to the floor.

"Why should you get to have all the fun?" Blanche asked, rubbing her sagging breasts with her bony fingers.

Alfred looked away from his sister into the mirror, where the slaughter continued. Vinny's bloody, gloved hands were in the process of pulling the head off the shoulders of one of the construction workers.

"Regardless," Alfred whispered, turning to Herman, "we have *you* to thank for getting us this far."

Rising to his feet, Alfred slipped off his dirty briefs, revealing a sweaty, discolored erection. Moving closer to the nightstand, he opened the drawer and extracted a medical-grade hole spreader.

Alfred looked back at the beast and grinned. "And thank you we will."

THE NIGHT SHIFT
REVISITED

"Compared to everything else we've done, tonight should be tit," Curtis said.

"Looks that way," Ryan replied with a smile. "Third floor should be painted when you come back tomorrow morning. I just checked on them. Martinez and the other five are right on schedule."

Curtis grinned. "That little gold-toothed hombre's been keeping the rest of the spics in line. And you're keeping *him* in line. That's exactly how it's supposed to go."

Curtis was hesitant about showing the kid too much gratitude, but he'd earned it. When he transitioned into the managerial role, the project was behind. Vinny's blurred vision fostered several setbacks. But somehow, Ryan had found a way to get them back on track. As he looked out the trailer window at the building, Curtis was grateful they were in good shape. He knew they couldn't have gotten where they were without his new protégé's assistance.

"You know what, hold on a sec," Curtis said. "Before I go, I've got something for you."

He disappeared into his office, only to pop back out seconds later. He held the golden Madison hammer he'd reclaimed from Vinny.

Even in the dimly lit trailer, the angelic tool sparkled.

Ryan's eyes widened. It was like he couldn't believe what was about to happen.

"I was gonna hold off, but seeing where we are, I want you to have this," Curtis said, extending the hammer toward Ryan.

"Really?" Ryan asked. "Are—are you sure?"

"Of course! You've earned it, kid. This building wouldn't have a chance to open on time without you. Still got a lotta work on the upper levels, but we're now officially back on schedule. Just do me a favor and keep that shit up. You've got serious potential."

There was a look of slight reluctance on Ryan's face. It was like he wanted to take Curtis' offering but also felt a certain measure of guilt. He looked up from the hammer at Curtis. "It's just, I . . . I feel kinda weird taking it. You know, seeing how you'd given it to Vinny—"

"Forget about that bum! He nearly screwed the pooch on this whole thing. Vinny was soft. His loss is your gain. That's the way the world works. Now set that hunk of shit in your toolbelt aside and slide this fucker in there already. People need to know that you're my top guy. It's important that they know."

Ryan smiled and stood up. Curtis could tell he still had some reservations, but the kid seemed smart enough to keep them to himself. Setting his old hammer on the filing cabinet, Ryan promptly slid the new prized piece into his weathered belt.

Suddenly, the loud cracking of an ignition turning over followed by the rough roar of an engine erupted outside. The men exchanged puzzled looks.

"The hell is that?" Curtis asked. He stepped toward the window and curiously peered outside. "Who the fuck's in the dump truck?"

Ryan followed and shrugged. "I don't know. We don't even have any debris to offload right now."

Curtis pulled the window blinds aside.

From where they watched, only the back of the truck was visible. The pair of men gasped in unison as the vehicle slowly turned around and started to accelerate.

"The hell is he doing?" Curtis asked.

The dump truck emitted thick black smoke from the top as it picked up steam. It glided across the parking lot—heading straight for the building.

"No!" Curtis yelled, rushing to the door of the trailer. "Brake, you stupid son-of-a-bitch!"

The King watched as the renegade dump truck crashed into the corner support beam of the beautiful building. A nightmarish dread filled his torso as the upper floor started to collapse. But it wasn't just the impact of the crash that caused a section to fail. A massive explosion erupted inside the cab of the dump truck.

"Oh, Jesus," Ryan whispered, sticking his head out of the trailer just in time to see the giant fireball ingulf the corner of the building.

"Get the fuckin' fire department on the line!" Curtis screamed. "Now!"

They both rushed back into the office and Ryan quickly snatched up the phone.

"What the fuck?!" he yelled.

"Call 'em!" Curtis yelled.

"It's—it's dead!"

Curtis took the phone from him and put it to his ear. "Goddamnit!" He smashed the telephone down on the desk. "We need—we need to get some fuckin' water on that building!"

"What about Martinez and the rest of the men?" Ryan asked. "They're still inside!"

"You check on them!" Curtis barked. "I'm gonna see if the power washer they were cleaning the walkway with can reach the fire!"

As the men ran out of the trailer, they took off in different directions—Curtis toward the flaming truck and Ryan toward the entrance.

Heart racing, Curtis couldn't be sure how volatile the fire was going to be, but if he didn't put it out and fast, it wouldn't just be the building that burned—his lofty aspirations would go up in smoke too.

As he approached the flaming rig, he was grateful to see that while the initial explosion came with a wave of fire, the flames were still mostly confined to the dump truck. If Curtis could get a handle on it, he might be able to prevent the fire from taking over the building.

He activated the power washer and immediately aimed the stream of water at the blaze. Luckily, the industrial-grade quality of the device allowed Curtis to project a powerful flow and start fighting the flames.

"C'mon, you bastard!" he yelled.

EVACUATION

Ryan ran up the stairs, screaming, "Martinez! Everyone's gotta evacuate this building now! There's severe structural damage and a fire on the first floor!"

He exploded out of the stairwell and onto the main floor. The area looked much different from the last time he'd visited. The baby-blue color the team had been focused on coating the entire floor with had been overshadowed in sickening fashion. Splotches of deep red were plentiful and splattered all over the wet walls and the canvas drop cloth that covered the floor.

The first body in his sight was severed in two at the waistline, a vomitous mix of viscera spilling out of his torn trunk. A cordless reciprocating saw lay beside the body, covered in blood.

Ryan shook his head, not believing his eyes as they found the next man. It seemed the saw had been run up from his groin all the way to his sternum. His legs and body splayed outward in an odd fashion, like a peeled banana.

Another worker lay headless in the corner of the room, baby-blue paint mixed with the blood on his detached cranium. The headless body was slumped over on its side awkwardly, void of the slightest hint of life.

A fourth had been dismembered, his hammy limbs stacked on top of his torso. The crimson pool surrounding the body continued to grow, signifying that the outpouring of carnage was relatively fresh.

Ryan's jaw dropped and slowly began to bob and chatter. As the scream ripped out of his throat, he turned and ran back in the direction he'd come.

FIRE AND PAIN

The flames had finally died down as Curtis kept the stiff stream of water on the vehicle the entire time.

Maybe this isn't as bad as it looks, he thought. *We'll find a way to finish the building. We always find a way.*

As the smoke started to dissipate, Curtis found himself doing a double take. He didn't know who he'd expected to find sitting in the cab of the dump truck, but it certainly wasn't the motionless man in front of him.

While the scorched tissues had burned up enough to create distended bubbles of skin in some areas and charred others to a hideous overcook, there remained a tell. Under the corpse's scalded scalp, melted nose, and liquified lips, a shiny golden tooth twinkled in the firelight.

"Martinez?" Curtis whispered.

"They're all dead!" Ryan screamed. "Fucking dead! We gotta get the hell outta here!"

Curtis heard his protégé's voice and furrowed his brow deeper as the dread set in. He stepped around the back of the dump truck and looked a few yards toward the entrance. Ryan was as white as a sheet.

"What the fuck are you talking about?" Curtis asked. "The fire's out, how can they be—"

"They were murdered!"

As Ryan replied, Curtis could hear a low, mechanical hum abruptly intensify. He gazed on in horror as a pair of wide, high-mounted headlights activated behind Ryan.

The forklift was moving forward with such speed that, by the time Ryan turned around, it was already too late. Upon impact, the girthy mass of steel shattered his chest plate, skewering his heart and cutting into his spinal cord. A steaming porridge of gore burst out of his back as the forklift elevated his bleeding body off the pavement.

"Ghhhhhaaaaaaa!" Ryan cried.

As the impact rocked him to the core, blood flew out of his mouth and the horrifying pressure inside his chest undoubtedly amplified. His trembling body dangled from the blood-drenched fork as it started to elevate.

"Ryan!" Curtis shrieked, the fear forcing him to hit an opera-worthy note.

As his protégé elevated higher away from the ground, Curtis watched Ryan's bodily fluids rain down onto the cement. The massive metal fork mashing through Ryan's back was easily the most gruesome accident he'd ever seen. The shock was electric, until he suddenly realized that it was no accident. The crimson forklift was now headed in his direction, zeroing in on him.

Curtis looked at his truck, parked in front of the trailer, and took off running. He'd never booked it so fast, but he was no match for the machine.

HAMMER TIME

Click . . .

   Click . . .

   Click . . .

The metronome was not currently around Vinny, but he could still hear its strange, echoey cycle bouncing around in his skull.

As the blood and spittle leaked down from Ryan's mouth, he felt the warm drizzle land on his face.

I killed them, Vinny thought. *How could I kill them all?*

A horrible feeling stirred inside him as he looked at the Madison hammer hanging from Ryan's toolbelt, shining in the moonlight. The feeling of horror swirling inside his guts was like nothing Vinny had ever experienced. As upset as he was with the men, and especially with Curtis, he didn't want them *dead.* He'd never have wished such harm on any of them, such feelings were foreign to him. But since he'd come into contact with the siblings, what *he* wanted was of little consequence.

Vinny eased off the accelerator, swung outside the forklift, and plucked the Madison hammer from Ryan's toolbelt. The deadness in his replacement's eyes suggested that he'd never be able to use it again.

Smashing his foot down on the gas, he sized up Curtis.

No, this isn't right!

His merciful thoughts did nothing to stop his body from cocking the hammer back. He flung the tool forward and watched it rotate before the heavy head cracked against the back of Curtis' skull.

When the hard steel connected with the back of his head, the King of construction stumbled. He fell on his side, laid out and motionless on the ground, as the blood began to puddle around his shoulders.

Vinny looked at the cluster of jackhammers lined up at the far end of the trailer. As he slowed the forklift over Curtis' body, it was clear that he had an idea. He just didn't know what it was yet—because it wasn't his own.

Vinny dropped the forks—along with Ryan's lifeless corpse—until they pinned Curtis' legs to the asphalt. He hopped out of his seat and connected a hydraulic hose to the jackhammer before activating the air compressor.

As he turned back around, dragging the device, Curtis was starting to regain consciousness. He rubbed the cavernous gash on the crown of his head while confusion lingered on his face. He looked up at the demonic representation of his former employee.

Vinny imagined the sharp nails poking out of his scabby gums were the stuff of nightmares. Under his navy-blue cap, the glowing garnet pupils within his blackened eyes were likely equally terrifying. His gloved hands hoisted up the jackhammer against his collared shirt.

"V-V-V-Vinny?" Curtis managed.

Vinny felt the dread and disgust flaring in his belly, but whether he liked it or not, he was along for the ride. But even as awful as he felt, there was a small part of him that was starting to enjoy watching Curtis squirm. The part he'd tried to suppress. The part that wasn't afraid of violence but attracted to it. Recalling how Curtis had treated him like a drunken stranger and kicked the shit out of him in front of the entire company changed something inside him.

For the first time since Vinny had donned the Handyman badge, he couldn't tell if the smile that he felt brandishing his abominable teeth was driven by his own emotions or by the metronome. And when he opened his jaw, he was even less sure.

"Working the spike is like fuckin'," Vinny whispered, grinning maniacally and showing all of his steel-spiked teeth as he looked down at the tip of the jackhammer.

Curtis pulled at his legs, only now realizing they were pinned. "What are you . . ."

He looked up at Vinny as he stabbed the flattened tip of his tool down into Curtis' chest.

"Nooooooo—"

His cries were swiftly cut short by the reverberations of violence.

The end of the cutter quickly made short work of his flesh. The steel tip was about the size and shape of a large paintbrush. The initial shot from the refined edge punched through his skin, fracturing his ribcage instantly. The follow-up collapsed his skeleton in on itself.

As Vinny applied more pressure, the relentless punches of the tool pulverized Curtis' organs, pushing so deep that it slashed gaping cuts into one of his lungs. The massive pool of blood filling the warm pit in his chest sprayed upward, projecting like a lawn sprinkler all over Vinny's face.

Curtis' body shook like he was possessed as he vomited crimson ropes from his mouth and over his face. His eyes started to roll up into his skull as a wet, ruby mask engulfed his face.

"Widening a hole in the ground is like widening a hole in a woman," Vinny continued. "You can't just stick it in her ass right away. I used to always tell the new guys that. You've gotta work your way up to it."

Part of Vinny wanted to stop, but another part of him didn't. The fact that he didn't have a choice only blurred the lines between his desire for revenge and the darkness that had taken hold of him.

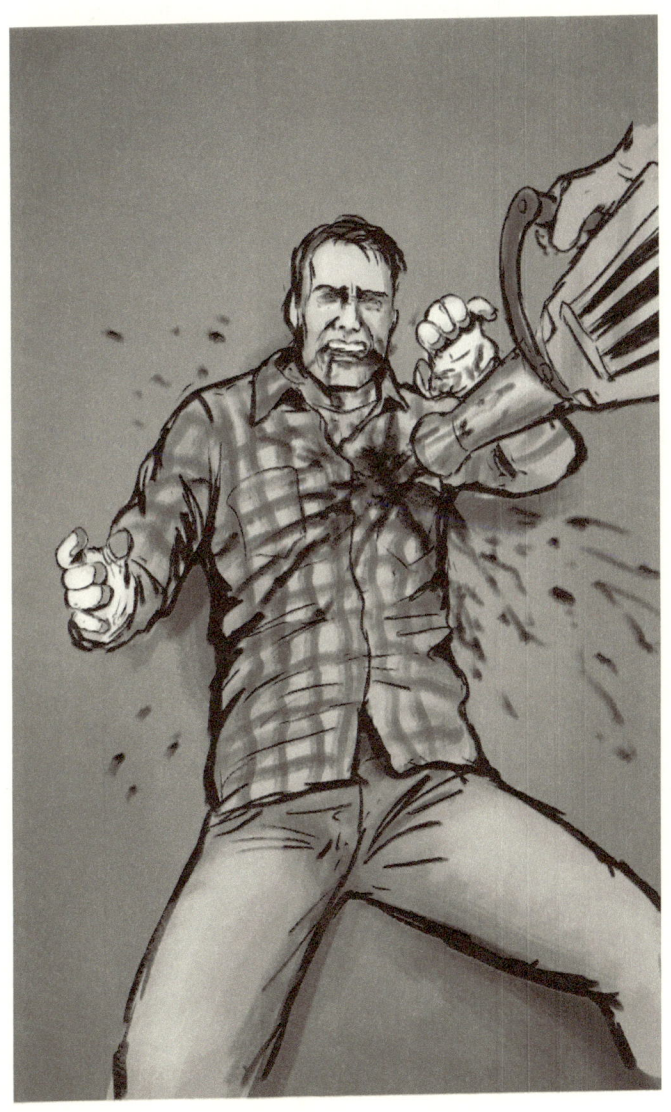

Everything was gray.

Bridging the jackhammer against the forklift, Vinny reached for the lever. He raised the forks off Curtis and lifted him off the ground. Repositioning Curtis' lower body, Vinny left him in an ass-up position. While his knees and head rested on the ground, Vinny brought the forks back down on his delirious boss.

As the bloody steel fork connected with the back of Curtis' head and pinned his skull against the concrete, the opposite blade held his calves in place. Taking hold of the jackhammer again, Vinny nodded as he watched Curtis, alive but in shock, spitting out blood and shaking uncontrollably.

"But now . . . I think you're about ready," Vinny said.

Curtis couldn't muster a word as Vinny dragged the jackhammer over his jeans. He positioned the steel tip just outside of his asshole. When Curtis' gurgling wails reached their peak, Vinny applied more pressure. The jabbing point pushed through his pants, ripping his taint open and stabbing into his rectal cavity.

As Curtis' jeans tore wider, the blood exploded upward like a human fountain. The stabbing revolutions bore deeper with each second. The red deepened to what looked like a mixture of dark brown and cherry as his fecal matter joined the fray. While the steel spike continued to sodomize, Vinny drove it deeper until Curtis' ass was butted up against the body of the jackhammer.

Despite Vinny being able to feel the rotating tip of his tool start prodding Curtis' guts, when it came to his own body, he no longer felt anything.

GATHERING MATERIALS

The dump truck's engine stopped sputtering and Vinny tossed the keys onto the passenger seat. He looked down at the cinderblock he'd placed on the accelerator, then back to his overcooked former coworker.

Martinez's flesh was burnt so severely that the many layers of duct tape holding him to the chair had melted and fused to his skin. As Vinny slid the box cutter down the gray, semi-dried goop, it felt like he was unwrapping a juicy mummy. Upon slicing into his flesh, a warm, translucent fluid oozed out. After freeing each side of his upper body, he did the same for his legs. While the man was no longer bonded to the chair, the liquified tape strips remained stuck to him.

Click . . .

Click . . .

Click . . .

With each stroke of the metronome echoing in his head, he continued to work. As Vinny pulled Martinez from the smokey truck, he was still trying to justify his actions. But no matter which way he attempted to stretch the truth, there were reservations and justifications.

Martinez wasn't even here when Curtis fired me, Vinny thought. *He wasn't one of the people laughing at me.*

219

As Vinny pulled Martinez to the ground, he continued to drag him toward the open sliding door of his van. The inside of his vehicle was far different than before. The few tools that he'd kept inside were mounted on the walls, but now a plastic, tublike interior accounted for most of the floor.

But he is one of Len Anderson's halfway house creeps. He couldn't have been that innocent . . .

The hacked-up bodies of Martinez's men, as well as Ryan and Curtis, were heaped up inside. The severed limbs, deep lacerations, and impalement holes all leaked copious amounts of blood, but the tub wasn't filling. The drain Vinny had installed before he left saw to that. It led below the van, funneling the drippings out until they disappeared into a flat black tank he'd fixed to the bottom of his van, so large it stretched the length of it.

Vinny tossed the last of his former coworkers inside and slammed the door shut.

A FRESH FOUNDATION

"This is just spectacular!" Blanche squealed. "We couldn't have asked for a better way to begin."

Vinny stood holding Curtis King's wide-eyed corpse at the main entrance of the black greenhouse.

"Do come inside," Blanche said. She stood beside Alfred in the main room brandishing a sinister smile.

As Vinny stared into the evil eyes of the depraved siblings, a chill ran down his spine.

Do they ever sleep? he wondered.

Alfred looked at the black toilet in the bathroom cubby at the far corner of the gore house. Willis' desecrated corpse sat slumped against the grimy bowl. "After you unload the other husks from the van and bring them inside, ensure Willis is stretched and bonded to the porcelain."

Blanche unrolled a substantial sheet of thin, white parchment. The red lines that dotted the entire document stretched out on the gore-stained table, revealing a house layout. The drawing was a blueprint, but not of the standard variety—it appeared to be crafted in blood.

Alfred tapped his gaunt finger against the blueprint atop the wooden table. Various knives, tools, and devices were either pinned or stabbed into the wall of flesh in front of it.

221

"Put this away," Alfred said. "We've already established where the exposed area lies. Have you gone senile?"

Vinny watched as Blanche blushed, the scolding from her smarmy brother clearly stinging. "I-I just wanted to double-check and make sure—"

"How about you leave the thinking to me?" Alfred asked. "I'm the one who's gotten us this far."

He turned to Vinny, not about to allow his sister to respond. "Anyhow . . . The Nexus will be where you do the bulk of your work this evening. But first, you'll need to strip the flesh from their bones and set it aside."

Alfred pointed toward the black curtains where the lone flimsy area of the building lay.

"I'm so close," Alfred said.

"*We're* so close," Blanche corrected.

"Anyhow," Alfred said, "their skeletons are to be fully dismantled so they can be used as the primary framework to support the lone weakened area of the structure. The entire exterior and interior—save for that single patch—is complete. But we must finish construction here before laying the final foundation."

Blanche patted the gleaming, bloody wall beside her. "But only once you've reinforced the vulnerable wall shall you be given additional instructions on pouring the final foundation."

"Poppycock," Alfred scoffed. "I will give you an advanced explanation near the general area first so you can familiarize yourself."

Vinny had the urge to vomit, but his body didn't flinch.

What the fuck are they trying to do with this place? What am I participating in?

Despite Alfred and Blanche carefully outlining their evil intentions, Vinny still couldn't exactly figure out what the purpose of their madness was. Helping to build a structure out of mangled corpses didn't exactly give him any hunches. He soon stopped trying to figure it out and was overcome by a wicked anxiety.

How . . . how do I get out of this?!

"Follow along," Alfred said, curling his finger toward Vinny several times.

Vinny dropped Curtis' lifeless corpse and trailed behind the siblings. They continued past the table and bathroom to the back wall, where two separate curtains met to obscure the doorway.

They moved through the drapes, revealing a spacious room. On the wall straight ahead, painted in black, was the same symbol from before—an ebony circle with a gray tuning fork overlapping it. The symbol in the room was much grander than the one Vinny had seen embedded on the metronome. Additionally, the mark didn't just appear on the wall; it also appeared on the floor, inside a deep rectangular pit nearly the size of an inground pool.

"Welcome to the dividing line," Alfred said, raising his hands. "Behold . . . The Nexus."

Stretching down from the ceiling and into the rectangular hole was the gravestone rod that poked out at the peak of the tinted greenhouse—the crux of Alfred and Blanche's abomination. The stone stuck right into the painted gray handle of the tuning fork.

Alfred looked down into the pit. "The blood collected into the drainage tank you fixed to the undercarriage of your vehicle will be siphoned to pool here, creating the base for the final foundation."

"Before Willis expired," Blanche interjected, "he was able to install these cooling coils. Once activated, the blood within will remain circulating and uncongealed." She turned and gazed into Alfred's eyes. "And that's just the way we want it, isn't that right, darling?"

Alfred seemed less annoyed with his excited sister as she unhinged her jaw and, with a hideous crack, a dollop of bubbly saliva slid off her tongue and dangled out of her mouth. Alfred leaned in and swallowed up the slimy muscle eagerly, and the two lapped at each other's faces with an incestual disregard.

When they finally pried themselves away from each other, a long rope of spit kept them connected before it slowly dissipated.

Alfred used his suit sleeve to wipe the ooze away from his mouth. "Of course, my sweet." He turned to Vinny. "And after you've finished your work this evening, a meal will be awaiting you in your chambers. Eat promptly, and then sleep through the day, because come dusk, we'll require a different type of labor from you."

Blanche pointed to Vinny's blood-soaked shirt. "And before you go to bed, be sure to discard your uniform into the laundry basket—it'll need to be cleaned prior to tomorrow's task."

"You shall meet us here at twilight," Alfred said, taking Blanche by the hand and leading her to the door.

What could they possibly want next?

Vinny still didn't fully grasp the horror of his situation—it was hard to believe he was a slave to such demonic beings. The violence they demanded, the twisted perversion they desired, it was all to a level that was previously unmatched, and to what ends he could only imagine.

THE CARNAL COMMODE

Vinny looked down at the fresh blood of the laborers. He'd used the saws and knives in his van to pull the red bones from the men. After stripping the meat, he installed them as the supports, just as he was told to. He then repurposed the meat and used a bonding adhesive to help reinforce the inside barrier.

The building was indeed finished except for the one small area that was still bare. It wouldn't have taken much flesh to fill the tiny void, but nonetheless, Vinny knew another body would be required before The Nexus was ready.

He wasn't sure if that was a good thing or not.

Once this godforsaken place is finished, they shouldn't need me anymore . . . right? he wondered.

They didn't seem like the kind of people that offered happy endings though. Still, the quicker the building was completed, the quicker he could stop slaughtering people.

What could this all be for?

He'd made use of his former cohorts, and while it wasn't something he would ever verbalize, killing them had felt good. They had taken enjoyment in his downfall. In some way, they were the tipping point for it.

I don't hear you laughing now.

As Vinny moved closer to the exit of The Nexus, the once lifeless gore, affixed to the wall he'd just patched, started to pulsate.

Vinny was glad he'd stuffed the facial meat and skin inside the area he'd built upon. Despite feeling they had some level of culpability in their demise, Vinny wasn't sure if he'd have been able to deal with staring at their faces while he finished out the room.

Was . . . was that my own choice?

"Vinny! Vinny, you fuckin' bastard," Curtis said, his voice muffled behind the marbled meat and skin.

Hiding the flesh was certainly what Vinny would have preferred, but he couldn't be sure of how it happened exactly. His free will was once the purest of pools, but now, the waters were beyond muddied.

Curtis is the last person I wanna talk to. I've gotta get outta here.

Vinny walked through the curtains, back toward the front of the gore house. Through the dividers he heard another voice.

"Please, don't go!" Ryan wailed.

Ignoring their pleas, Vinny proceeded into the bathroom, where his final task of the evening remained. The idea of regaining his free will was a nice thought, but he wasn't sure that would change anything.

Where would I even go? What could I possibly do?

The horrors he'd unwillingly inflicted upon himself weren't going anywhere. Vinny's gaze shifted from Willis' rotten body to the slab of mirror hanging on the wall of maggoty skin. The ruby pupils within his black sclera glowed whenever the droplight above flickered. The hot drool coating his pointed steel teeth glimmered along with the bloodstains upon the uniform he donned.

You're a fucking monster. Not just a monster, but their monster.

He wasn't sure there was even a path back to society for him. Surely, without the shielding of the siblings, he'd be found out—locked up for life or put to death.

Is that a better alternative? I'm so tired . . .

Vinny's brain swirled with endless amounts of awful information. He imagined his body might ache if he could still feel pain, but that was no longer the case. Still, the mental burnout lingered. He looked back to Willis' rotten body, ready to be done with the dreadful evening.

Plucking the box cutter from his toolbelt, he pushed the razor under Willis' necrotic facial tissue. A blackish ooze and clear fluid leaked from the laceration as Vinny clamped down on the ghastly skin. When he yanked the flap, he discovered that the pockets of bugs squirming on the corpse's exterior were nothing compared to what lay beneath. The plump, pulsating larvae frolicked excitedly, tails wiggling like an army of tiny dogs about to be walked.

How do they expect me to make him part of the fuckin' toilet? They're crazy with all this. Crazy.

With the sheet of decomposing skin sliming his glove, Vinny retrieved the superglue from the workbench and returned to the bathroom. He set the face and glue on the toilet tank and cut the remaining garments off Willis' body. Once all the clothing had been removed and set aside, Vinny continued to cut down the seams of the dead handyman's decaying vessel.

He ripped up the rotten sheets of skin, as large as he could keep them, from all different regions of his body. Sheet by sheet, inch by inch, Vinny used the superglue to fix Willis' nasty casing to the toilet. Until—just like Blanche and Alfred had requested—the entire porcelain bowl and tank was covered in spoiled tissue.

Vinny had even bonded some wads of maggoty meat around the seat to serve as cushioning. As he flipped up the lid and rested it against the tank, he knew there was only one area of the toilet left to finish. He grabbed the mask of skin off the top of the bowl's tank and squeezed a healthy amount of superglue onto the side that was once attached to Willis' cranium.

Vinny pressed both of his gloves firmly against the underside of the lid and looked into the holes of deadness where the man's eyes previously rested.

228

Ironically, just as it felt like the face had finished bonding, nature suddenly called. Within his stomach, he felt a deep pinch, triggering Vinny to unbuckle his pants and plop down. The meat he'd implanted under the skin of the seat felt like heaven to his cheeks, despite the squirming bugs still wedged inside the hunks that tickled his legs and ass as they twisted about. It took some getting used to, but the soft, human touch allowed Vinny to feel at home and his rectum retracted with ease.

As the log of grayish fecal matter slid out, he couldn't help but think about how ludicrous the moment was—he was most likely shitting out the woman he loved into a toilet decorated with human flesh. Vinny grabbed some toilet paper and wiped his ass, trying his best not to concentrate on the absurdity of the moment.

Instead of thinking about the undead turd leaving his body, he switched his focus to the flesh he rested upon.

"Willis, huh?" he grumbled. "You poor son-of-a-bitch."

But as he cleaned himself, Vinny suddenly felt a vibration behind him. The part of his back that rested against the lid suddenly started to twitch.

"Me?" a voice asked. "The worst of it's over for me. But *you've* got some shit to look forward to."

"What the fuck?!" Vinny shrieked. As he felt the rubbery lips tickle his back, a new terror found him. Instinctually, Vinny vaulted off the toilet and hit the floor face-first.

THE LIBRARY OF SOULS

The shock of the skin mask reanimating and attempting to converse with Vinny had caused him to fall forward, leaving his rump partially exposed.

Willis' ghastly face continued to twitch. "I can't imagine too many people'll be shittin' in here. That's about the worst I gotta deal with. But you? It's Vinny, right?"

Vinny was speechless. Instead of responding, he nodded at Willis in disbelief while scrambling to pull his pants and boxer-briefs up.

"Well, Vinny, I'm afraid the worst is just the beginnin' for you. I wasn't the first, but hopefully you'll be the last."

"You—you're alive?" Vinny stammered.

Willis laughed. "You just glued my goddamn face to a toilet, so definitely not."

"But you can talk?" He paused, starting to comprehend another odd difference. "And . . . so can I."

Willis grinned, the black porcelain of the toilet seat behind his eye holes looking freaky as hell.

"Wait a minute," Vinny mumbled, astonished to feel his own personal intent once again powering his body and actions. He paused, scratching the side of his face, feeling the confusion swell inside his body.

"In case you haven't noticed, a lot of weird things seem to happen 'round those two old creeps. Some inexplicable, impossible things."

Vinny felt the long-overdue emotion boiling inside him. It had been bottled for far too long. His eyes glistened. "What have . . ." He paused, struggling to get the words out. "What have they done to me?"

"Same thing they done to me, I imagine. They found a man in his darkest moment and they sank their teeth into him. Once you put on that uniform, you're nothing more than a tool. A tool to be used and—regardless of what they tell you—eventually, discarded."

A tremble ran through Vinny's body. "When I'm doing the bad things, it's like I . . . I can feel them inside me or something. I can't stop it."

"I bet you can hear it too. But not right now, right?"

Vinny squinted. "Hear what?"

"The metronome," Willis whispered. "You see, that's how they control you. That old witch uses it to tune into you, then your molecules, then your soul, and then—click, click, click—your body just goes right along with it. All the sudden, you're a slave to the tempo."

"Before," Vinny said, "when I was hurting myself . . ." He paused, running his tongue over his rusty teeth. "And then the other people . . . I felt like I couldn't stop. Like I had no choice—"

"Because you didn't."

"But why isn't it like that now?"

"When you wind a normal metronome, on average it lasts about twelve minutes. But their mechanism must've been manipulated. It lasts about twelve *hours*. The dark incantation presides over their intended target with great strength initially, but like anything, over time the spell grows weak. Also, the farther you are from the device, the less influence it holds over you. The power of suggestion is mighty, until we realize that it's *only* suggestion. Some never do, others eventually come to the epiphany over time. But you, you're very lucky."

Scoffing inside, Vinny found that assertion ridiculous. There was absolutely zero luck on his side.

"How the fuck you figure?" he asked.

"Because, they made a mistake," Willis explained. "Out of spite, they brought back the guy that figured them out. Apparently, humiliating me in death is more important than the madness they've been chasing since they were children."

Vinny's eyes widened. "All this is . . . it's too much. It's insane."

Willis' lips quivered. "It's not quite as insane as having your face nailed to a toilet."

"None of this feels real. It's like I'm trapped in some horrible dream."

"In a way you are, but with one very, *very* important distinction."

"What's that?"

"It's not *your* dream. It's theirs."

The depression that had been confined to Vinny's mind now poured out in his body language. He felt the wrinkles in his face fold under the profound misery they held. Still, he pressed on, forcing himself to drift away from his internal anguish.

Forget about your fall from grace, he told himself. *You can't change any of that.*

Vinny looked around the gory bathroom. The once gray and decaying flesh that hung raggedly from the walls was now far livelier. It gleamed with a fresher moistness and subtly throbbed with a growing vigor. It was as if the fresh blood and bodies added to the foundation had breathed new life into the putrefying structure.

It was *his* hammer and nails that had revitalized the house of gore.

"What even is this place?" Vinny asked.

Willis smiled. "It's just what the creeps said it was—a nexus. A union of flesh. A library of souls. But what it actually is and the potential they see for it are two completely different things."

Vinny's brow furrowed. "How so?"

"They think when this is finally finished . . . that it's gonna be some kind of portal."

"A portal?"

"Like a gateway."

Vinny scratched the side of his face. "To what?"

"To absolute power and control over the universe. To agony and depravity the likes of which no mortal mind could ever imagine."

"They sound like devil worshipers or something."

Willis laughed. "It's nothing as simple as that."

"Then what is it?"

"They don't worship the Devil . . . they envy him. They aspire to replace him."

Biting his lower lip, Vinny was afraid to ask the question. Finally, he loosened the tension to talk. "Does . . . does this mean there's something after we die?"

"Yes. But these bodies of ours, they hold a certain level of connectivity, of power. Man has an instinctual urge to lay the dead to rest, and that's no coincidence. It's those timeless rituals that serve to finally set us free. They allow us to venture on to where we must. But there are things, things like this sick place, that can pull spirits back from their final destination."

"But why? Why would they want to create this place, to . . . to disturb so many spirits?"

"They believe if they can pull back enough human energy from the other side, they can use it to harvest *everyone's* energy— even the living. And then they'll be powerful enough to overthrow the pits of Hell. At least, that's what I've put together."

Vinny felt stupefied by the revelation. No longer was he merely participating in the sick fantasy of the old weirdos; he was potentially helping them overthrow the universe and beyond. He didn't want to believe it.

"H-how do you know all this?" Vinny whispered.

"Don't forget, I wore that uniform before you did. It took me years to put all the pieces together. But when your only purpose is killin', there ain't much else to do besides listen."

Vinny put his hand on his forehead, overwhelmed by the responsibility that now rested on his shoulders.

"You'll see," Willis said. "Soon you'll understand my plight. And you'll find out very quickly if you have what it takes to face that darkness inside you—to snuff it out. And it'll need to be fast, 'cause if you take a look around, this place is just a few bodies away from being finished."

Sighing, Vinny was unsure how to respond. He rubbed his eyes and stood up, looking into the filthy mirror. Staring at his red eyes and glimmering teeth, he thought about the walking chaos he'd become.

"This . . . this can't be real . . ." he whispered. "This can't be real!"

"Vinny!" Willis yelled.

"What?!"

"Get ahold of yourself! You've gotta accept it."

"It's too much! This is too fuckin' heavy!"

The tears were streaming down Vinny's cheeks as he focused on the pointed nails protruding from his enflamed gumline. He looked like a monster.

"I know it's a lot," Willis said. "It was a lot for me too. I'm not sure how I woulda responded if someone dropped all this madness on me instead of learning it over time. I'm sure I'd have probably flipped my shit too. But you know what I'm saying makes sense. You know these two ain't right."

"Makes sense?! None of this fuckin' shit makes sense!"

"What doesn't make sense about it?"

"Well . . ." A thousand thoughts ran through Vinny's brain all at once. "Why me?"

Willis sighed. "Because you've got *it*. Just like *I* had it. It's like that symbol inside The Nexus—the black circle and the tuning fork. Not every fella walking his dog in the morning is a candidate. In fact, a candidate for something like this needs a special kind of darkness—because they can only tap into the *darkest* ones."

"No! No! No! That's . . . that's not me! I don't want it!" Vinny punched the mirror and backed away.

"The only way to even challenge those creeps is to first gain your free will back. But to do that, you've got to be fearless. To do that . . . you've got to face it."

"What are you talking about?! Face what?!"

Vinny was screaming at him, hiding from the truth behind his emotions. He knew what Willis meant, but playing stupid was easier than confronting the demons.

"When I was sixteen years old, I lit an abandoned building on fire," Willis said. "My friends and I were just stupid kids doing stupid shit. I didn't know there were five homeless people living inside, including two children, until I saw it on the news. That was a secret I kept every day of my life. It took putting on that uniform for me to face it . . . for me to acknowledge what I'd done. To accept my guilt and stop living a lie. To let go."

More tears beaded down Vinny's cheeks as he clenched his bloody fist. He slid against the glistening wall and plopped down onto the floor. As a shiver ran down his spine, Vinny tried to suppress the wicked memories, but they were unignorable.

Willis paused, as if selecting his next words carefully. "So, I guess what I'm saying is, it doesn't matter if you want it or not. It chose you. And for that to be possible . . . you must have some kind of darkness inside you."

1988

JUST SOME PICTURES

"C'mon, babe," Vinny said. "I think you're overreacting to something silly."

As he sat slumped on the couch, Vinny knew he should be scared, but the copious amounts of whiskey he'd consumed had left him deeply confused. Truthfully, from one minute to the next, Vinny wasn't sure what he was anymore.

"I don't care what you say," Linda said, pulling the cord closed on her duffel bag.

"Look, I-I get that you're angry—"

"Angry? I stopped being angry a long time ago. But this is different than the drinking or anything else. This is . . . it's just fucking sick, Vinny. Sick, and weird, and I—I don't want anything to do with it. Who even are those girls? Are . . . are those photos *real*, or—no, just forget it, I don't even wanna know."

Vinny shot up off the sofa and picked up the bottle of whiskey from the coffee table. Before he knew it, he'd launched the glass in Linda's direction. As the television behind her shattered, his tirade commenced.

Linda shrieked and dropped the duffel bag.

"You don't know what it was like!" Vinny yelled. "You got no fuckin' clue! You think I chose this?!"

Grabbing Linda by the shoulders, Vinny slammed her up against the wall. As the spittle launched from his mouth, he could feel his eyes widening. The rage inside had been stewing deep down since he was a child.

"He kept them," Vinny whispered. "I could keep you. I could show you exactly what it was like."

"W-what are you talking about?" Linda asked, on the verge of tears.

"Wouldn't you like to fuckin' know."

"Please, Vinny, I'm begging you . . . just let me go. I don't want any trouble. I—"

"It's just some fuckin' pictures!"

"You're scaring me. I-I know you're upset. I tried—we both tried to make it work. But after this, there's just no way for me to unsee it. Please, you know I tried my best. You know I did."

The broken neck of the whiskey bottle on the carpet next to them glimmered under the lamplight. The desire to pick up the sharp glass dwelled in his broken heart. He pictured what he might do with it. He felt like the idea of sliding it along her dainty throat was trying to seduce him. As Vinny keyed in on the terror in his girlfriend's eyes, a series of flashes erupted in his head.

The rotten car.

The trunk of filth.

The violent pornographic images.

Among the perverse contraptions his legless mother was hooked up to, Vinny had found familiarity. That same glimmer of pure dread in her eyes was now in Linda's, and a profound feeling of sickness overcame him.

His grip loosened on her shoulders as Vinny watched the tears roll down her cheeks. Jaw slackening, he took a step back toward the couch and sat down.

Still paralyzed by her fear, Linda remained in place, as if waiting for a command. She was trying to keep her howling cries as quiet as possible, seemingly afraid that she might upset Vinny further.

With his own eyes starting to glisten, Vinny looked down at the source of their argument. While the pornographic behavior displayed on the page was of an extreme nature, it wasn't the bondage or rough sex the women were partaking in that had spooked Linda.

It was their faces.

Just like in his dad's issues, in place of the heavy makeup and modern hair styles were superimposed images of brutalized women. They were all clearly dead, but mutilated with concerning variety. The woman he stared down at was missing an eyeball and ear. Gaping lacerations, a puffed cheekbone, and swelled lips sat atop a beautiful tan body being held by a muscular man in a full-nelson position while he stuck his cock in her asshole.

"I'm . . ." A tear rolled down Vinny's cheek. "I'm him."

Linda continued to sob quietly while carefully picking up the duffel bag. She stood frozen another moment before finally mustering the courage to ask Vinny the question he knew she'd been waiting to.

"Can I go . . . please?"

Vinny's gaze drifted to the other page, where a girl lay bent over beside a man in a cooking apron with the crotch cut out. His cock bulged while he inserted the wide handle of a saucepan inside her cunt. The face overlaid on this woman was more corpse-like. The maggots and decaying tissue could be seen in the photo—and like all the others, it was real.

Looking back at Linda, Vinny nodded. "Go . . . go as far away from me as you can."

THE ROOT OF REPUGNANCE

The bar was the only place Vinny could ever seem to think. As the bartender dropped a glass of bourbon in front of him, there was only one thing on his mind.

You left her behind, he thought.

Linda was gone, just like all the others before her.

Funny how sometimes you can run away, but no matter how far you go, that place you're trying to run away from is still right there with you.

Vinny hoped that wasn't the case for Linda. While she and the other women who'd bounced in and out of his life had left scars on his heart, there was only one woman who pained him in a way that was almost unbearable.

"You left her in the fuckin' trunk to rot," Vinny mumbled.

"What'd you say?" the bartender asked.

"Nothing."

The bartender walked away to service another barfly at the other end of the counter.

It had been nearly fifteen years since the last time he'd seen his mother. The image of his cock in his hand and the horrifying recognition in her eyes haunted him.

Those eyes. They're all I have to remember her by . . .

After his dad took him out in his muscle car that evening and they escaped the police, that was somehow the last outrageous activity his old man forced him to endure. In the years beyond, Dennis had stuck to his word. As far as Vinny knew, his father never picked up another girl for the rest of the time Vinny lived under his roof. And every day that went by, Vinny saved money, hoping to move on to something better. Hoping to escape from his twisted past.

But wondering what had become of his mother tormented him.

Even as he sat at the bar, Vinny had no idea if she was still alive. Based on her condition and the methods of upkeep that his father was employing at the time, it was doubtful. But one thing surely wasn't doubtful.

You allowed her to continue being tortured. You allowed everything you hated about your old man to become the very fabric of your existence. You're a fuckin' coward.

It ate at him then as a boy, and it ate at him now as a man. Vinny was a full-blown alcoholic, pushing thirty, without a single successful relationship—romantic, professional, platonic, or otherwise—to show for it.

He took a massive swig from the glass, the bottles behind the bar catching his eye. The split second when he'd thought about putting the broken one to Linda's neck revisited his mind.

What the fuck was I thinking?

Vinny had done plenty of messed-up things in his time. The fantasies of having sex with mutilated or dead women was a vice that normal people didn't share. The debilitating alcoholism and constant memories of his warped childhood that continued to terrorize him weren't easy to live with. But the actual thought of killing someone—someone who'd gone above and beyond to try and make things work with him—was a new low.

The idea of jamming the broken bottle into his own throat crossed his mind.

I've lived like a coward, why shouldn't I die like one?

243

The television behind the bar transitioned from local news to a commercial. The ad for a local auto body shop showed a friendly-looking mechanic using a lug wrench to remove a tire. The man's smile was captivating.

What if he's still doing it?

It wouldn't have surprised Vinny if his father had fallen back into his old ways. After all, his only promise was not to involve Vinny in any of his depravity after Beverly's murder. He'd never vowed to stop.

Maybe I don't gotta go out like a coward. If can finally put an end to this, then maybe I can have a normal life. Linda don't deserve to die . . . Dad does.

Vinny pushed the empty glass in the direction of the bartender.

"Another?" the bartender asked.

"I don't think so," Vinny said.

"Wow, early night for you."

Vinny's face felt blank. While he might've appeared despondent, a switch had flipped. "The first of many."

ON THE ROAD AGAIN

The stretch of highway was all too familiar. As Vinny passed a big pop-up sign advertising fireworks for sale, he wished he could spend the holiday doing the normal things families usually did. Have a few beers, cook up a barbecue, maybe play some cards.

But that wasn't what life was like for him. Vinny was on his way to see his father, but the difference was he wasn't planning on a nice, relaxing afternoon.

He was going there to kill him.

Vinny could relate to the fireworks advertised on the exit sign—he too felt like he was just a tiny spark away from exploding. But he wasn't quite there yet. He still wondered if he could actually do it.

As he drew closer to his destination, his heart pounded. His hands were also a little shaky, since he'd cut back on drinking. After thinking about all the details for several days, Vinny felt sure he was making the right decision.

The afternoon sky was appropriately dark, and a drizzle of rain started to dot his windshield. The sedan in front of him was driving slowly, and he liked that. Normally he would be racing down the highway, but with what lay ahead of him, he preferred taking his time.

He was so close.

Activating the wipers, Vinny went over his reasoning in his head again. Killing his father would do many things—some things for certain, others might've been wishful thinking. It would make the world a safer place—for women in particular. Even if his father had stopped the killing, he deserved to pay for his sins of the past—for what he'd done to Vinny's mother, for what he'd done to Vinny.

But deep down, Vinny knew this noble motive wasn't the reason he was making the drive. It was a selfish one. At his core he believed that to avoid becoming the monster, he needed to slay it.

Vinny had spent over a decade trying to bury his past trauma, only to have it resurface again and again, ruining whatever little good he'd been able to accumulate and resetting him back to square one.

The idea that after his road trip there might be hope for him romantically was a tasty carrot.

After this, he would put all those rotten and brutalized faces behind him. No combining pictures from old medical books with fetish magazines. No more taking out his internal anguish on the people who were trying to help him. He would forget about the darkness once and for all.

Can't just think about yourself, he thought.

It wasn't just about freeing himself. It was also about burying everything that happened in the past. One of the reasons he'd drank so much after moving out on his own was the thought that if his father's true identity was to one day be discovered, he might still be implicated in his atrocities. Vinny didn't have a clue how the law worked. The fact that he'd only been a teen, that he'd been intimidated into participating in the crimes, didn't change the fact that he'd participated. With that fear of being revealed constantly looming, it would never be possible for him to start a normal life.

Lastly, it was to find out what had become of his mother. *She was your mother . . .*

He'd failed her in the worst way, there was no changing that. His extended silence on the dark matter compounded his anxiety and guilt with each passing birthday. Vinny had tried to justify his exodus, tried turning his head the other way, but it never worked.

You left her to rot in that fuckin' trunk.

Vinny focused on the music coming from the droning radio in the background, but it was no use—distractions only worked for so long. Part of him wondered if he was about to discover that she was still alive. That would certainly throw a monkey wrench into his plans.

In that condition, it's impossible . . .

He hoped that solving the mystery of his mother's fate would help him put everything in the rearview. Maybe then he'd stop seeing her rotten face every time he had sex with a girl or looked into their eyes romantically. Maybe then he could find a way to lead a halfway normal life.

Gotta fix all this. Gotta finally make things right.

"Fix" was maybe a poor word choice. There was no way to amend the past, but he hoped to at least make his future livable. After everything his father had taught him, he was good with his hands. And while he'd gone out of his way to avoid becoming a mechanic, Vinny's current job—working construction—had been the lone bright spot on a path of extreme darkness.

I'll just stay on that. Bust my ass, focus on the work.

There was talent on the jobsites. Vinny stood out among the other men. His boss seemed to acknowledge that much, but if he didn't present him with any other opportunities, then maybe it was time to find someone else who could.

As he drew closer, the thoughts of his personal life dissipated, being replaced with the frightening responsibility that lay ahead. Despite Vinny having driven all the way back to his old stomping grounds, he wasn't sure he could do what he'd come here to do. There was a wide void of doubt in his guts resting alongside his fear. Thinking about it was one thing, but actually doing it was another.

He'd been sporadically thinking about such things for many years, but he'd never believed himself capable. Was Linda leaving the straw that broke the camel's back, or would his next stop be where he made a U-turn and reverted to his cycle of torment?

The sedan in front of him suddenly jerked right. A few seconds later the car straightened out but started to slow down. Vinny yielded behind the car. Thankfully they were the only two on that stretch of lonely highway.

As the car pulled into the breakdown lane, Vinny coasted past, catching a glimpse of the woman driving. She was stunning, and as he noticed the look of concern on her face, he felt sad inside. He could see in the rearview mirror that her passenger-side tire was nearly flat.

She looked so sweet.

Shaking his head, Vinny approached an old sign he'd forgotten about: *Fowler Automotive Next Exit ½ Mile.*

Disgust curled his lip as the realization dawned on him. *He's still doing it.*

FATE OR FATALITY?

Vinny parked his car beside the sign and gazed back through the mirror. He recalled the many times his dad had parked on this very stretch of highway feigning a breakdown while he sent Vinny off with a handful of nails.

"Not too many in one spot," Dennis would say. "Gotta spread them out. We want it to look random."

His father was a smart son-of-a-bitch. Whenever he wanted to avoid suspicion, he used Vinny as a buffer. Kids are innocent, and so he could always come up with some kind of harmless explanation.

The tactic his father used was not only to drum up business from out-of-town clients, but also to collect their keys. In Vinny's experience, this method worked about as often as Dennis wanted it to. His dad had been using it for decades. He didn't even have to look at the poor woman's tire to know there was a nail stuck inside.

Some things never change, Vinny thought.

Vinny opened his door and started walking in the woman's direction. She was already hunched over outside the car, inspecting the tire while trying to shield herself from the droplets of rain.

"What's the damage?" Vinny asked.

"Damn!" she cried, looking at the rusted piece of metal sticking out of the tire. "Another flat. How is there a nail on the highway?"

"Another? So, I'm guessing there's no spare then?"

The woman shook her head dejectedly, looking at Vinny initially, then past him. She pointed at the sign. "You think you might be able to give me a ride to that mechanic?"

"I'll give you a ride, but how about I take you somewhere else? There's another guy just a couple miles up the road. Much cheaper, and he specializes in wheelwork."

The woman scrunched her face, somewhat uncertain if she should accept. "What's wrong with that place?"

"Well, people from around these parts know he's just a bit . . . unethical."

Vinny hoped the proposition didn't sound too creepy. Helping the pretty lady out was all he wanted to do.

The woman looked him up and down. "Are you from around these parts, Mister . . . ?"

"Fowler. Vinny Fowler." He gestured back to the sign. "Yeah, that's my dad's garage, actually. I'm just back to visit though. Thankfully I escaped this place."

A little smile curled her lips. "Well, congratulations." She stuck her hand out. "I'm Kelly, by the way. I appreciate you giving me a ride."

The rain started to come down harder.

"But . . . what do you say we continue this conversation inside your car?" she asked.

"Sure."

Kelly grabbed her purse and locked her doors, then the two of them made their way to Vinny's car. Once inside, he turned the key.

"Thanks again for the ride," she said.

"Happy to do it," he replied. "I hate to see someone get stranded. Out in these parts, sometimes the help is few and far between."

"I guess it's kind of ironic. I'm actually taking a bit of a road trip to see my parents too."

"Oh, really?"

Vinny pulled back onto the highway and started to accelerate.

"Sounds like you've already traveled quite a bit if you're unlucky enough to have a second flat. You're pretty close with your folks, I'm guessing?"

"You could say that. I am driving all the way up from Stoneville, so it's definitely a hike. But I don't get to see them much, and they're worth it."

"Stoneville?!" The crackle of excitement in Vinny's voice was obvious. "I . . . I live like twenty minutes away. That sure is a nice little town."

Kelly was breathtaking. From the moment he'd laid eyes on her there was a nervousness and thrill rumbling inside him that was undeniable. He was doing his best to play it cool. A woman of her beauty and sweetness didn't just stroll past him every day. There was something different about her, something that had captivated him instantly.

"You've gotta be kidding me!" Kelly said. "This is so random. Small world, I guess."

"Seriously," Vinny chuckled.

"So, what about your dad? Outside of his 'unethical' business practices, are you guys close?"

A dead silence filled the car.

Don't make it weird.

"I'm sorry, if I'm prying too much, just—"

"No, you're not. I'm just not sure *close* is the right word to describe us."

"Well, when you figure out that word, just let me know."

Vinny could see in his peripheral that she was eyeing him up and down. It seemed to him that their excitement and attraction were mutual—and when she continued, Kelly confirmed his suspicion.

"In fact, maybe when we each get back from our little trips, we can maybe get a drink. That'll give you some time to think. If you haven't figured out what to tell me by then, I'll be concerned."

Vinny grinned and flicked his turn signal. It felt like a storm of butterflies had invaded his belly.

From the corner of his eye, Vinny could see Kelly biting her lip. She looked so cute, out on a limb, awaiting his response. He couldn't believe that *she* was suggesting they get together. But deep in his mind, if he was to break the cycle, he knew there was something he needed to fully commit to before her. And her sweet words were *just* the thing he needed to give him the strength to do it.

Vinny tried not to sound overly enthused—he needed to play it somewhat cool. "I'd say that's about the best idea I've heard in a long, long time."

CREEP

The nightfall helped Vinny blend in with the trees. He'd left the car a ways down the road to keep a low profile.

Far enough away to avoid attention, but just close enough for a quick exit, he thought, recalling his father's wisdom.

There was a reason Vinny had decided not to just walk in and confront his old man. That would look quite strange, and such an unexpected drop-in might potentially hint at what he had in store. His father might be older now, but that didn't change the fact that he was a very dangerous man.

While his heart thrashed, and reservations still swirled inside him, his exchange with Kelly helped push him along. If he hadn't met her, it was possible he might've turned his car around and headed home. But with the rusty nails on the highway having all but confirmed his father was up to his old tricks, picturing that sweet, innocent girl ripped to shreds inside his father's ghastly storage container enraged him. It was the bit of extra fuel he required to do the unspeakable.

How many people like Kelly has he killed?

Vinny had been waiting for some time. The same lights inside the house remained until, finally, he heard the door creak open. With a black garbage bag by his side, Dennis crept out from the back of the house.

Watching him closely, Vinny saw his father enter the side door of one of the garage bays in his yard. Tactfully, he tiptoed up to the structure and looked through the door that remained partly open.

Beside the bench stood his father, hunched over a vintage hubcap with a bottle of superglue. Once he'd finished applying a healthy amount to the chrome center, he removed what appeared to be a human heart from the garbage bag. A vintage radio sat beside him playing some oldies as he worked.

Using a box cutter, Dennis spliced the organ with a long cut, allowing more of the carnal material to connect with the adhesive. Turning his back to Vinny, his father pressed it against the glue, holding it in place and waiting for it to dry.

Vinny snuck through the ajar door, watching each step he took. He spied a bulky socket wrench on the bench beside him. When he swiped the socket, he did his best to mask it with the beat of the music.

As he inched closer, his father remained in place, bobbing while Dion belted out the lyrics to "The Wanderer." There was no song that could've better encapsulated his depressing odyssey any better. Vinny had always felt like a mindless zombie—moving from one horror to the next, feeding on the agony he inflicted on those around him, just as his dad had taught him.

I'm all done wandering. This is where it ends, he thought.

As he moved past the two-post vehicle lift, Vinny found himself in striking distance. He raised the socket just as he saw a change in his father's posture.

Dennis straightened up but didn't turn around. "I knew you'd come back eventually, Son. I'm just surprised it wasn't sooner."

"Well," Vinny said, bashing the heavy socket into the back of his cranium. "Better late than never."

SAYING GOODBYE

Vinny had been watching over his father for some time before he'd finally awoken, all the while considering what he might say. But when his eyes finally came open, he hadn't come up with much.

Staring at his son, dumbfounded, Dennis slowly noticed the chains around his wrists and ankles. He tried to adjust his body from the awkward position, only to realize the steel was tightly wound around each post of the hydraulic vehicle lift. His ankles were secured to the steel arms on the left post while his wrists were chained up to the steel arms of the opposite. His body was strung out on the ground and there wasn't a thing he could do about it.

"So, how you been?" Dennis asked.

Vinny shook his head. "Not good. Thinkin' about the past a lot. But at least I've finally found the guts to deal with it."

"Sure seems like it. I can't say I blame you."

"If you know you're wrong, then . . . then why'd you do it? Why put me through that?"

Vinny thought about the frog getting crushed by the rock. The horrible magazines that he was ashamed to say excited him. The ghoulish car made out of rotten body parts. His legless mother in the trunk.

255

"That's a great question. I'm not gonna bullshit you, I don't have some magical answer. I guess abuse is a strange thing. It's cyclical. I was just doing what I know, what I was taught. Isn't that what we all do?"

Vinny shook his head. "You never stopped and thought you might've had a bad teacher?"

"Son, I'm not gonna lay here and make excuses for myself. What you're about to do ain't wrong. But you asked. The answer ain't what you wanna hear."

"Oh, no? Why's that?"

"Because my answer will sound like it's trying to minimize your plight. And that's not—"

"Trust me, you're not gonna say anything worse than making me think Mom left because of me, when in reality you cut her legs off and kept her in the trunk of that sick, rotten car."

"It sounds pretty fucked up when you say it that way."

Silence filled the garage.

Dennis grimaced. "I didn't even know you knew about your mother."

"Yeah, you would've let me suffer and think I was to blame until the day I died. Father of the fuckin' year."

"I lived a life of rage and selfishness. I ain't dancin' around none of it." Dennis shook his head. "You didn't deserve what you had to deal with. And I ain't just saying it because you got me at your mercy neither. I've thought this for some time, reflected on it for years. For all I put you through, for the terrible shit I shown you . . . I'm sorry."

Vinny's gut felt like it had been hit by a rocket. He'd have bet on the Second Coming of Christ over getting an apology from his dad.

"What about Mom and all the girls?"

"Those fucking cunts got what they damn well deserved. If I could carve them up every day for the rest of my godforsaken life, I'd sharpen my knife every sunrise."

Shaking his head, Vinny exhaled.

"What?" Dennis asked.

"It's just sad," Vinny said.

Dennis grimaced—the awkwardness of his position was clearly starting to hurt more. "The more of them you let get close to you, the more obvious it'll become."

Vinny's life hadn't shown him much different than what his father was saying, but he knew that was the result of not being able to be self-critical more than a conclusion about the women in his life.

"So it's everybody else's fault but you?"

"I guess so," Dennis replied.

Vinny was having a hard time deciding if he believed what his father was saying. While figuring out a psychopath didn't so much matter to him any longer, there were still some things he needed to know.

"Why Mom? What did she do?"

Dennis furrowed his brow. The question had struck a nerve. "What do you mean? She turned her fuckin' back on me! Not even just me, but you too!"

"But why'd you hurt her? You could've just been single parents, like so many other normal people. But instead, you tortured her and kept her like a fuckin' animal."

Dennis smiled. "No one walks out on me. She tried, so I took her walking sticks."

Reliving the situation made Vinny feel sick to his stomach. There was nothing he could say that would get through to his father. He was an absolute narcissist. But there was one more question he needed answered. One that, without his old man, he might not get the answer to.

It took Vinny another moment to muster the courage to ask. "Where is she?"

"She's gone," Dennis said, then added, ". . . or is she?"

Vinny shook his head and approached the hydraulic control. "I guess you're just gonna be a son-of-a-bitch right to the end."

"You said you were ready to deal with the shit," Dennis said. "Good luck dealing with what's inside that container, Mr. Perfect. Good luck explaining everything to the cops."

"Wasn't it you who just said you were only doing what you were taught?"

"Damn right."

Vinny hit the lever for the right post, which began to elevate his father's legs. "I give a shit about the cops. This sickness ends tonight."

"Fuck you!" Dennis yelled. "Shit ain't stoppin', this shit'll never stop! It's inside you, Son. Christ, look at you!"

The tension in Dennis' body reached the breaking point. His legs were nearly six feet in the air, while his arms remained shackled to the other post that was still on the ground. Wailing in agony, the old man's brittle bones started to crackle and pop like mini fireworks.

"All right!" he cried. "I'll—I'll tell ya! She's dead!"

"How?" Vinny asked, stopping the lift.

"A fuckin' infection! What's it matter?"

"It matters to me," Vinny growled.

He pressed the button and watched as the lift put a new level of stress on his father's frame. The popping coming from Dennis' joints resounded throughout the garage. A wet, sickening splitting noise accompanied it. The primary stress looked to be on his elbows. It looked like his forearms might detach from his body until suddenly his father told him otherwise.

"M-my bad hip!" Dennis howled, accompanied by a series of horrified wails echoing in the garage.

The socket exploded, causing his jeans to rip away along with the flesh and bone. Blood rained down as the old man's moans amplified. A gory gulch where his leg formerly resided quivered.

As Vinny continued to lean on the lever, the intensity moved on to his father's remaining leg. The knee joint sounded like popcorn exploding in the microwave. Listening to his father shriek, he hoped it was louder than all the tortured women combined.

When the bone snapped and the veins and torn tendons became visible, Dennis passed out.

While his father's legs were elevated toward the roof of the garage, his broken body remained gushing on the ground. He'd gone white as a ghost from the sheer agony and blood loss.

Vinny hadn't planned on having his father's legs ripped from his body, but the poetic justice was well received. While he still felt mostly numb, he'd be lying if he didn't admit he'd gotten at least a smidge of joy from how it all worked out.

Suddenly, he felt a stir of emotion inside. It was his father's body destroyed before him—by his own hand, no less. As horrible as the man had treated him, it still hurt.

The small moments that every boy remembers came back to him. The times—however warped—when he'd made him proud. It wasn't something he'd ever cared to admit to himself until that very moment, but there was some good mixed into the predominantly gruesome timeline.

Vinny looked at the hubcap with the human heart affixed to it, then back down to his father's mangled body.

Suddenly, Dennis' eyes shot open.

"I . . . I can see the darkness now," he whispered. "Thought this might happen." He looked at his destroyed hip socket as the blood poured out. "Ain't got much longer . . ."

Vinny took a step closer, eyes glossing over. It felt like his dad was trying to tell him something important.

"In the . . . the t-trunk of the car . . ." Blood oozed from Dennis' mouth as his eyes grew wider. "There's a little b-b-black box. It's f-for you, Son. I wish I could've been what you wanted. I wish I could've . . . been . . ."

Vinny looked at his father as the profuse blood loss started to slow. Sobbing hysterically, he watched his father's eyes roll back and the life drain out of his body.

TAKING OUT THE TRASH

Vinny dragged the construction bag containing his father's corpse through the yard before slowing to a stop in front of the huge storage container. Cleaning up the murder scene and inspecting the rest of the property had taken several hours, but there was still plenty of night left. Still, he wanted to ensure he wasn't there for more than two days.

He had specifically picked the Fourth of July as his old man's kill date. It landed on a Monday that year, and his father always took the following day off. It would only be when Dennis didn't show up at the garage on Wednesday that people would start asking questions.

Plenty of time to get this entire place scrubbed, Vinny thought.

While the initial sweep had taken more time than he would've preferred, he was still on schedule. The real concentrated effort lay beyond the doors in front of him. Any evidence or traces of murder on the property currently sat bagged up outside of the storage container. Disposing of a few trash bags and the gore car was his final task.

Almost free . . .

As he opened the massive doors, Vinny's heart pounded. He wondered about his mother and what he might find inside the storage container.

No time to be scared.

Clearing his mind, Vinny dragged bagged pieces of his father's corpse up to the car. Pushing his way through the hordes of agitated flies, he did his best to ignore the pests. After stuffing the pieces of Dennis into the backseat, Vinny returned to the entrance of the storage container and got each of the additional bags. He was grateful everything fit into the backseat of the muscle car. The thought of going into the trunk made his stomach turn.

Backing away from the car, he tried to corral his distress but found himself looking at the wall of death. The last time he'd been inside the storage container, the most recent news article was Beverly's.

An image of Beverly, wide-eyed and gagging on motor oil, popped into his head. Sickened, Vinny rubbed his hands. He recalled the resistance of her shins against his palms when he'd held her down as his father murdered her.

But equally as horrifying as the memory of Beverly's assassination were the many cutouts of news clippings that had been put up *after* hers. They all stared back at him—the eyes of the dead victims glaring, as if trying to stir up the guilt of a thousand sins. Vinny knew that if he would've just told someone what his father was doing, if he'd had the courage to face the demons, those clippings wouldn't exist.

They're all dead because of me . . .

Eyes glossed over, Vinny pulled another trash bag from his pocket and started ripping down the clippings and copied keys underneath them.

Just push through.

After getting all his father's trophies into the bag, he took a deep breath. Vinny turned his attention back to the outside of the gore car. His eyes darted to the skin, rotten flesh, and faces covering the headlights.

I can't get rid of it like this.

DO WHAT YOU'RE TAUGHT

As Vinny pulled the car onto the road, he cringed. The sound of the old skin and meat ripping still resounded in his head. The many pieces of the mutilated women stuck to the car's exterior had been torn off, bagged, and stuffed into the backseat. He still hadn't had the guts to open the trunk.

The outside of the car still wasn't perfect, but it would have to do. He was grateful to at least have all the gruesome evidence out of immediate sight.

Just another few miles and I'll be there, Vinny thought. *It's over . . . it's finally—*

Suddenly, like a ghost in the darkness, blue and red lights lit up behind him. The cop car's siren came to life at a deafening pitch.

"Fuck!" Vinny yelled, heart pounding in his chest like a deranged monkey in a cage.

But just as quickly as the lights appeared behind him, they were gone. The cop car blew by Vinny, heading down the road doing at least eighty.

Looking down at his right hand, Vinny saw that he'd instinctively been ready. His trembling fingers had already found their way to the nitro switch. Exhaling a deep breath, a tiny smirk found his face.

"Let's see if this fucker has nitro," he whispered, eyeing the black bag that contained his father's dead body via the rearview. "Right, Dad?"

An unexpected, melancholic feeling overcame Vinny as well as a tingling sensation in his nose. In a weird way, he'd *wanted* the cops to chase him. Maybe getting one last crazy hurrah with his old man was something his subconscious desired.

"I guess it just wasn't in the cards, Pop . . ."

Wiping the tears off his face, Vinny forced himself to control his emotions. He couldn't fall back into the pit of despair when he finally was so close to climbing out.

Flicking his turn signal, Vinny drove deep into the woods. He'd been down the route enough times with his dad that it was burned into his memory.

While the swamp was massive and remote, he still wondered how many cars and carcasses his father had dropped in it by then.

There's gotta be room for one more. After all, it's only fitting that Dad be left here. It's only fitting . . .

Vinny pulled the car up to the embankment and left the windows cracked. He did it just like his father had taught him—only open enough to allow the water in but not enough to let any of the bags or bodies escape.

As he popped the car in neutral, Vinny got out and bridged his body up against the door hinge. He gazed down into the murky water, then back in the direction of the trunk.

There's a little b-b-black box. It's f-for you, Son, Vinny thought, recalling his father's last words.

He took a deep breath and popped the trunk. Biting his lip and clenching his fists, he made his way around the car.

His mother's body was in the most advanced state of decay Vinny had ever seen.

Countless pests peppered her dried, jerky-like carcass, filling the caverns of her gaping mouth and pitted eye sockets. A large percentage of her skeleton was now exposed. The pan of old piss and shit sat beside several condoms hardened by crusty semen.

The tears rained down from Vinny's face as a profound wave of shame hit him. When he sensed the erection throbbing in his pants, he felt defeated.

"I-I'm sorry, Mom . . . I never meant for it to be this—this—"

Several clusters of thunderous bangs and pops echoed out into the night. Startled, Vinny looked up at the tree line, taking notice of the beautiful fireworks off in the far distance. His gaze dropped back down to the black box inside the trunk. It sat beside his mother's corpse with a tiny key jammed into the lock like it was waiting for him to turn it.

"I love you, Mom . . ."

Vinny wiped away more tears, realizing that this was the first time he'd ever watched the fireworks with his mom and dad. As his eyes returned to the black box, he hesitated.

Do I even want this thing?

He took hold of his father's final parting gift and pulled it out, despite being stumped by his internal question. Closing the trunk, he pushed the vehicle forward and watched it go racing down the embankment.

As the dark water swallowed up all of Vinny's problems, along with his sadness, he felt some relief. But he had no way of knowing how far that would take him. Grabbing hold of the key stuck inside the black box, Vinny faltered. Until the faint glow of the taillight finally disappeared inside the cloudy swamp. Just as the light died, he locked the box and slipped the key inside his pocket.

SICKER THAN BEFORE

It had only taken Vinny a short time before he'd jerked off thinking about his mother's maggot-infested corpse. And it didn't end there. As he lay on the bed beside Kelly, gently stroking her stomach, Vinny knew he was still sick.

"I love you," Kelly whispered, eyes closed and resting.

Their relationship had taken off in the fast lane ever since getting a drink. While Vinny felt a weight lifted off him in the several months that had passed since murdering his father, the darkness was still with him.

"I love you too, sweetie," Vinny replied.

He thought it would be different—that slaying the man who imbedded all the warped ideology in his mind would somehow break him of his patterns. That wasn't the case. Vinny was probably even worse than before, but just better at hiding it.

As his fingertips felt Kelly's bulbous stomach, he cringed inside. Knowing the truth about what it took to extract the seed from his body that created the baby inside her fucked with him. Having to live with the fact that he'd thought about his mutilated mother's insect-riddled corpse before he was able to cum inside her wasn't something he was sure how to do.

Vinny's eyes drifted away from the back of her head to the closet. He thought about the black box he'd pulled out of the trunk that night he'd dumped the car in the swamp. Despite not ever wanting to open it, he now related to it. A dark box of secrets was all he'd ever be, but the least he could do was hold it together for Kelly and the little one inside her.

She's so fucking wonderful, Vinny thought. *I'll find a way to make it work. To protect them . . . to give them the normal life that I never had. They never need to know.*

"Vin, I'm thinking more about names," Kelly said.

"Oh, yeah? Come up with anything good?"

She rested her hand over his. "What do you think about Ashley?"

Vinny continued to stare at the closet, still lost in the pool of darkness inside his mind. "I . . . I think that sounds like the name of our daughter."

1996

LIKE FATHER, LIKE SON

Slumped on the floor, Vinny shook his head in disbelief. He felt utterly lost. He'd been staring at the fleshy wall for some time, drowning in his thoughts. But there was still one question that was eating him alive.

How can things be this *fucked up?* Vinny thought.

"Hey!" Willis yelled. "Wake up, man!"

"What the hell do you want?" Vinny asked.

"Just promise me something, okay?"

"I . . . I ain't making no promise to a fuckin' toilet."

The sheer lunacy of not only his past but the situation before him was beyond daunting.

Willis furrowed his brow. "I know you're not there yet, but once you've had a little more time to . . . digest everything that I told you, come back and see me. To defeat darkness, you have to be free of it. I'm afraid you've still got to face what's inside of you before you're ready. But when you are, I'll tell you how to finish this once and for all."

"Whatever," Vinny said, shaking his head.

"If I was you, I'd listen carefully. Don't forget, they take our teeth for a reason. As long as that witch is wearing that little necklace, you won't be able to talk to no one outside of this place."

Vinny's memory of murdering Curtis quickly came to mind. "That's bullshit! I've already talked outside of this place. You're lying."

"No—that's not what I mean," Willis said, now sounding frustrated. "It's hard to explain it all. Sure, you can talk, but you can't talk about this place—where it is, what's happened to you, anything about those creeps. It's like a built-in safety mechanism, so even if someone on the outside happens to interact with you, no one can trace what you're doing back to them."

Not knowing whether to believe him or not, Vinny turned his back on him.

"Wait!" Willis said. "Go ahead, try to tell me where we are right now. Just try it and you'll see I'm telling the truth."

1 Bovine Drive.

Vinny recalled the address with ease. It was simple enough to remember when he'd jotted it down on the sticky note on his fridge. But as he tried to speak the words from his mouth, they failed to manifest.

"See?" Willis said. "You can't do it. But you can say whatever else you want—"

"What does it even matter?" Vinny asked, peeking back at the toilet.

"It means they probably didn't think about me being able to talk to you," Willis said. "It means you better damn well exploit this loophole while you still can, 'cause no one else but me can help you!"

He looked into the broken pieces of the mirror on the ground. Vinny's monstrous reflection was unrecognizable. As much as he wanted to believe there was someone who could help, the image that confronted him in the mirror told him otherwise. The deflated feeling in his chest left him unable to find the slightest motivation.

"I'm telling you," Willis pleaded, "you think it's bad now, but things can get worse. I was under their hex for years—this is just the beginning!"

Glancing up from the mirror, Vinny shook his head. "Feels more like the end."

Vinny staggered out of the bathroom, wanting to be anywhere but inside the house of gore. Anywhere that wasn't going to remind him of his enslavement and the absolute nightmare that his existence had devolved into.

"Hey, Vinny, wait!" Willis yelled. "I'm not messing around! Those two have very few weaknesses, but during my time under them I figured out that—"

"I don't want your goddamn help!" Vinny yelled. "I just want to be left alone!"

"You should be happy I'm trying to help! When I was doing this shit, I didn't have no one! I was alone, for years! Aw . . . damn, wait! Before you go, can you at least flush this thing?!"

Vinny paid him no mind. As he placed the bottle of glue on the workbench, he felt exhausted on every level—he could do no more. He made his way away from The Nexus and headed toward his resting chambers.

The walk didn't help him figure anything out. Once inside, he collapsed in his resting space. He thought about his father and how he'd reached the point of pure madness— the same point that Vinny now found himself facing. He'd come full circle and become everything he'd hoped he'd never be.

No, you're worse.

At least his father had killed people on his own terms. Vinny knew he was just a miserable meat puppet—even more pathetic than his old man.

When Vinny closed his eyes, he saw the black box in his mind. His body trembled at the mere imagining of it. He was still too frightened to find out what was inside. And while Willis claimed that was the only way to regain his freedom, he hoped that wasn't the case. Because if there was one thing Vinny didn't believe he had the strength to confront, it was the unknown. The possibility that his past could be even worse than he remembered.

WAITING PERIOD

When she awoke, Sara could still see the explosion of gore in her mind. Michael visited her in her dreams often, but they were never happy visits. And worse, the visions had been intensifying as of late.

Ever since meeting with Vinny, Sara couldn't stop thinking about the past. Every time she wondered how he was doing, or when he might call, her own demons found a way to creep up in the back of her mind. She knew she needed to stop thinking about Vinny so much, but she couldn't. Not until she knew he was on the right track again.

There was also another dimension to her desire to speak with him. For the first time since Michael had passed away, Sara found herself attracted to another man.

It probably had to do with how much in common Vinny seemed to have with Michael. Not only the personal trauma and the guilt they'd both been forced to grapple with. They also had the same rugged, manly demeanor and humble kindness that seemed impossible to pair together. Vinny even had an overgrown beard just like Michael's.

Sara got out of bed, trying to control the excessive thoughts and curiosity. Her optimism helped wash away the aftertaste of her nightmares, but she wasn't trying to get her hopes up. Despite Vinny acting a bit flirtatious at the diner, she still hadn't gotten the call he'd promised her.

Well, he didn't actually promise it, Sara thought, having to remind herself for the hundredth time.

Was she just going to wait around forever for him to make the move? It wasn't even just about making a move—the primary concern remained his well-being, although the romantic elements she believed to be forming between them certainly did complicate things.

She wandered out into the living room and approached the answering machine—zero messages.

Taking a deep breath, Sara tried to push away the violent images from her nightmare. How many times would she have to watch Michael put that gun to his head?

Should've kept a few pills for myself.

Sara's half-closed eyes darted to the clock on the wall.

Would've had to get up for work in an hour anyhow.

Looking at the bathroom door, she thought about taking a shower, only to turn her gaze back to the phone.

If he won't call you, then it might be time to call him.

"Just do it," she whispered, as she walked to the phone and lifted it off the wall.

ANOTHER PLOT

"Get as many as you can fit in the van," Blanche said. "But be sure these particular bodies are located." She handed Vinny a list. "Grayfield has its share of historical deviants."

Click . . .

Click . . .

Click . . .

The sound of the metronome rattled in Vinny's head as he took the paper and mindlessly nodded. He couldn't help but internally focus on his collected enamel—it once again encircled Blanche's neck. The swaying metronome that rested in Alfred's gloved hands propelled him.

"They shall make for a powerful addition, my dear," Alfred said with a smirk.

"That they will," Blanche replied. She redirected her lustful leer at Vinny. "And be sure to implant all of the new bodies tonight, *before* you return to your chambers."

As if the morbid atmosphere in The Nexus wasn't disconcerting enough, it appeared the rest of the flesh had awoken. The amalgamation of deformed bodies from the previous handiwork, and even the fresher corpses, moaned. The wet walls pulsated with pain. Vinny could hear the unmistakable wails of Curtis King infused with all the rest.

They weren't happy to be there.

"Please! I want to go back!" one cried.

"This . . . this can't be it!" another wailed.

"Vinny! What have you done!" Curtis screamed.

Vinny couldn't have answered them even if he wanted to. The mash of throbbing humanity wasn't calm like Willis had been in the bathroom the prior evening. He wondered why that was. It could've been because the souls reawakening in horror that he'd installed in The Nexus were gaining a knowledge of what they were becoming. Willis had been there and done that. Still, Vinny found himself debating if being a piece of the hell over his head was a better alternative to the role the siblings had enslaved him in.

The pleas of desperation seemed to not even faze Blanche or Alfred. The orange in their eyes glimmered faintly and their grins remained wide.

The fury rumbling inside Vinny was staggering—he hadn't realized that he could hate with such intensity. Thoughts of his teeth gnawing into Kelly's decomposed flesh haunted him. He daydreamed about what he might do to them if he had his free will again.

I'd beat both your fuckin' heads in! Vinny thought.

But in reality—as much as it didn't seem like reality—his burning desire couldn't come to blossom. All he could do was head to the graveyard, so that's exactly what he did.

THE GATES

Vinny parked the van in front of the tall ebony gates at the entrance of Grayfield Cemetery, the headlights fixed on the length of chain locking them up. He slid the side door of the van open and removed the bolt cutters.

Of course they'd fuckin' send me here, Vinny thought.

He pictured his sweet baby girl, with her childish smile and curious eyes. She had been so happy.

Ashley . . .

The lovely face was replaced by a muddle of meat and garbled skin. He could still hear the incessant gnawing sound in the back of his head as the beast feasted on her. Rage flourished throughout his chest as he considered what he might do to the beast if he ever had the opportunity to face it again.

While his emotions were stirring, they had no impact on his bodily movements. The bolt cutters chomped down; the chain broke free. Vinny gazed into the darkness and considered how different the circumstances were now from the last time he'd visited.

Should've just fuckin' killed myself.

He pushed open the pointy gates and they cried out into the night.

278

Upon returning to his vehicle and pulling it into the cemetery, many other thoughts crossed his mind, particularly concerning the details Willis had explained to him the prior evening.

Over time it grows weak, Willis had said. *The farther you are from the device, the less influence it has over you.*

Vinny didn't want to dig up bodies for the siblings. He wanted to visit his family—or at least the memorial of them. He battled internally as the incessant click of the metronome echoed in his skull.

Click . . .

Click . . .

Click . . .

As the van approached a fork in the road, Vinny looked toward the left-hand path where their gravestones lay. He wanted nothing more than to veer down that road. Gradually, his steady hand started to pull, and he was able to make the turn his heart desired.

A micro smile crept up one corner of his mouth, but quickly melted away when he approached their gravestones.

Kelly's probably not even there . . .

Vinny got out of the van. The oddly fresh soil on her plot the day he sat drinking and crying suddenly made sense. Flashes of Vinny sitting at the table with the siblings appeared in his mind. The memory of Kelly's gray meat being torn into by his eager jaw made him shudder. He recalled the gamey, necrotic tissue creating resistance against his teeth with each of his aggressive chews.

Did they take all of her?

Vinny fell to his knees, starting to sob.

"I'm sorry . . . I'm sorry I couldn't protect you," he whispered.

As he stared into the dirt, he envisioned the many horrified faces stuck inside the walls of The Nexus. They were entrenched in anguish, but at least they existed. At least they were approachable. A dark idea wormed its way into his mind, posing a question that Vinny was afraid to answer.

I . . . I could bring Ashley back . . .

Blanche and Alfred had already shown their hand to ensnare him in their insidious activities. When he looked at the well-kept ground in front of and surrounding Ashley's tombstone, Vinny felt with a degree of certainty that his little girl's body remained buried.

The only question was, should she stay that way?

THE GRAVE GRIFTER

I could never make her part of that monstrosity, Vinny thought, picturing The Nexus in his mind. The pulsating, bloody mass looked nightmarish. *I'm not that selfish.*

Despite deciding against it, he'd thought about what it might be like while digging up each of the graves on his list, and the picture in his mind was far from pretty. He pushed the idea away and shifted his focus to finishing the work he needed to finish inside the cemetery.

The van was already full of rotten meat when it pulled up to the last grave on Vinny's list. But as his shovel struck soil, his emotions started to toy with him again, continuing the internal argument over who or what he was now. Part of him just wanted to try and drive away from it all. It felt like he had enough willpower to move on, but even if he did, many questions remained.

Where would I even go? What would I do?

Furthermore, the responsibility Willis had thrust upon him remained on his conscience. Vinny had seen enough nasty and impossible things already to know that not only was Willis' theory possible, but it was probable.

Maybe I can make a difference. Could stopping them be a way of making amends for what I did with Dad?

As Vinny lifted another shovel of dirt, he thought about Kelly's grave.

Can't let those fuckin' creeps get away with killing my family and . . . and what they did to Kelly.

Whether he'd regained some of his free will or not, there was no way Vinny could just coast off into the darkness, washing his hands of the atrocities that Blanche and Alfred had committed against him. Such a choice just wasn't a spiritual compromise that Vinny could accept.

They've gotta pay.

As he pushed the shovel into the dirt again, he wondered what kind of vile acts the name on the tombstone must've committed to become a blip on Blanche's radar. As the pile of dirt beside him continued to grow, he rekindled his rage.

The siblings and their blueprint of depravity needed to be stopped, but so long as Vinny was in close proximity to them, he would remain their meat puppet. The only path to retribution was regaining his free will. But that entailed something that Vinny wasn't sure he was capable of. He pictured the black box in his mind.

No . . . I can't—

"Hey!" a voice yelled from behind. "You can't be—what the fuck are you doing?"

Vinny whipped around and saw an older man wearing a flat cap. The flickering lantern in the groundskeeper's hand illuminated the look of dread on his face. Even through the darkness, Vinny imagined that he must look like a demon to the man.

The groundskeeper glared into the van beside him, full of decaying bodies that were stacked up like flapjacks.

"W-what kind of sick shit is this?!"

By the time he turned his head back to Vinny, the shovel already had landed upside it. The steel connected with his facial bones, triggering a loud ping, and sent the old man to the ground in front of a tombstone.

Vinny didn't think or wait. Before the groundskeeper could get his bearings back, his boot collided with the heavy stone, sending it toppling over.

What have I done?

The weight and size of the rock was large enough to account for the groundskeeper's entire skull. A sickening crunch erupted along with the blood that pissed out from the circumference of the stone.

I-I had no choice. Can't let him get in the way of stopping the siblings.

Looking back into the van, Vinny knew he'd have to squeeze in one more. He bent over and took hold of the groundskeeper's legs. As the death tremors found his fingertips, another strange sensation hit him.

Sadness.

How could I have been so quick to extinguish a human life?

Vinny didn't even know the man from a hole in the wall. But he was probably someone's grandfather.

What the fuck am I doing?

As he pushed the headless corpse inside the van, he couldn't be sure if it was the spell he was under that killed the man or if it was his daydreams of rage. But if he hoped to face the darkness, it might be a question that was better left unanswered.

VULNERABILITY

Alfred stood in front of the dresser in his bedroom, looking into Willis' eye holes. He grinned, stretching the mask of skin taut with his crimson-caked fingers. As the wrinkles of dread curved the former Handyman's flesh, he was grateful that it still clung to life in his hands.

"W-what are you doing?" Willis asked.

Alfred looked down at the glass container of acid atop the dresser.

"I'm doing what I must," Alfred replied.

"What *we* must," Blanche corrected.

Alfred looked back at his sister as she sat on the bed, gazing into the standing mirror. As the metronome clicked away on the nightstand, Blanche watched the mirror's glass offer a window into Vinny's activities. Alfred observed along with her as Vinny drove the van and parked it outside of his residence. Shifting his glare back to Willis, he dangled the mask of skin over the acid.

"It seems you've shared some of our secrets," Alfred said. "That was a very careless thing to do. You were right— it was our mistake to humiliate you . . . and now, we must ensure that you don't do any further damage."

"We shall ensure that you hold your tongue," Blanche said. "Permanently. It would be a shame if we allowed you to foil what we've worked so hard for right as we approach completion. It cannot happen. It *will not* happen. The final foundation is about to be set. It is within our sights."

"The two of you creeps will never finish!" Willis yelled. "You're both insane! You're both—"

Alfred dropped the mask of skin into the large jar of acid and put the cover over it.

"Go where you must," Alfred whispered.

The fluid started to cloud and change color as it ate away at the skin and gore. The fizzing bubbles eradicated the tissue as it twitched, and it seemed like the flesh could somehow feel pain in its every molecule.

Alfred's grin widened like that of an evil jack-o'-lantern. "You shall be a part of my army one way or another, fool."

"*Our* army!" Blanche yelled. "What is it with you? Always trying to cut me out!"

"Sister, we've had this discussion before and nothing's changed," Alfred said.

He pointed to Oswald Hitchens' worn journal where it rested on the nightstand beside the metronome.

"The writings are very clear," Alfred continued calmly. "It can only be one who stands in the pool of The Nexus when the final foundation is laid. If we're to succeed, then we must obey Hitchens' commands."

"We could try it with the both of us," Blanche said. "There's no reason—"

Alfred smashed his hand down on the dresser, rattling the glass lid on the acid jar. "There can only be one! *One*, damnit! Do you understand me? I didn't work my entire godforsaken life to raise The Nexus in its totality just to watch your ego piss it all away in the final moments!"

Blanche stood defiantly. "Oh, *my* ego?! Why should it be you and not me?! What have you done that should grant *you* opportunity over—"

The back of Alfred's hand collided with Blanche's jaw, sending her tumbling back onto the floor. A jagged line of blood oozed out of her busted lip as she gazed up at her brother, shocked.

"Ever since we were children, *you* followed *me*! It was *me* who tainted Uncle Rooney's tobacco! It was *me* who translated Hitchens' work! And it's *me* who allowed you to tag along for the ride! I act and you *re*act! It shall be the same over these final days! Understood?"

Blanche remained stunned but nodded.

Calming himself, Alfred felt his boiling emotions drop to a simmer. He quickly realized that he'd gone too far. As he got down on one knee, Blanche raised her arms as if to block a punch.

"I . . . I'm not going to hit you," Alfred said. "I'm sorry. I lost my head."

Placing his hand on his sister's shoulder, he helped her up and brought her to bed. As they sat on the edge of the mattress, he rubbed her knee as she sobbed.

"You must forgive me," Alfred said, rubbing his hand against his forehead. "With Willis spilling the beans, my brain's been in a whirlwind. I just have this dreadful feeling that this might all have been for nothing."

Finishing her sniffle, Blanche locked eyes with him. "Don't say such things. Although, why should I care? It's *you* who shall be the backbone of the final foundation."

There was an uncomfortable silence between them.

Alfred sighed, grabbing hold of her hand. "But that doesn't mean once the ritual is complete that your presence and attitude shan't be required." His pruned finger coasted over one side of her wrinkly face. "I would be lost without you, my sweet, sweet sister."

Gazing into the mirror, Blanche watched carefully as Vinny discreetly approached the door to his apartment and found a key. As he entered the apartment, Vinny walked up to the refrigerator, and a wicked smirk found Blanche's face. She turned back to her brother, licked the blood off her busted lip, and swallowed it.

"Then don't you worry about what Willis told our little Handyman," Blanche said, her tone emitting a crude confidence. "I know exactly how to keep him motivated."

Excitement knocked around in Alfred's ribcage as his confidence was restored. He could always count on his sister's twisted mind to solve a problem.

He leaned forward, kissing her deeply, tasting the iron-strong blood that he'd caused to leak from her face. As the siblings suckled upon each other, he could feel the erection in his pants intensifying.

It wasn't long after taking their vow to finish what Uncle Rooney had started that Alfred and his sister realized something about their relationship. They'd not only committed to the darkness but to each other.

The sex initially came out of isolation from the outside world due to their supreme focus on the sinister task at hand. But the older they grew, the more Alfred realized that it wasn't just lust that lit his loins ablaze; the fire was in his heart too. Despite his annoyance with her at times, he loved her. His sweet sister was only second to their common goal.

Alfred felt guilty after striking her, and as his warm tongue wormed deeper into her bloody mouth, he wanted nothing more than to show her how much he cared, and to make up for his hotheaded actions. But as Alfred started to massage her droopy breast, Blanche pushed him away.

"As much as I'd love for you to lay with me right now, if you want to truly alleviate your stress, we don't have time," she said.

"I trust you, my love," Alfred said. "Since we took this bond in darkness, regardless of bloodline, our love was inevitable. Know that once I reach the pinnacle, I shan't leave you behind. And in the meantime, I trust you to guide me—no, *us* . . . to a resolution."

Blanche grinned, some of the blood from her lip staining her teeth. "Then be a dear and fetch Herman, along with a shovel."

A FORGOTTEN FACE

There was still plenty of time to make the stop. Since visiting her grave, Vinny needed to see Ashley's face as he remembered it—not the garbled mess that no funeral parlor could make passable for an open casket.

I miss you, he thought.

Envisioning the photo of her playing in the park magnetized to his fridge, Vinny's heart raced. As he pulled into the parking space, he looked around and was glad to see there was no one in sight. He didn't imagine there would be anyone at such an ungodly hour, but he still had to be careful. There was no telling how his neighbors might react if they ran into him.

Under the guise of darkness, he quietly exited the van and slipped into the apartment building. The hallways remained dimly lit, and Vinny walked briskly with his head down until he reached the end of the hall. Having no clue where his own keys were, he lifted the spare key from its hiding space on the tall corner of the doorframe.

As he closed the door behind him, Vinny started to feel overwhelmed. Countless awful thoughts circled his mind, but the one that brought him home was the one he struggled with the most.

How could I even consider making her a part of that vile place?

Still, when he'd reminded himself about how The Nexus reanimated the souls of the fallen, he couldn't resist considering the idea of one last conversation with his baby girl. All the things he would've told her if he had the chance.

Vinny leaned against the wall, feeling the dread continue to unfold in his gut. Flashes of what Ashley looked like with the ravenous beast gnawing on her face.

That beast will pay too . . .

The police had been no help. With his family already dead, there was little incentive to try and locate the "animal" that they claimed was responsible for the attack. Due to all the other personal trauma, self-blame, and loss Vinny was constantly dealing with, he'd not had much time to even think about the creature that left them unrecognizable.

His mind shifted from Ashley's muddled meat-flap face and the creature's glowing eyes, back to the wet walls of The Nexus. He pictured what Ashley's ribbons of skin and torn flesh would look like if they contorted like Willis' had. Would her spirit be able to see him? Would that be the parting snapshot she was left with? The nightmarish rendition that wasn't Daddy at all, but instead, the nail-toothed maniac—Handyman?

There were too many questions to even justify the thought of bringing her back, yet it was difficult to let go of. Such sickness left Vinny weighed down with the burden of guilt. He stepped around the counter and up to the fridge. More than anything, he wanted to remember his sweetheart as she was in the picture before him—to preserve her innocence and forget about the horrible way things had ended.

Vinny gazed into the happy eyes in the picture. The joy on Ashley's face in the playground that day was something he'd assumed he would see for countless years to come. The assumption felt so foolish now. As he stared at her, tears welled in his blackened eyes, and he realized it was joy he'd taken for granted.

"I'm sorry, baby," Vinny whispered.

He carefully plucked the picture off the fridge. Holding it against his chest, he tried to compose himself. He couldn't believe that his life had turned into such a revolting pile of carnage. Once he calmed himself, he slipped the snapshot into the back pocket of his pants.

Click . . .

Click . . .

Click . . .

The faint sound of the metronome interrupted his thoughts. His eyes drifted back to the fridge, where his sticky note remained.

First Job Back. 1 Bovine Drive, Wickford.

As he reread the note, he quickly realized what a mistake it was to take the job. With his family gone in such gruesome fashion, he didn't believe it could get worse.

Boy, was I fuckin' naïve.

As the metronome continued to echo in his brain, Vinny shuddered. It wasn't close enough to completely control him, but even from afar, it made sure he was reminded of his spiritual slavery.

But a red flicker in the corner of his eye distracted him yet again.

Just a short distance away the answering machine displayed a flashing number one. Vinny shook his head. The fact that he'd only received one message since he'd become Blanche and Alfred's Handyman saddened him.

The only people who cared about you are gone.

He sighed and shook his head again. "Probably just another creditor or telemarketer . . ."

As he wiped the salty streaks from his cheek, he figured it was probably better that way. If he had anyone who cared about him, they'd be crushed by what was happening to him. At least the way it was, he wasn't a burden—he took the brunt of everything.

Still, his curiosity nagged. While it hadn't even crossed his mind prior to entering his apartment, he needed to know who had tried to contact him.

Vinny walked over to the table and pressed the play button. The sweet voice he heard was one that—amid all the madness and commotion—he'd almost forgotten about entirely.

Sara's tone sounded just as kind and caring as it had when she'd sat across from him that time at the diner—a meeting that, after everything he'd been through, now seemed like a lifetime ago. But unlike then, the concern she expressed now sounded much more urgent.

"Vinny, it's . . . it's Sara. I was just calling to check up on you. I wanted to see if you got any leads on the work stuff we talked about, and if the pills are helping. Speaking of help, I could use a little myself lately. Been having some nightmares again and—sorry, I don't mean to ramble on. I just—I hope everything's going well. If you get a chance, give me a call back. Bye."

Sara . . .

Just hearing her voice and thinking about seeing her again made Vinny's knees feel weak. The chaos he'd been ensnared in had all but eradicated the warm, comforting thoughts that he'd felt prior to donning his new uniform.

He'd forgotten his promise.

He'd forgotten the plan they'd devised.

He'd forgotten there *was* someone who cared.

Even as a monster, Vinny somehow felt human again when he thought of Sara. He had no idea what the future held for him, but he instantly knew it couldn't involve her. She didn't deserve to be dragged down beside him—he couldn't endanger her in the risky game he was playing with the siblings. But at the same time, he felt awful ignoring her.

Should I call her back? Who knows if I'll ever get a chance to make another . . .

It felt like a circular saw blade was being run up against his heart as he realized what needed to happen.

He walked into the bedroom, flung the closet door open. Tearing through several bins, he finally located the one he needed. Pulling the top off, he sorted through the contents until his gloves found the dark steel.

His mother's maggot face flickered in his head, causing him to immediately drop the box.

I . . . I can't do it.

The thought of opening the box, of potentially learning that things had been even worse than he could've ever imagined, was too much. He didn't have the strength to fight off such a hypothesis.

This isn't about you. This is about Kelly and Ashley . . . it's about Sara . . . it's about everyone.

If he was to avenge his family and get the opportunity to thank Sara, the only way was by facing his fear of the unknown. Vinny reached back into the bin and retrieved the box. He clenched it between his fingers tight. He didn't plan on letting go. Even if he wasn't ready to open it yet, Vinny knew he had to eventually.

BODY BUILDER

Vinny pulled the van deep into the woods before coming to a stop outside the nightmarish greenhouse that encapsulated The Nexus. He glanced over at his father's black box on the passenger seat, wishing he had the willpower to open it.

I . . . I can't, he thought, shaking his head.

He snatched up the box and shoved it under the passenger seat of the van, then got out. When he pulled the headless groundskeeper's body from the van, he felt terrible. The thought of the black box he'd just hidden entered his mind.

You're him . . . you're—

"Handyman," a man's voice whispered.

Vinny turned to see Alfred grinning and Blanche aiming the swaying metronome at him.

"Don't bother bringing them inside," Alfred continued. "There was only one tiny spot left to patch in the house, and we decided to do that ourselves."

The two seemed overly gleeful about the work they'd accomplished. Seeing their vile smiles made Vinny angry. He would've loved to have sunk his spiked teeth into their flesh and rip them to pieces, but while in such close proximity to the metronome he had no way of controlling his bodily movements.

Vinny stared into the maddening device, a feeling of uneasiness taking hold of him.

Click . . .

Click . . .

Click . . .

"Don't worry," Blanche said. "They won't go to waste. Come 'round this way."

Vinny remained silent and obediently nodded.

As the siblings led him around the side of the massive greenhouse, the tension in Vinny's chest ramped up. It only took a moment to see what they wanted to show him.

The massive, black and red cement truck was parked beside the building. At the rear of the truck, near the ladder, stood a forklift and pallet. The pallet was mostly empty, but also held several large jars of acid. One of the containers looked murkier than the others and still bubbled. Next to the forklift was a professional table saw.

"With the inside of the building complete, we will begin preparing the final foundation," Alfred said. "You will bring the dead here and cut them down so that they fit into the barrel of the truck." He pointed to the massive, black and red drum beside him. "Once they're cut down to size, stack the pieces on this pallet and elevate it. You will then drop their body parts into the drum along with the containers of sacrificial liquid."

"We've already seen to it that some of the spare parts we've had laying around be used to fill part of the barrel," Blanche explained.

Alfred grinned and winked at Vinny. "We try to help out as much as we can."

"That we do," Blanche said with a snicker. "In addition to the limbs of the long-departed, we shall also require a mass offering of flesh that's more . . . recently deceased. As far as the contributors of this final offering, we'll leave that up to you to decide. So, after you've completed your tasks this evening, be sure to get your rest. Because tomorrow night you'll most certainly need it."

"And just to ensure you're adequately motivated to complete the project," Alfred said, "we have one more thing that we simply must show you . . ."

Blanche aimed the metronome at Vinny from behind as he followed Alfred around the structure and into the entrance.

As Vinny passed the bathroom, he couldn't avoid looking for Willis. But when he glanced at the toilet, the face that he'd affixed to the seat was no longer there.

Shit, where is he?!

Vinny recalled when Willis had told him to circle back and visit him once he was ready. While Vinny still wasn't sure if he had the courage to open the black box and face his darkness, even if he did, Willis would no longer be there for him to gather intelligence from.

Guess I'm on my own . . .

Alfred snapped his fingers at Blanche and pointed toward the black curtain. His sister grabbed hold of the cloth and peeled it sideways.

Vinny's heart might've stopped when he gazed through the opening if it wasn't a slave to the rhythm of the metronome. He hadn't heard the sadistic snarl of the beast since the car accident, and it was now mixed with the bubbling groans of his little girl.

Ashley!

"Yes, Mr. Fowler," Alfred said, "while she might be a little difficult to recognize after her last encounter with Herman, that is in fact who you think it is."

Vinny wanted to jump out of his skin and pounce on the beast, burrow his fingers into the creature's neck, and rip its throat out. To break its face down punch by punch and turn it into a soup of crimson chunks. But he was helpless, fully at the mercy of the metronome.

Eyes drifting off the beast he loathed, he studied Ashley in horror. The tiny area on The Nexus wall in need of mending had been filled with her mangled body.

No!

Her head was still the same garble of gore that he vividly remembered. Her fizzy, unintelligible groans escaped from the ribbons of meat, the throbbing mass glistening with each twitch. Drool and blood oozed from the puncture wounds as the flesh pulsated with the rest of the bodies in the area.

"D-D-D-Daddy," Ashley moaned.

Vinny looked on in horror, unable to show emotion, unable to grieve. Blanche stepped beside him, holding the metronome in one hand and caressing the necklace comprised of his teeth in the other, and he was unable to respond.

"Do not forget, we see all," Alfred said. "After your little conversation with Willis, we had no choice but to repurpose his flesh. He shall be an ingredient of the final foundation."

"Since he can't seem to keep his mouth shut—"

"I've got this," Alfred said, glaring at Blanche.

She stopped talking, blankly staring forward.

"But I will credit my dear sister with pointing out the obvious," Alfred continued. "Now that you understand that, outside of these walls, a certain measure of your free will is reinstated, we needed an incentive to ensure that you will stay committed to finishing the job."

"I can't think of a better one," Blanche said, laughing to herself.

"Nor can I," Alfred concurred, eyes darting from his sister back to Vinny. "Because, should you decide not to finish what you've started, our nasty pet, Herman, shall see to it that your daughter relives that night in the car for every waking minute of her purgatorial existence."

"Better yet, we can make it even worse for her," Blanche said, dropping down to her knees and resting her hand on Herman. "Change."

Herman's hairy features started to melt away and the beast transitioned to the woman Vinny had seen standing in the road the night of the accident. He stared into her black eyes, yearning to respond with violence, but remained restrained like an indolent child in a car seat.

"No . . . change again," Blanche commanded.

The beast went through another metamorphosis. While Herman now resembled something similar to the woman, the creature now had male features and genitalia.

Son-of-a-bitch!

As Blanche reached out and stroked Herman's cock, causing it to solidify, Vinny thought back to the dining room. The strange cook, the one who'd brought out the disgusting stew comprised of chunks of Vinny's dead wife, was unmistakable.

"We can have him defile every little hole on whatever's left of your little girl's body," Blanche said.

Alfred looked down on his sister, smiling approvingly.

Taking notice of her brother's enthrallment, Blanche stroked the cock more vigorously and took it a step further. "We can even have Herman rip open some new ones and sully those too."

"So it would behoove you to be smart about this," Alfred said. "If you simply follow through and do as we've instructed, we can spare your daughter any further torment. But if you don't . . . well, we can't be blamed for what she endures."

"I'll fuck her too," a man's voice said.

Vinny glance at the patch of wall beside Ashley that he'd installed previously. The face of his perverted replacement, Ryan Clements, bubbled to the surface of the wall.

"I've been thinking about sliding into her from here this entire time," Ryan said. "Oh, the things I would do, the things I would—"

"Silence!" Blanche yelled. "Herman, silence him!"

Herman quickly shifted from his manly form back to the beast. Using its thick claws, the beast raked the dagger-like tips across the patch of flesh where Ryan's face was. Thick pink gashes burrowed into the wall of gore as Ryan wailed in agony.

"No!" he cried. "Please, stop!"

Alfred held up his hand. "Enough!"

Herman immediately ceased the onslaught.

Turning to Vinny, Alfred locked eyes with him. "Let this show that we can be trusted. We don't aim to cause harm to your daughter without cause. In fact, we'll even protect her. So long as you hold up your end of the bargain . . . I shall have Herman see to it that this perverted soul's meat is migrated."

Alfred looked at the beast and pointed to the clawed patch of gore where Ryan's face had surfaced. "Ensure that this degenerate is fully extracted and transported far away from Mr. Fowler's daughter. Replace him with someone who's less . . . enthralled by adolescence."

The beast snarled, immediately starting to claw and rip up the area. Ryan's screams of agony once again resounded throughout The Nexus.

Drawing closer, Alfred placed his hand on Vinny's shoulder. "Now return to your van and do what you must with those bodies. And when you've finished, while you rest this evening, think about where you're going to find the rest of the flesh that will comprise the final foundation."

Blanche moved to Herman's side, petting the beast's hairy coat as it continued to pull the bloody wads of gore off the throbbing wall.

"You have nothing to fear," she said. "Herman shall watch over your baby."

Rage had bubbled inside of Vinny at the sight of Ryan's face and sound of his perverted comments. But despite his anger, Vinny was almost glad to have seen him. He felt like he'd been hit in the gut by a sledgehammer after everything the siblings had dropped on him, but with it all stacked against him, it reminded him of something.

Ever since Vinny became a man, he didn't just sit around and take shit from people. He adapted, calculated, and executed. The creeps had sought him out because of his darkness—because he'd been through hell. Because he'd stared the devil in the face and tore him limb from limb. Because he was strong.

It's time . . .

He looked at the mutilated, gurgling mass that was his daughter. She hadn't spoken another word to him. Whether that was a choice she'd made as a result of his appearance or just because of the extreme shock she was in was anyone's guess. Either way, maybe it was for the best. Vinny wasn't sure if he could handle listening to her tortured words in such a state any longer. He instead tried to focus on the anger stewing inside.

It doesn't matter if you're scared anymore. It's not about you now. It's about her.

As his gaze shifted from his daughter to Ryan's maimed face, Vinny smiled inside. He knew exactly where to get the rest of Alfred and Blanche's materials.

INSTINCT

As the sunlight shone through the window, lighting up the nurse's station at Lakeland Hospital, Sara sipped her coffee and reached for the phone. After returning for another short stint to the building Vinny had been taken to after his accident, it was hard not to think about him, but she did her best not to dwell on her sadness and curiosity. As Sara punched the number in, the scene across the hall caught her attention.

A middle-aged father knelt on one knee holding his little boy and girl, one in each arm—the thick beard on his face again reminded her of Vinny.

"Don't worry about the car," the man said. "What's important is that we're okay."

"But what about Mommy?" the little girl asked.

"Mommy's gonna be fine," he replied. "She just hurt her arm a little bit is all."

As Sara patiently listened to the phone ring, she continued to wonder about Vinny. He seemed to be doing so well after their meeting, but then it was total radio silence. The longer the gap in communication, the more she worried about him. But earlier that morning, she'd woken up with an absolutely horrible feeling in her belly.

Something's wrong, Sara thought. *I can feel it.*

When she dialed the number, she wasn't sure if she was jumping to conclusions or being overprotective as a result of her own life experiences. But as she watched the man interact with his family, it reassured her that she'd made the right decision.

"Hello," a female voice finally said.

"Hey," she said, "Dr. Marrow, it's Sara. I'm sorry to call out of the blue like this, but I think I'm going to have to cancel our meeting this afternoon."

"Oh, I'm sorry to hear that. Is everything all right? I have a few minutes now if you need to talk."

"I appreciate that, but for once, it isn't about me. I'm lucky that I have you to lean on. But the man I'm trying to help . . . he doesn't have anyone. And I'm a little concerned that he might be going down a dark path again."

"Well, it's very noble of you to look after someone going through a difficult time. If you're in a good place aside from worrying about him, then it seems the most logical thing would be to lend your support. Have you told me about this man before?"

"No . . . we've only seen each other a couple of times." Sara exhaled deeply. "But I think what he's going through is a lot similar to—"

"What you went through. I kind of imagined that might be the case. If that's so, then I'm glad he has you. I'll cancel the appointment—free of charge. We can just catch up the following week, and you can tell me all about how much better he's doing. Sound good?"

"That'd be wonderful, thank you for understanding," Sara said.

"That's what I do. Take care," Dr. Marrow said.

As Sara hung up the phone, she continued watching the grateful father across the hall comfort his children. She wanted nothing more than to do the same for Vinny. But the nasty feeling in the pit of her stomach made her wonder if her conversation next week with the therapist would be as cheerful as Dr. Marrow assumed.

She picked the phone back up and dialed an internal line. It was answered almost immediately.

"Hey, Lauren," Sara said. "I'm not really feeling so great. Would it be okay if I take off a little early today?"

As the head nurse gave approval, Sara reached for the filing cabinet.

"Okay, thanks," she said, hanging the phone back up.

She passed her fingers over several files until she came upon the one labeled *Fowler, Vincent.*

"Bingo," she whispered to herself.

Prying the cover open, Sara scanned the document until she located the address field.

If you won't answer your phone, then I'll just have to come to you.

THE DAY THE WORLD CHANGES

Alfred stood completely nude, facing the mirror alongside the metronome. Inside the reflective surface he saw Vinny at the workbench outside of The Nexus. He held the golden hammer in hand, driving nails through a large, rectangular patch of wood.

"Today is the day that the world changes . . . forever," Alfred said, feeling a tickle of emotion in his nose. "I can't believe I'm finally here."

"We still need to ensure that our Handyman follows through," Blanche said, chewing her fingernail while seated on a chair in the corner of the room.

"We've already seen that he is properly motivated." Alfred pointed into the mirror at Vinny. "He's hard at work focusing on securing the materials. And he'll do as he's told if he knows what's good for him."

"Still, it would be wise not to underestimate—"

"I'm not underestimating anyone." Alfred turned and glared at his sister. "Do you think I would be so foolish as to jeopardize the most important day, not just of my life, but of man's existence? I think it's best that you leave the strategizing to me today."

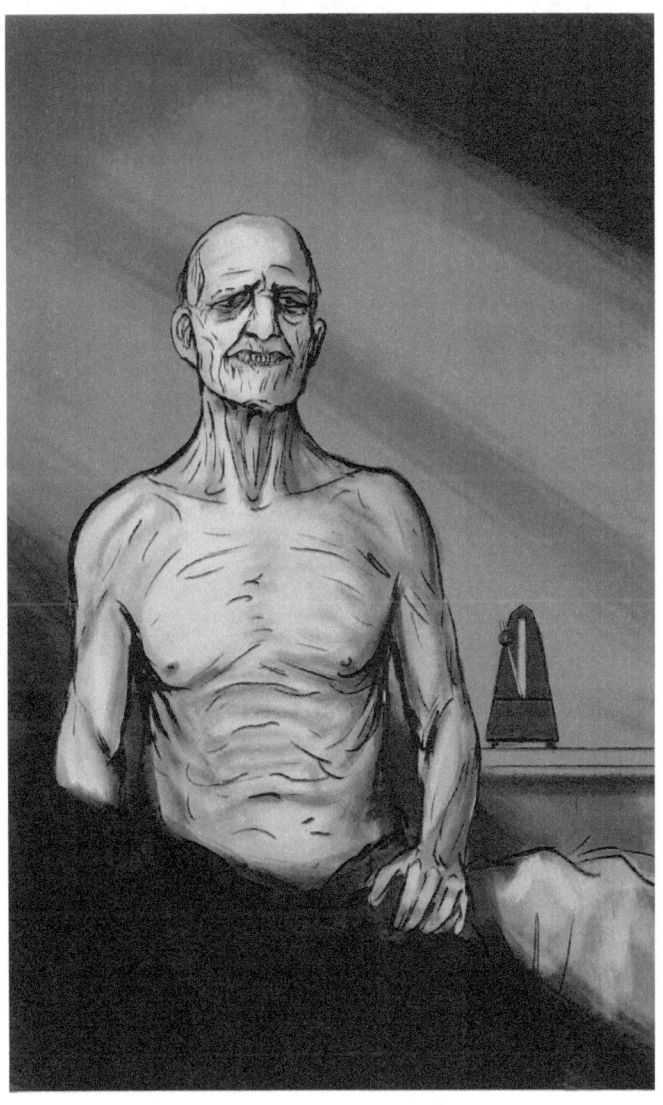

Blanche nibbled on her finger more aggressively.

"Now would you be a dear and fetch me my robe?" Alfred asked.

The echo of Blanche chewing on her nail resounded. She didn't answer him but did as she was told. Rising from her chair, she disappeared into the closet momentarily, returning with a white robe.

The front of the garment bore the symbol from The Nexus—a black circle with a tuning fork overlayed on it. Shuffling the robe over his head, Alfred adjusted himself until it hung evenly on his body.

"How do I look?" he asked.

"Like the master of man," Blanche replied.

Alfred smirked proudly. "It's good to know that I shall fit the part."

IN PLAIN SIGHT

When Sara pulled up to Vinny's apartment building, she was already starting to second-guess herself.

What are you doing? she thought.

Looking at the handful of cars parked outside, she wondered if other people might see her creeping around and find her presence strange.

Am I going too far? Maybe he just wants to be left alone. Is he going to think I'm some kind of psycho stalker?

That thought, however, didn't stop her from parking and turning off the engine. The feeling in her gut continued to urge her onward.

You've got to trust yourself. The last time you had a feeling like this was when—

She saw Eric's crushed head in her mind like it was yesterday. Her nervous and apprehensive feeling turned into a sickening one.

"You're doing this," she whispered to herself.

She got out of the car and approached the entrance of the apartment building. Grateful that the front door wasn't locked, Sara quietly slipped inside. She looked at the apartment number layout, seeing that Vinny's was just a few doors down.

When Sara approached the door, she was glad to see that his apartment was separated from the others. She made a fist—but hesitated. Closing her eyes, she took a deep breath and forced herself to knock.

After a few quiet taps, there was no answer.

Shit.

She knocked several more times, a bit more aggressively, and suddenly the door popped open. It must not have been closed properly.

The unexpected entry spiked her concern. It was one thing if Vinny wasn't home, but it was hard for her to think of a reason why his door was left unlocked and ajar.

"Vinny?" Sara said, taking a half step inside. "Anybody home?"

Again, there was no response.

Now believing something was truly wrong, Sara stepped inside and looked around. She crept around the apartment, calling for Vinny in the other rooms, before eventually making her way back to the kitchen.

"What the hell happened to you?" she muttered.

As she glanced at the refrigerator, she noticed the lone yellow sticky note on it. She moved in closer and read the heading *First Job Back* scribbled on it.

Maybe they know something.

Sara approached the fridge, peeled the note off, and looked at the address. The light bleeding in through the window was starting to turn orange and the sun was beginning to droop.

Wickford . . . It's still early enough to pay them a visit.

THE LAST HARVEST

Vinny sat in his van thinking about the black box under the passenger seat. He still couldn't believe that he was finally going to pry it open. Even though he still couldn't look at it just yet, the idea that it was going to happen felt monumental.

The siblings might be watching—they were *always* watching. With time running out, Vinny felt it would be wise to approach the situation with extreme caution.

Get what they want done first, he thought. *Maybe then they won't feel the urge to keep an eye on me. It's better if they don't know. Besides, it's probably best if I wait. I might need the darkness inside me to get through this anyhow.*

Vinny was on edge as he stared at the halfway house Len Anderson had created in the middle of nowhere. The sun had just set, and Vinny knew it was time to get moving.

They're all creeps. Kid-fuckers and perverts like Ryan . . .

He recalled the nasty words his work replacement at King's Construction had hurled at his daughter the night before. Using that memory as fuel, Vinny tried to convince himself that he was doing the right thing. Being so far outside the circumference of the metronome's influence, Vinny knew that any blood on his hands would be his doing.

They deserve it. It's time.

Vinny had parked on the side of the road a sizable distance away from Len's house.

Just like Dad taught me.

Under the cover of darkness and nature, he opened the van door. His toolbelt lay on the bloodstained floor, various other apparatuses hung on the wall above it. As he tightened the belt around his waist, Vinny loaded a duffel bag with various tools from the wall, as well as several boards, but left the bag in the van. His eyes darted to the stack of nail beds that he'd created back at the estate.

After dragging the last nail bed out of the van, he stealthily crept around the perimeter of the house. He carefully positioned the spike strips outside each of the windows before making his way around to the back door.

Vinny removed a length of steel wire from his toolbelt and fastened it around the doorknob before tying it to the axle of a sit-down lawnmower being stored under a tarp.

As he made his way back to the front of the house, Vinny glanced inside one of the windows. Several men and a woman sat at a table playing cards.

"You think *you* can't control yourself," a male voice said, "you should talk to Julia."

The man's voice was unmistakable—Vinny had spoken with him on the phone many times, and he'd hated every sickening minute of it.

Len Anderson grinned, brandishing his yellow teeth, and nodded in the direction of the woman sitting across the table from him. "How many'd you get to taste?"

Julia blushed as she looked at the other men at the table and around the room and adjusted her eyeglasses.

"How many did I taste, or how many did they charge me for?" she asked.

Len laughed. "I never thought I'd have so much in common with a woman."

"How many *was* it?" one of the other men asked.

"Eleven," she said. "But, full disclosure, I'm a teacher, so it makes it a little easier."

The rage inside Vinny started to stir violently. There was a certain amount of self-loathing that was accompanied with the anger. He'd folded to Curtis—allowed himself to become a pawn in his perverted chess game. These were the people who Vinny had helped support.

But tonight, the support stopped.

The only fuckin' support they're gonna get—if they're lucky—is life support.

He quickly dismissed that idea.

No way. They're all *coming with me.*

"Teacher?" Len continued. "You're a woman—I think *that's* the biggest advantage you have. This is the first time I've *ever* had a woman stay here."

"Well, hopefully it's not the last," Julia said with a grin. "I love this place. I feel . . . right at home."

"Which one was your favorite?" another man asked.

Julia put her cards down and looked up at the ceiling, as if she really had to think about it. "It's hard to choose, but if you had a gun to my head, I'd probably say this fourth grader, Nilton Waters. I didn't teach fourth grade for long, so most of the others were just out of middle school. But there's something special about them when they're *that* young."

"Tell me about it," Len said. "Sweet as pie."

"This is the first time that I've been able to talk about it openly," Julia said. "I'm so glad to finally share with others who understand."

"That's the whole reason I started this place," Len said. "While I've never been convicted, I know many have. And they have nowhere to turn and no one to listen to them. Just those fuckers trying to tell them that their natural attractions are somehow sick. It's no different from being gay—if we were born like this, then how can it be wrong?"

They're all pure fuckin' scum.

"Amen," one of the other men said.

Julia clapped and nodded, as if what Len had said should be obvious to the world.

"I wasn't about to let you"—Len looked at Julia, then to the rest of the men—"Peter, Sam, Carlos, Doug, or anyone struggling outside of this house, be brainwashed into believing that there's only one school of thought that exists on this topic."

Vinny watched each of the sick men nod as Len called out their names. The sense of unity between the brigade of deviants disgusted him. Len's little peptalk was starting to wear on him.

He thought about Ryan and what a piece of human garbage he was. The vile things he'd expressed to his child with such ease. Seeing all his comrades engaged in this twisted way of thinking made Vinny thirst for their blood even more than before.

"They're all the same—none of them have a goddamn clue," Len continued. "And one day, in the not-so-distant future, we won't be falsely imprisoned and forced to meet in the shadows. One day, things will change. But it takes a village. It starts with us."

Several of them cheered on Len in agreement, excited by the fiery rhetoric being spewed. There was a true sense of unity between them.

"Well, looks like we might not get to finish the game though," Len said. "We've gotta get some rest."

As he tossed his cards in the center of the table, the rest of the players followed. Julia gathered up the entire deck and started putting them back into the box.

Len yawned and wiped his eyes. "After whatever kind of accident happened with King's Construction, we've gotta be on our best behavior. I've got a couple of other companies on my radar that are willing to try us out, but tomorrow is a big deal. I had to leave a few things out about some of your histories, of course. Not every company is as understanding as King's was."

Len's statement made Vinny cringe. The sick son-of-a-bitch wasn't wrong. A wave of shame washed over him that he forced himself to convert to rage.

The various men in the living room all nodded in agreement along with Julia.

"So, let's get some early rest," Len said. "Almost all of you are scheduled for tomorrow, and you've gotta be out of here by four a.m. to reach the jobsite on time."

This'll be the last time you fuckin' sleep.

As the people in the house dispersed into various rooms, Vinny crept around the front of the house. He took note of the two work vans parked outside and moved to the rear of them. Taking the drill from his belt, Vinny attached a one-inch bit. Slipping under the backside of the van, he pulled the trigger on the drill and pressed it against the gas tank until it pushed through.

No one's gettin' out of this one.

After creating several small holes in both tanks, Vinny watched all the gasoline drain out. Seeing the final drips hit the puddle of accelerant made him grin for the first time since he could remember.

As the lights in the house started to go out, Vinny returned to his van and opened the sliding door. He grabbed hold of the duffel bag and turned back toward the house. All the light had died—the house was now completely engulfed in darkness.

I'll show them how dark it can get.

WHEN STRANGERS MEET

As Sara exited the car, she continued trying to convince herself that she'd made the right decision. If Vinny hated her for showing up at a client's house to ask about him, then so be it. One thing she wasn't going to do was stand by and ignore the situation. She'd done that once before and it cost Michael his life.

Taken aback by the extraordinary manor, Sara couldn't avoid being intimidated as she approached the door. The glow of the lantern outside was dim, cultivating a spooky aura around her, but the unsettling vibe didn't stop her from ringing the bell.

Here goes nothing, she thought.

It took several moments for the door to be answered. The elderly woman had a curious expression as she stuck her head over the threshold.

"May I help you?" she asked.

"Hi, I'm . . ." Sara shook her head, trying not to let the awkwardness stop her from asking what she needed to. "I'm sure this is going to sound weird, and I apologize for showing up unannounced at such an hour, but I'm wondering if you might've seen or maybe talked to a friend of mine."

"I'm sorry, dear," the woman said. "Who are you?"

Sara's cheeks grew hot. "Oh, forgive me! My name is Sara—Sara St. James."

"And who are you—"

Click . . .

Click . . .

Click . . .

The woman's response was cut off by an older man who manifested out of the darkness behind her. He was dressed in a white robe and holding a strange triangular device. The black and red eye sat on a pendulum stick. As it swung side to side, Sara couldn't take her eyes off it.

"Don't be so rude," the man said. "I'm Alfred, and this is my dear sister, Blanche. Please, do come inside."

Before Sara could even decide if she wanted to join them, her feet were moving. As she entered the house, she felt something awful in the pit of her stomach.

"Now tell us, who is this friend of yours that you're looking for?" Alfred asked.

"Vincent Fowler," she said.

While Sara felt herself replying, it wasn't her actions piloting her body. Her heart began to pound, fear taking hold of her. With her pupils glued to the wave of the metronome, Sara remained motionless.

"Oh, a friend of Mr. Fowler's," Alfred said with a smile. "How lovely. Why, he should be returning in just a short while. I think it's best you stay here until then."

Sara nodded, but inside, staying with them was the last thing she wanted. She tried to speak but couldn't. Fear took over her as she suddenly realized the truth: it was no longer her choice.

Alfred turned to his sister and grinned. "Blanche, why don't you close the door?"

MEASURE TWICE, KILL EVERYONE

The house was dead silent as Vinny set the duffel bag on the ground. He unclipped the tape measure from his toolbelt and used it to check the length of the doorframe.

Perfect, he thought. *That's about just what I figured.*

Snagging his gold Madison hammer, he laid the first board across the doorway. As he drove the long nails through the wood and deep into the wall, it was like Vinny had returned to the job. In that moment, all that mattered was finishing the task as quickly as he could.

The loud pounding continued with the second board, but by then people in the house started to awaken. The familiar voice was the one who objected first.

"Hey, what the hell's going on down there?" Len yelled down the stairs. "People are trying to sleep!"

Vinny didn't answer the question. Continuing to pound away on the door, he moved on to the third piece of wood.

"Who . . . who the fuck are you, dude?" another man asked in confusion.

This man sounded much closer than Len's voice had been. Despite his certainty that the man was in the same room as him, Vinny continued to hammer away.

"I'm the Handyman," Vinny said, removing the fourth and final board. He saw Carlos' reflection in the window.

"Yo, Peter, Sam," Carlos called. "Come and take a look at this!"

"Hey, we didn't ask for no handyman, asshole!" Peter yelled. "And if you know what's good for you, you'll fix this mess you started."

Once Vinny drove the final nail into the wall, he used his tape measure to check the gaps between the angled boards.

Nah, no one's gettin' through these.

"Hey, retard!" Sam yelled. "Are you fuckin' deaf or something? He said you better fix it."

Vinny clipped the tape measure to his toolbelt and stood, still keeping his back to them. "Or what?" He finally turned toward the men.

"Or we'll—"

Peter stopped midsentence as Vinny glared at the trio, brandishing his rusty grin and black and red eyes.

"My . . . my God . . ." Carlos tried to swallow the lump in his throat, looking to his friends for guidance.

"Right now I am," Vinny growled. "And unfortunately for you, I'm not feeling very benevolent."

In a blink, Vinny flung the hammer at the man across from him. It moved with such velocity and force that it did several revolutions before the tip caused a horrible crack to echo when it collided with Carlos' forehead. He dropped to the floor, body spasming. As blood rained down Carlos' face, frothy saliva bubbled over his lips.

"You crazy motherfucker!" Peter yelled, picking up the hammer and turning to Sam. "Let's get his ass!"

As they charged toward Vinny, he pulled out a corroded screwdriver the size of a short sword. Lunging into Peter's swing, Vinny dodged the hammer and thrust the tip of the flathead into his abdomen.

"That's what you get for screwing around with me!" Vinny yelled, elevating the man's entire body off the ground with the lengthy screwdriver.

A wet hiss rattled inside Peter as his wail turned into a final groan of death.

Under the weight of Peter's carcass, Vinny forced the bloody steel forward, skewering it completely through him. As the tip of the tool worked its way out of Peter's lower back and poked against his T-shirt, Sam took his shot.

As the punch flew toward Vinny's face, he leaned into it. His mouth made short work of Sam's fingers, shredding them down to the bone. He bit down harder, and as the horrified man instinctually pulled back, a mangled mess was returned to him.

"Ahhhhh!" Sam screamed, falling onto the floor holding his destroyed digits. "My—my fuckin' hand! You chewed my fuckin' hand!"

As Vinny let go of the bloody screwdriver, the impaled sex offender thudded to the ground. Looking up the staircase, he saw the shocked expression on Len's face.

"V-V-V-Vinny?" he whispered.

"Hang tight, Len," Vinny said, picking up the Madison hammer. "I'll be with you in a sec."

The man in Vinny's sights had already made his way to the back door. Crying haplessly, Sam pulled and yanked on the doorknob, cursing through his wails of agony.

Vinny plucked the chisel from his belt and knelt beside Carlos, still frothing at the mouth from the hammer blow. Vinny set the unforgiving edge of the chisel deep inside the gash on Carlos' forehead and raised the tip of the hammer behind his ear.

"Night-night," Vinny whispered, driving the tool into the handle of the chisel.

As the flattened steel caved in his already fractured skull, Carlos' eyes rolled up in his head. Vinny smacked the handle again, pushing it several inches deeper. The pink globs of corrupt mind oozed upward around the gaping hole as Vinny grabbed the handle of the chisel and twisted. While the man's brain got further scrambled, his limbs flailed about, and he lost control of his bowels.

"I'll be right up, Len!" Vinny screamed.

He stood up from the quivering man as piss and blood started to unify in the growing puddle on the ground. Turning his attention to the back door, he saw Sam still cradling his mangled hand and crying against it.

Click . . .

Click . . .

Click . . .

The sound of the metronome was still in the back of Vinny's mind, but for the first time since he'd donned the uniform, he wasn't thinking about his duty. The only thing he was thinking about was killing every single person inside that house.

As Vinny closed in, Sam reached for a pan on the kitchen stove with his good hand. The hammer smashed his fingers before Sam even had a chance to raise it. Vinny slipped the hammer into his belt and picked the thickest nail he had. Pulling Sam away from the stove and pinning his arm to the door, Vinny used his raw strength to push the tip of the nail halfway through his wrist.

"Pl-please! Whatever I did, I-I'm sorry!" Sam wailed.

As Vinny held his wrist against the door and grabbed hold of his hammer again, he shook his head. "It's not me you need to apologize to."

The head of the hammer smashed into the nail, causing blood to explode all over the door. The shredded fingers shook; ribbons of meat and bone dripped crimson. As Vinny finished hammering the spike snug against his arm, he positioned Sam's other limb against the wall beside the door.

"God, no!" Sam begged. "God help me!"

But as another nail was drawn and hammered through Sam's other wrist, Vinny knew the spur-of-the-moment crucifixion was probably what God wanted most.

Vinny added several more nails into his wrists before pulling out the duct tape. After wrapping it several times around the weeping pervert's head, Sam's face and hair were no longer visible. The gray-headed mummification trembled, still held up by the nails driven into his wrists as he slowly suffocated.

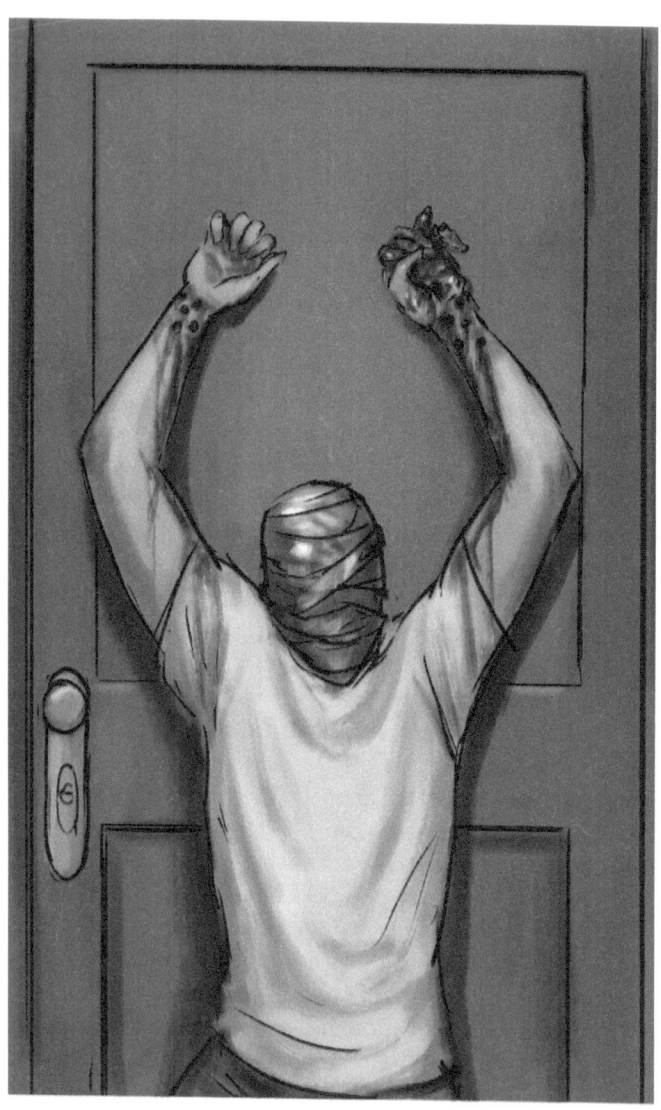

"Don't worry, you'll be back soon," Vinny said. "And it'll be a thousand times worse than how it ended. It'll—"

Blam! Blam! Blam! Blam! Blam! Blam!

Vinny felt a handful of bullets enter his body, but just as the siblings had explained, he felt no pain. One of the bullets landed square in Sam's duct-taped head, causing crimson gore to splatter all over the door.

Click . . .

Click . . .

Click . . .

The clicking of the metronome was drowned out by the empty gun in Len's hand. As Vinny turned, he saw him standing in the doorway that connected the kitchen and the living room. Len continued to pull the trigger despite the piece being empty, as if he didn't want to believe it was so.

"You shot your little pervert pal," Vinny said, as his ghoulish grin oozed blood. "Who you gonna talk about fuckin' kids with now?"

He felt the blood start to leak out of the holes in his torso. But as his glove coasted over the wounds, he felt the open flesh in his chest close.

"But me?" he said, stepping toward Len while holding up his bloody glove. "Don't worry about me. A few holes ain't nothing. I'll be just fine."

Removing the drill from his belt with the large bit, he revved it up. As Vinny closed in on the doorway, Len back-pedaled.

"But maybe I can return the favor," Vinny said, aiming the drill at his head.

"Now, Dougie!" Len yelled.

As Vinny stepped through the doorway, Doug swung the chair. The wood shattered into pieces, thudding against Vinny's shoulder and carving a wide laceration into his eye-brow.

"That the best you fuckin' got?!" Vinny screamed.

Lunging at Doug with the drill, he stabbed the point deep into his Adam's apple.

The twisting steel burrowed into the thyroid cartilage, mauling the tissue and violently ripping through the meat. But Vinny's force didn't stop with the bit penetrating his gullet. He continued using his momentum and pushed Doug through the glass window.

As the pane shattered, Doug went tumbling back-first onto the bed of nails. Upon impact the pointed steel penetrated his back, pushing through to his lungs before the glass shards showered his entire body. Vinny looked down at the massive void in his throat and the nasty lacerations that the panes of glass made—so deep that pieces of his skeleton were visible. While blood jumped out of the hole in Doug's neck, Vinny listened to his gurgles as the life left his eyes.

"Not as much fun when it's your own holes, is it?" Vinny asked, lifting the blood-soaked drill and pulling the trigger.

The battery pack died, causing the drill to no longer rotate. Letting the power tool drop to the floor, Vinny walked over to his duffel bag and opened it. Pulling out the large socket, he turned his attention to the stairs.

"Just like I promised, Len," he said.

"Don't come up here!" Len yelled, appearing at the top of the staircase. He held a knife to Julia's throat, pressing it firm enough against the skin to draw blood.

"Please, don't!" she shrieked. "I-I didn't even do anything!"

"Take one more fuckin' step and I'll cut this bitch's goddamn throat, so help me God!" Len threatened.

Vinny continued forward without hesitation. In a calm and calculated manner, he extracted a long socket extension from his belt. As he added it to the ratchet, his bloody smile widened.

"Well, if you don't, then I will," Vinny said.

"Please, no—"

A look of defeat overcame Len as he cut off Julia. "What . . . what the hell do you want, you crazy fuck?!"

Vinny continued to close in on them. "One way or another, you're gonna find out."

"Fuck you!" Len yelled, tossing Julia down the steps at Vinny.

As her body crashed into his, Vinny somersaulted backward. He landed at the bottom of the stairs, feeling several bumps expand on his cranium. But just as quickly as they rose, they fell. Julia was groaning in pain as Vinny mounted her holding the oversized ratchet.

"I-I'm just a woman," she pleaded. "I'm not like them!"

Vinny aligned the tip of the ratchet with her eyeball—it was big enough to fill her entire eye socket.

"I can see through you," Vinny whispered, ropes of blood and drool leaking through his sharp, steel teeth.

Plunging the ratchet into her eye, a garble of sclera sludge and translucent liquid gushed around the socket. Vinny twisted the wrench around frantically, putting all his weight on her head until it was too deep in her cranium to dislodge.

As the blood pooled around the crater of gore in her destroyed face, Vinny stood tall. After tearing through the rest of the scum, he was ready for the climax.

"And now, for the man of the hour!" he screamed.

When he reached the top of the staircase, Vinny passed each of the bedrooms but found no one inside. As he approached the bathroom, he could see Len hanging halfway out the window, trying to will himself to jump. Vinny didn't want that. He wanted to get his hands on him.

"There's no escaping it," Vinny said. "One way or another, tonight's your night."

Bare chest popping in and out like a terrified bird, Len looked at Vinny then back out the window.

"What the fuck do you want?" Len said, fear flooding his voice.

"It's not about what I want," Vinny said, closing in on him. "It's about what you deserve."

After what Len just witnessed, Vinny couldn't blame the creep for taking his chances with the window. As Len jumped through the opening, he let out a wail of terror.

Vinny made his way to the window and looked through the opening. Len had managed to clear the nails on the ground outside the first-floor window, but now had a new obstacle to deal with. As evidenced by his horrifying shrieks and the compound fracture just below his knee, walking wasn't going to be in the cards any longer.

Vinny grinned, waiting by the window for another moment to savor his screams. They were extra enjoyable because he knew the worst ones were yet to come.

IN HORRIBLE HANDS

"Where did you have Herman repurpose that one pervert?" Alfred asked as he broke the threshold of the greenhouse.

"In the bathroom, close to where Willis was," Blanche replied. "I figured he'd be far enough away from the girl in there."

Alfred grinned. "You figured right." He turned back to Sara and waved her over as the metronome bounced back and forth. "Right this way, my dear."

As he looked at Sara's stare of blankness, he could only imagine what was going on in her mind behind the scenes.

"Where?" Alfred asked.

As they entered the nasty room, Blanche pointed to a patch of relatively fresh gore. "Right there."

Ryan's face pushed its way out of the wet wall, a grimace of concern taking hold of him. "I-I'm sorry about before. Please, don't hurt me anymore!"

"I suppose we could spare you any further torment," Alfred said. "But only under one condition."

"Of course, whatever you want!" Ryan pleaded.

Alfred gestured toward Sara. "You see this lovely little peach? I want you to hold on to her tight. She doesn't get hurt and she doesn't leave this room, understood?"

"Anything to keep that beast at bay!" Ryan said.

"Wonderful," Alfred said.

A pair of glistening, blood-caked hands emerged from the amalgamation of gore. As the wall pushed outward, Blanche guided Sara into the mass of violence and shook her head.

"Maybe a little old for you," Blanche said, "but hold on to her nonetheless."

The grimace on Ryan's face turned into a distorted smirk. "You can count on me."

His bloody hand slid over Sara's mouth, while the other wrapped around her waist. Blood smeared over her skin and clothing, tainting them.

"That had better be the case." Alfred turned to Blanche. "Let us go now and ensure our preparations are in order for the final foundation."

As the siblings exited the bathroom and made their way to the black curtains, Alfred's pulse accelerated. Imagining the culmination of over fifty years of hard work caused a euphoric feeling to spike inside him.

When he penetrated the black curtain and entered The Nexus, Alfred looked to the left. Vinny's garbled little girl remained affixed to the throbbing wall.

"The building is different today," Alfred whispered. "It's like it can sense what's about to happen."

Blanche remained quiet and at his side.

Looking down into the massive rectangular pit, Alfred noticed that it was already partially filled with blood. He gazed down at the gravestone that stretched from the crimson pit all the way up to the exposed steeple of The Nexus and poked out past the dark greenhouse shell.

"So when I'm inside, you shall stand over me here," Alfred said, pointing to the emblem on the stone floor. "And after you finish the incantation, you shall then give Herman the signal."

He pointed to Herman, who'd chosen to don Jack's persona while finishing up some work on the exterior window of the greenhouse.

Standing beside the pane of shattered glass, Herman positioned the cement truck's chute through a hole in the greenhouse and beyond it past the lone void cavity in the wall of The Nexus. Gazing back at Alfred, Herman nodded, acknowledging the plan.

"When she gives you the signal, activate the control and pour the final foundation down the chute," Alfred added. "But under no circumstances will you take your eyes off that Handyman. Understood?"

Blanche and Herman both nodded.

"Excellent," Alfred said. "The time is near. Activate the mixing drum."

Herman picked up the control and pressed a button.

Eyes lighting up like a child, Alfred watched as the black and red drum started to spin.

WHEN DEMONS DIE

As the blade of the saw moved over Len's shoulder, his eyes looked like they were going to jump out of his head.

"Puh . . . please," Len whispered, "k-k-k-kill me."

Vinny grinned, the bloody nails in his mouth drooling all over the destroyed joint as the moonlight illuminated it. The massive pool of blood on the floor spread out wider as he pulled off Len's limb and tossed it in the pile with his other arm and his leg.

Standing, Vinny looked down at Len's mangled body—the lone limb he'd left attached was the leg with the compound fracture that was shaped like the L-square in his toolbelt. He returned to the duffle bag and dropped the bloody saw inside.

"I'm not sure you deserve to die just yet," Vinny said.

He took a few steps closer to Len and extracted a wire brush from his toolbelt.

"I think, after all those things I heard you say, there's one more thing that needs to happen first." Vinny squatted down over Len's face and held the wire brush over it. "What do you think?"

The only sound to escape Len was a groan of anguish.

"Glad you agree," Vinny growled.

As he dragged the brush over Len's lips, the unforgiving steel wires sliced deep. After just a few of Vinny's scrubbing motions, the blood ran and the flesh rubbed away. It tore through the mouth's surrounding skin and cut open Len's lips. It didn't take long for the pressure of the steel brush to reach the teeth and gums.

"A dirty mouth like yours should be scrubbed clean."

The sickening sound of the wire tips scraping against Len's enamel and opening up his gums didn't bother Vinny. As he continued to work the gore-caked brush, gurgles of desperation and agony fluttered from Len's mouth. Angling the bristles up, Vinny used all his weight to drive the coarse metal into Len's esophagus.

When Len finally stopped breathing, the anxiety hit Vinny full force. He'd thought about it while breaking down the front door and dragging Len back inside the house screaming.

Once they're all dead, I have to open it, he had thought.

Maybe that's why he'd taken his time with Len—quite a bit more than he had with any of the others. Maybe that's why he'd pulled the van around the house already and cut up all the other bodies and stacked them inside. The fear of what his father had in store for him loomed, and it was unavoidable.

Just get it over with. It's not about you . . . it's about Ashley.

Vinny dragged Len's body from the house and tossed it inside the van. He then gathered the bleeding limbs, the duffel bag, and his toolbelt. But before sliding the door shut, he removed the Madison hammer and a flathead screwdriver. Making his way to the driver's-side door, Vinny slipped inside and took a deep breath.

There's no other way.

When Vinny grabbed the steel box, it sent a shudder down his spine. Having no idea where his keys had gone, he arranged the box on the van's console and aligned the screwdriver with the lock. After just one swift strike the container popped open—as if it had been dying to be open for years.

Fuck . . .

Vinny felt his eyelids close. Pushing past his fear, he forced them back open.

Inside the box was a weathered photo sitting atop a folded sheet of paper. When he saw it, Vinny felt his eyes well with tears.

In the picture, his father and mother sat side by side in rocking chairs with big smiles on their faces, while Vinny rested on his mother's knee between them. He'd never seen his father in a suit before. He couldn't have been more than four or five years old in the photo, but unfortunately, he didn't recall it.

It made him sad to think there were maybe a handful of happy moments that he wasn't able to hold on to. But on the other side of the coin, it was nice to know they existed at all.

Damn . . .

He saw her face the way his father had left her—the dried husk of a woman in a trunk. Shaking his head, Vinny tried to push it out of his mind and savor the rare tender moment.

She was so pretty.

When he picked up the note, Vinny's hands were shaking. It took him a minute to pry it open; all the while his fear spiked as another tear rolled down his cheek.

What could Dennis possibly have to say to me?

Vinny didn't like consciously calling his father "Dad" anymore—he didn't feel it was appropriate. When he looked at the penmanship and recognized his father's handwriting it made his stomach turn. Popping open the door, Vinny vomited on the ground before calming himself down.

Just get it over with . . . it's almost over.

Even then Vinny knew he was lying to himself. It wasn't like once he read the letter that would be the end of all the baggage attached to his psyche. Not by a longshot. There was no doubt in his mind that the words he was about to see would forever haunt him.

But something strange happened. As he started to read, he realized that—despite the penmanship—it wasn't his father's words in the letter.

Mom?

With his eyes starting to water again, Vinny took another deep breath. Trying to get the little extra push to finally uncover what he feared was the most difficult feat he'd ever attempted. Forcing his eyes open, he hung his head and glared at the writing.

Dear Vinny,

Your father has decided to show me a rare act of kindness. He's offered to pen this letter to you, as I am in no condition to do so any longer. I want you to know that I have and always will love you. And that no matter how big you get, you'll always be my little munchkin.

While I can't tell you exactly what became of me, just know that every day I was away from you, my heart ached. You were and are everything a mother could ask for. I only wish I had found a way to spend more time with you, regardless of how challenging the circumstances were.

You will know these are my words because I'm including a moment that only you and I shared—the very last moment we shared. Please know that I don't blame you for doing what you did. I understand what you were left with, and more specifically, who you were left with. Do not hold any shame or regret from our last time seeing each other. I know that you didn't recognize me. I could see it in your eyes.

None of this is your fault. You were just a child.

Please remember that I will always be looking down on you. I know that you will find a beautiful woman and have a child of your own one day.

And I know that you'll make all the right decisions, since you know what the wrong ones are. Thank you for making me whole again. Seeing you that one last time is what's gotten me through. And for that, I can't thank you enough.

I love you, Son,

Mom

The crushing weight on Vinny's shoulders was suddenly less. The decades of guilt and shame washed away in a matter of seconds as he reread the words again.

You were just a child.

And while the note was from his mother, in a way it meant even more because his father had not only allowed it but transcribed it.

Even the deepest darkness fades occasionally.

While he couldn't put into words what the letter meant in totality just yet, he felt an immediate shift. As the darkness transcended his body, Vinny knew he was once again in control of his own destiny. A buzzing magical feeling warmed his body and soul.

But his newly reclaimed free will wasn't merely about him any longer. The fates of his loved ones and so many others hinged on whatever he chose to do next.

FINAL INSTRUCTIONS

When Blanche watched Alfred guide Vinny toward The Nexus, she felt a supreme sense of excitement. After watching their Handyman load the dismembered bodies into the cement truck, she knew the final foundation would soon be poured. But as they approached the bathroom, she wondered how he would react when he saw what came next.

"Don't be upset with us," Alfred explained. "She came here looking for you. It was not as if we sought her out. We had no choice but to hold her here."

As Vinny gazed upon Sara's blood-smeared body, she stood, wide-eyed and silent, gazing at the black pyramid in Blanche's hands.

Continuing to study every detail of Vinny's expression closely, Blanche felt a sense of satisfaction in what she saw. Their Handyman remained emotionless as the metronome rested in her hands, pupil pivoting back and forth.

Ryan kept quiet while Alfred talked, but Vinny's rival spoke to him with his motions—bloody hands groping Sara's supple breasts, rubbing her curves with a perverted lust. Still, Vinny had no words or reaction.

"It seems she cares enough to track you down," Alfred said. "How . . . sweet."

Seeming pleased by Vinny's reaction, Alfred led his Handyman through the curtain and into The Nexus.

"And as promised, your child remains safe and free of harassment," Alfred explained, pointing to the bloody jumble of flesh glued to the wall of gore.

The gurgles of the girl's voice echoed inside the chamber of throbbing humanity as Alfred turned to face Vinny.

"I show you all this again to remind you that if you finish the job without incident, you, your little girl, and even your new lady friend don't have to be part of what transpires after our ritual is complete."

The lies Alfred told with such confidence made Blanche feel warm inside. They were so close she could taste it.

"Under no circumstances will you reenter this room during or after the ritual," Alfred commanded, pointing in the direction of the cement truck chute lingering above the pit of blood. "You shall remain with Herman, ensuring the final foundation pours smoothly into the pit of The Nexus."

Alfred nodded, as if he'd finished his piece, and turned to Blanche. "Now, before we begin, is there anything that you're uncertain about?"

"Just one matter," Blanche said.

She walked around the bloody pit to the wall the truck chute ran through. Leaning up against the glistening flesh was a long, aluminum rod with a half-moon shape at one end. Blanche set the metronome on the ground and reached for the handle.

"What is this for?" she asked.

Taking hold of the tool, Blanche glared down at the curved edge.

"Be careful—it's sharp," Alfred said. "The last thing I need is you getting hurt."

Despite her brother's warning, Blanche carefully ran her finger over the edge anyway. She let the sharp aluminum slice into her skin ever so slightly. As a little row of red pushed out of the tip, she stuck her finger inside her mouth and sucked on it.

334

"That's the chute shovel," Alfred said. "While the contents inside the truck have been blending for some time, there will be new bodies added into the mix. As a result, there may be some parts that are a bit . . . chunky. Should the chute become clogged, you shall use it to clear the bits."

As the chrome glimmered in the dim lighting, Blanche grabbed the shovel tight. She looked down at the shiny half-moon edge and then up at her brother. The grin on her face widened as she considered how close they were.

"After all these years . . ." Blanche said. "It appears that it's finally time."

FREE WILL

Vinny stood by, silently watching the beast the siblings called Herman listen from outside of The Nexus. Currently, Herman displayed the upper body anatomy of a woman, the lower body features of a man, with beastly teeth, overgrown body hair, and claw-like nails.

The siblings had told Vinny to activate the control when Herman gave him the signal, but it was taking everything inside him not to pounce on the creature and rip it to pieces. When he pictured the jumble of gore stuck to the wall in his head, Vinny knew it was Herman who was personally responsible.

Ashley . . . Vinny thought

Still, the element of surprise was his best asset. He was on their turf. If he fought them up front, they would most likely have another trick up their sleeve to thwart his efforts. But if he allowed them to believe everything was fine and waited until the ritual started to make his move, he'd catch them off guard.

Through the hole in The Nexus, Vinny heard Blanche talking in what sounded like gibberish. And while the words meant nothing to him, clearly they meant something to the universe. In the night sky, above the steeple of The Nexus, gray clouds started to swirl. A crackle of lightning erupted.

Despite all the madness and chaos that he'd already witnessed firsthand, there had been a part of Vinny that didn't believe whatever incantation the siblings had planned was going to work. The endgame that Willis had explained to him was so fantastical—even more so than what he'd personally experienced.

He was right. My God . . . it's happening.

The responsibility of his family had been weighing on him, but he'd convinced himself to believe that was the only responsibility he had. But as the clouds inflated in the darkness, Vinny knew that wasn't the case.

Herman turned and snarled at him, aggressively indicating that Vinny should begin the pour. Activating the switch, he did as he was instructed. As a steaming sludge of gore and partially melted bone slid down the chute, Vinny dropped the control. The sound of it smacking against the ground drew Herman's attention.

Vinny turned his back on the creature and started to walk toward the front of the building, when a roaring hiss escaped Herman. Upon hearing the patter of Herman's footsteps behind him, Vinny reached for the Madison hammer in his toolbelt. But before he could retrieve it, the creature had already pounced on him.

As Vinny dropped the hammer and braced for impact, he watched Herman's head transform into that of a full wolverine. The beast bit at Vinny's face, the unforgiving fangs pulling a small piece of tissue away. Using its claws, it raked its razor nails down Vinny's chest, shredding through his torso and some of the Handyman uniform alike.

Vinny still didn't sense any pain, but he could feel the damage he was taking starting to weaken and tire him. As he battled with Herman, he was shocked by the power of the creature. It was as though it harbored the strength of two, maybe three people combined.

The image of Ashley's mangled face flashed in his mind again as the beast latched onto his arm and tugged at it like an attack dog. Vinny's eyes bugged as he found an inner vigor, funneling his rage.

337

He could see it in the creature's eyes as he overpowered Herman's neck strength and pulled his arm close to his face. For the first time, there was doubt. Vinny grinned, eye to eye with the beast, brandishing his own teeth.

"This time . . . I can bite back," Vinny whispered.

Plunging his teeth into the face of the beast, Vinny felt the rusty nails in his mouth pierce Herman's eyeballs. The creature's blood and eye liquid oozed all over Vinny's tongue as he bit down harder.

Herman flailed wildly, limbs shifting back into human form as it attempted to pull away. But as Vinny slipped the box cutter out of his toolbelt, he bit down even harder. Slipping the blade out, Vinny set it against the edge against Herman's neck and sliced.

A warm surge of blood rained all over Vinny's clawed chest as he pressed the tip of the cutter so deep that it broke off in Herman's flesh. Tossing the whimpering animal to the side, Vinny mounted it.

He quickly realized the beast had morphed. Picking up the golden hammer from the ground, he stared at the same disturbing face that he'd seen in the middle of the road that night. The strange woman who caused him to swerve and changed his life forever.

Flipping the hammer around, Vinny raised up the claw points. He drove it down, sickening thuds resounding as the backside of the tool punched into the creature's cranium.

"Time to put you down," Vinny growled.

As he landed blow after blow, crimson spatter painted Vinny's psychotic expression. He watched as the twitching pieces of the shapeshifting face continued to transform. The blood-soaked chunks of man, woman, and animal were all represented.

Seeing the beast in pieces made Vinny feel like another weight had risen off his chest. But as he reminded himself of the situation, there was no time to savor his vengeance. Sara and Ashley were still inside the abomination, and he needed to get them out.

Got to get them out of there. Vinny slipped the hammer back into his belt. *Got to stop those creeps.*

Looking down at the bloody box cutter, Vinny quickly snatched it off the ground. He used the screwdriver in his belt to open the knife and flipped the broken blade over. As he tightened it up, he pushed the fresh metal tip out of the tool and raced around the building.

When Vinny entered, he realized all the materials inside the house of gore were now quivering. The shredded humanity under the spell screamed as blood rained from the walls.

Click . . .

Click . . .

Click . . .

While Vinny was no longer impacted by the incessant click of the metronome, he could still hear it. And looking at Sara, he recognized that she was now wholly entranced.

"Sara!" Vinny yelled as the walls and foundation started to rumble. "Hold tight, I'm gonna get you out of this!"

"Like hell you will!" Ryan's voice sounded demonic. His hands held tight on Sara's bloody body, squeezing her breasts and rubbing between her legs.

Vinny raised the box cutter and started to slash Ryan's hands. Creating wide gashes and carving ribbons of flesh off his fingers, he quickly freed Sara and dragged her out of the quaking structure.

As he laid her on the ground outside, Vinny caressed her face gently.

"Are—are you okay?" he whispered.

Seeing her expression so vacant and hollow hurt him deeply. Sara was a special woman. The fact that she'd even shown up blew him away. She was selfless, an advocate for others.

"Please, wake up," Vinny continued. "I need you . . . I-I can't do this without you."

Vinny knew it wasn't just him who needed Sara—the world did. The lifeless husk in front of him couldn't be her final sentence.

He wiped the blood away from his mouth, pressed his lips together, and closed his eyes. As his lips touched her cheek, suddenly he heard a gasp. It sounded like someone who'd been holding their breath underwater for five minutes taking in air again.

"Vinny!" she shrieked. "W-what happened to you?!"

The look of shock and horror on her face frightened him. He'd been their puppet for so long that he'd forgotten how nightmarish he must've looked.

"I know this is crazy," he said, "but there's no time to explain."

"We've got to get out of here!" Sara cried, tears running down her face. "Those people, they're—"

"I can't leave yet," Vinny said. "If I don't go back in there then it won't matter where you run. What they're about to unleash will find you. It'll find everyone."

Trembling uncontrollably, Sara looked up at the gray clouds above the steeple and stayed quiet.

Vinny retrieved the bloody box cutter from his belt and handed it to her.

"W-what's this for?" she asked.

"I need your help . . . Ashley needs your help." Vinny looked back at the demonic structure. "She's stuck inside. They made her a part of that thing—like they did with you. I need you to get her out of there while I handle those two."

Looking into Sara's warm and glossy eyes, he watched her slowly nod.

"I'll help you, Vinny," she whispered.

Vinny stood, turned in the direction of The Nexus, and cracked his neck.

"Don't go in right away," he said. "Wait a few minutes after I go inside."

"What the . . . what the fuck is happening?" Sara whispered to herself.

Vinny paused his stride but didn't look back. "I'm about to finish the job."

LIKE LIGHTNING
FROM ABOVE

Blanche stood over Alfred, watching as the bumpy sludge continued to pour down the chute and fill the blood pool. As Alfred held on to the wall of the pit, he wailed in agony. The acidic slush was up to his waistline, and as the vapors rose up, Blanche could smell his flesh dissolving, becoming one with the foundation.

As the walls around her continued to spasm, Blanche paused her recitation just before the final few words.

"Wh-what are you doing?!" Alfred cried, extreme agony lacing his tone.

She pointed up to the chute, high above, where he couldn't see. "I've got to clear it! Before the rest of the foundation is prevented from reaching the pit!"

"Be quick then!" Alfred yelled.

Blanche set Hitchens' journal on the ground beside the metronome and took hold of the half-moon shovel. But instead of approaching the chute, she returned to her place and stood over her brother.

"Being quick is the only kindness I can offer you," Blanche said.

Alfred's eyes widened and his face turned ghostly white.

"What are you doing?" he asked.

"It's like you said," Blanche replied. "There can only be one."

"Nooooooo—"

The sharp aluminum flashed downward like lightning from above, the edge slicing deep into the back of Alfred's head. As he stared up at his sister, the metal pushed through his brain stem. The flap of tissue added a fresh surplus of blood to the pit. She wiggled the razor half-disk so that the blade made its way deeper, forcing the top half of Alfred's head to fall forward. Cranium hanging on by a clump of tissue and cartilage, he looked like an open Zippo lighter.

Dislodging the edge, Blanche raised the chute shovel once more and brought it down on Alfred's fingers. The death grip that he'd clawed into the wall with was soon no more. The edge cut through several of his fingers, and the digits fell into the carnal soup.

Quickly she dropped the shovel and reached down. After pulling the blood-drenched, half-dissolved robe from Alfred's trembling body, Blanche began to strip. She slipped the steaming cloak over her wrinkled, sagging body just in time to see her brother vanish in the pile of violence.

As Blanche watched Alfred get swallowed up by the bubbling porridge, she could see the crimson pit had almost reached its capacity. But her focus was interrupted by a man's voice.

"With family like you in this world, I'm glad I don't got any left," Vinny said.

"What . . . what are you—well, I suppose it doesn't matter, anyhow," Blanche said, grinning as her furrowed brow smoothed out. "You're too late."

She looked above her head and screamed the final words of the incantation before diving headfirst into the final foundation.

TEARING DOWN THE HOUSE

When Vinny saw Blanche come up from the pit, the ruby slop pouring out from the chute was directly over her head. The acidic gruel was burning away her hair and the skin on her face as she shrieked. A thunderous boom echoed inside The Nexus as the gravestone that ran up to the steeple was electrified.

As the lightning connected and shocked the gumbo of gore, Blanche ripped off an even louder, bloodcurdling scream. The power from the bolt caused the contents of the pit to sizzle and congeal. The gruel of humanity bonded with Blanche, forming around her. The sick amalgamation of bodies came together below her melted head, which ballooned outward. Her nightmarish face continued to distend as Blanche became one massive blob of death.

Stupefied by the twisted sibling's new horrifying form, Vinny froze. From the corner of his eye, he saw Sara behind him cutting away the final bits that held his daughter's remains to The Nexus. Just before Blanche's metamorphosis, he'd pointed her out. Vinny was impressed that Sara had been able to put aside her fear and focus enough to free her.

As Sara lifted Ashley's limp carcass off the ground, she yelled at Vinny over the explosions of thunder.

"What now?"

"Now, go!" he yelled. "I've gotta finish this! I'll meet you outside in—"

A glob of bodies crashed into Vinny. Shards of hard bone, muscle, and meat sent him crashing into the wall.

"Vinny!" Sara shrieked.

Lifting his head up, Vinny got his bearings back enough to shout, "Run!"

"I'll swallow you up," Blanche wailed, laughter echoing off the shaking walls. "And your little friends too!"

As Sara made a break for the curtains, Blanche sent a slimy appendage comprised of dozens of legs, arms, and eyes in her direction. But as Sara cleared the curtains, the demonic limb crashed into the wall behind her.

"She may stray for now," Blanche said. "But they shall all be mine. Soon, there won't be anywhere to hide!"

The distortion in her diabolical voice rattled Vinny's bones. He watched as part of The Nexus started to mesh with Blanche's new, disgusting form. The area where Ashley had been was now an extension of the abomination. The entire house of gore throbbed in harmony with Blanche's glistening mass.

Shooting forward, Blanche's disgusting limb lifted Vinny off the ground, the gunky broth of humanity clamping around his body like an octopus' tentacle.

"You really fucked this one up, didn't you, Vinny?" Curtis King's voice said.

As the torrent of tissue continued to thump, his former boss' face manifested in the appendage.

"You had to drag me into this fucking mess!" Curtis yelled. "Didn't you?!"

Vinny now saw the faces of all the people he'd killed and the others he'd dug up from the cemetery. As he sat helplessly, engulfed by the crimson goo, Vinny tried to free himself. When he was almost completely covered in the blob, he saw another face right in front of him. Through the sliver of light above, he recognized the kind expression.

"Your stubborn ass should've listened when I first tried tellin' you," Willis said.

"What . . . ?"

"It's the metronome!" Willis yelled. "That's what powers all this! That's what can stop it!"

Vinny felt himself fading, slipping into a state of dread and confusion. "The . . . the what?"

"The metronome! Don't stop fighting, damnit! You can't let them win!"

The words resonated with Vinny as he somehow found the strength to start fighting through the sludge. Reaching for his toolbelt, he was able to retrieve the folding saw.

"Finish it!" Willis yelled.

Unfolding the blade, Vinny stabbed the teeth into the meld of flesh. The hole started small, but as he continued to cut, he finally saw more light. On the floor of The Nexus, beside the truck chute, he saw the metronome bobbing side to side. Slipping through the void he'd carved, Vinny tumbled forward.

His leg landed against the chute of the cement truck and a loud crack erupted, sending him tumbling to the floor on his back. While he didn't feel the pain of his injury, it still hampered him. As Vinny shook off the disorientation of the fall, his eyes searched for the noise.

Click . . .

Click . . .

Click . . .

Staring down the black pyramid and its swaying pupil, Vinny tried to muster the strength. But as he sat up, a new appendage from Blanche's body slithered toward him like a hungry snake. As it wrapped around his leg, Vinny reached for his toolbelt.

"There's no way out but in," Blanche said, laughing nefariously. "You're mine, Handyman. Forever."

Sitting up, Vinny whipped out the golden Madison hammer from his belt and cocked it back.

"Consider this my early retirement," he said.

Slinging the hammer forward, he watched it spin through the air. It felt like it took several minutes before it finally reached its destination.

"Noooooooooo!" Blanche wailed.

The point of the golden hammer crashed into the metronome with extreme force, collapsing the tiny pyramid and shattering the black and red pupil on the pendulum.

As Oswald Hitchens' magic box came apart, a strange black oil leaked out of it. The sickening version of Blanche, along with the entire house of gore, transitioned from the vivacious colors of human insides to a deathly gray. The limbs, heads, and body parts liquified as infernal shrieks echoed within the walls of the greenhouse. It sounded like an army being slaughtered all at the same time.

Suddenly, Vinny felt extreme pain—everything he'd endured was hitting him all at once.

As he started to nod off he thought, *You did it. You did it for them.*

HOPE

When Sara saw Vinny on the ground with his eyes closed, she rushed to him. Sliding to his side, she cradled his head. As the body pieces continued to dissolve around her, she watched the cloudy red and black colors fade from Vinny's eyes, like a storm clearing in the sky. Soon after, the rusty nails wedged inside his gums glided out of his mouth. She turned him on his side and cleared the bloody spikes from his breathing passage.

"Vinny, stay with me," Sara said. "Hang in there!"

His chest began rising and falling. A huge wave of relief washed over her.

"Ashley . . ." he whispered. "Where's . . . Ashley . . . ?"

"She's gone, Vinny," Sara said. "I'm sorry."

Vinny started to sob.

"You did what you had to," Sara said, rolling him back over so she could look him in the eyes. "You protected her. Anything's better than her being a part of whatever this was. Now . . . she's where she's supposed to be."

It didn't take long for Vinny's mouth to fill up with blood from the holes in his gums. He spit up a pool of red on the floor.

"I . . . I feel cold," he whispered.

Sara took off her sweater and wrapped it around him.

"I don't care how cold you feel," she said. "You're not leaving me tonight, okay? Not tonight, not ever."

Vinny's exhaustion was evident as he stared forward without saying a word.

"I said, okay?!" Sara yelled this time.

Vinny nodded. "Y-yeah."

As the emotion ran through Sara, a strange feeling of accomplishment manifested in her heart. While the void Michael and Eric had left in it may not be completely filled for a long time, perhaps never, keeping Vinny alive helped her feel like that might change someday.

"We've gotta get you to my car," she said. "You've got somewhere to be."

"Where's that?" he asked.

Wiping a tear from her eye, she smiled. "The emergency room. And I promise, you're going to get the best care any hospital can offer."

Vinny forced his grimace to contort into a smirk. "I'd like that."

1998

TOGETHER

Checking the adhesive paste on his dentures, Vinny tugged on them gently. The grip was satisfactory.

Not a single gray hair on your head or in your beard and you already got fuckin' dentures, he thought.

"Babe, can you come in here for a minute?" Sara asked.

Leaving the bathroom, Vinny ventured down the hall and into the living room.

"Where are you?" he asked.

"I'm in the basement."

Opening the door, Vinny headed down the stairs until he met her below.

"What's up?"

"Did you feel that?" Sara asked.

"Feel what?"

"The stairs are wobbly." She pointed at the support beams under the staircase. "We should probably just cut up a few more boards and reinforce this before it ends up becoming a bigger problem."

A flicker of that night back at Len's house erupted in his mind. The saw blade hacking through his shoulder as he dismembered the man alive. He shook his head, trying to forget about the carnage.

"Vinny?" Sara said.

"I thought we agreed on this already," he said. "No home improvements. That's why we didn't buy a fixer-upper, right?"

"Oh . . . sorry," she said. "I can't believe I didn't even think about that—"

"It's fine," Vinny said. "I'm not trying to be a wimp about it. If you really think it's urgent, we can just hire a handyman. But I'm permanently retired."

"Of course, babe."

She closed in and wrapped her arms around him. Kissing him on the mouth, Sara leaned back into the washer and grabbed his crotch.

"I'm glad you're retired," she whispered. "You're much more handsome this way."

"Is that right?"

"Damn right." Sara moved in again and kissed him with a pent-up passion.

As Vinny caressed her, he realized that he could handle the occasional flashback of horror. He'd faced his darkness and moved on from the black box. Having grown to understand that no one moves on from trauma by forgetting about it entirely, he considered himself lucky. And as he kissed her deeper, Vinny was just grateful that when he made love to Sara, her face was the only one he saw.

ABOUT THE AUTHOR

Aron Beauregard is an author who is not handy. Largely a waste of flesh, he has been known to easily get super-pissed while assembling basic items like lamps. Why is he so useless at stuff? Laziness is believed to be mostly responsible, while lack of attention span rides ass at a close second. Beauregard is a man, however. His penchant for swallowing pickled eggs whole and the penis that rises up from between his hairy legs each morning indicates that much. Still, sadly, even though he looks kind of handy and manly in this above photo . . . he will never be a Handyman.

COMING IN 2025

PLAYGROUND

ARON BEAUREGARD

DELUXE EDITION

FOR SIGNED BOOKS, MERCH, AND
EXCLUSIVE ITEMS VISIT:

ABHORROR.COM

FILM & TV RIGHTS

Handyman was written with both the big and small screen in mind. For inquiries on obtaining film or television rights, please email:
AronBeauregardHorror@gmail.com

SERIOUS INQUIRIES ONLY.